The All-American Boy

by

Michael John Sullivan

I thought I was awake, but I was dreaming. I was just dreaming. But now I'm awake. I'm sure of it. I'm awake.

Balancing myself up on my left elbow, I opened my eyes and squinted at the soft sunlight on the empty bed across the way. I sat up and flexed my back and gave this really gigantic yawn. Everything seemed to be floating every which way in my head. Yeah - floating - just drifting and floating and moving all over the place. Yawning again and blinking, I started trying to remember my dream.

But I couldn't. I tried. I tried really hard. But I couldn't remember it at all.

What was I dreaming? I could still feel whatever it was right in the pit of my stomach. At least, I thought it was the pit of my stomach, or whatever that thing is down there that hits you dead cold like a fucking punch in the gut when you're not looking. You know - the feeling you get when you're falling backwards off a tall building or when you look up all of a sudden from the steering wheel and see some heavy shit right in front of you about to smash into you head-on.

Yeah - it was sort of a feeling like that.

I just sort of rolled over onto the floor and started doing my 50 morning push-ups. It felt really good. All I could think about was how nice and warm the sunlight coming through the parted window curtains felt on my back. I've always loved the feeling of heat on my body. Long as it's not too hot. You know - like I don't want to be burned or anything like that. But this was just right. Perfect. I didn't even notice the awful smell of the gray carpet every time I dipped my face down close to it.

1

When I was done with the push-ups I hopped up on my feet and stepped over to the window and looked out at the four huge pine trees to the left. Our room has this colossal view of the whole damn city and sometimes even the ocean when it's really clear, Usually I can stare almost a whole damn day at that fucking awesome view. But today I didn't feel like looking at it. I don't know why. It was a really clear day too. But for some funny reason, I didn't want to look at the view.

I just kept looking at those four thick pine trees and I seemed to be trying really hard to keep a lot of stuff out of my mind. In fact, I was really trying to make it completely empty and blank, like those hypnotist guys tell people to do in those phony movies.

It worked pretty well. I was feeling pretty blank. Had some wandering hypnotist come in the room right then, they could have easily had me flapping around like a bird or jumping all over the place like a rabbit.

After a minute or two, I took a really deep breath, sort of like I was standing next to the rec center pool and getting ready to dive in. I could feel both of my hands balling up into really tight fists, and it gave me a weird feeling. I wondered why I was doing that. I know I hadn't meant to. It just happened.

Today was going to be a perfect day! That's what I told myself.

It was going to be the best day of my life!

And that's what I kept saying to myself.

It was going to be the best fucking day in the history of my entire fucking life!

I was going to score the most points in the league championship match this afternoon, and I was going to ace my history exam, and I was going to give the best speech ever since Socrates in my philosophy class.

Today was going to be magic!

And I didn't even think any more about that damn dream I had last night. The memory of it was totally all gone. It was gone for good. Well - almost.

I remember giving this huge, happy smile, and, then, swinging my arms and kicking my legs as if the soccer game had already begun, I charged over to the bathroom door and quickly slipped out of my boxer shorts, getting ready for a nice, warm shower. It was just then that I noticed the sizzling sound of the running water inside. My roommate Josh had beat me to it. I was hoping that his empty bed had meant that he had already left the room. But he was still in the damn shower!

Christ! That guy showers at least four or five times a day! I swear to God! He lives in that fucking shower. Every time I want to take one, he's already in there slathering away. And it's never the hell a short rinse or anything. He's always in there a half-hour or longer. Minimum! I don't know what the fuck he does, but I do know there's hardly any hot water left all the time. Josh the Jerk! Shit - what is this guy? Part goldfish? Does he have to keep himself wet all the time to survive or something? I honest to god expect to see gills on his sides when he takes his shirt off. I'm gonna give him a much better look next time and really check it out when he's getting dressed. I'm sure he must be some kind of fish or something.

But I guess I have to admit that it could be a hell of a lot worse. Old Josh could have been like my roommate last year in Whelan Hall. He was a guy named Danny, and I swear to god he never took ONE damn shower the entire year. Not one damn shower - I swear it. Least I never saw him or heard him take one. And, god! He really stunk! He stunk so bad you could smell him all the way down the hall. Fuck - you wouldn't believe what that guy smelled like. Sometimes I couldn't even fucking sleep at night. My girlfriend finally had to give me some of her perfume so that I could put a slab of it under my nose above my lip when I went to bed. It helped a little, but not all that much.

So I guess I really shouldn't complain about Josh. At least he's clean and he doesn't stink. And he's also on the soccer team with me, so ya gotta suck it up and make allowances and cut him some slack and be a team player and all that other rah rah crap.

Thinking of all this, I waited about two second and then began loudly pounding on the bathroom door. I could hear Josh yell something from inside as he turned the water off, and a few moments later the door opened and he was standing there soaking wet with a towel wrapped around his waist. Seemed kind of stupid - I mean, there I was all naked and everything and this character is carefully hiding behind a towel. So like what was the big deal?

"Shit!", he exploded in a high, excited voice. "Where the fuck have you been! When did you finally get in last night?"

That really hit me in the gut. Took me completely by surprise.

I didn't want to even think about last night or yesterday, and I DEFINITELY didn't want to talk about it. I really didn't. No way!

And fuck! The memory of it started coming back all of a sudden and I bit down hard on the side of my tongue without even realizing it. Turning away from him, I stared at my bed.

"I don't know," I mumbled.

"You don't know where you've fucking been?", Josh asked me incredulously - if that's the right word you use when you're totally amazed and don't believe some shit that's just been shoveled at you.

4

"No - I don't know when I got in. It was late."

"Fuck, you're telling ME it was late! It had to be after three. Fuck! What were you doing?"

"What the fuck are you - the jerk-off police or something?", I answered him with a really pissed-off expression. "Mind your own fucking business!"

"Okay, okay," Josh instantly backed down. "Chill, bro. Don't get all bent out of shape. Chill out."

"I'm chill, bro," I said almost challengingly as I spun around and stared him directly in the eye. "I'm chill. Stop acting like a nosey turd."

"Forget it. Big deal. I just wondered, that's all. You didn't even show up at the reception yesterday afternoon. You just disappeared and nobody's seen you since. I thought you'd want to talk to Kyle's parents."

FUCK!

Why did he have to go and say Kyle's goddamned name? Why? Can't anybody just go one goddamned day without saying his name and talking about him? Just one goddamned day!

"Did Beth come by last night?", I weakly asked him, still standing there naked in the center of the room, smoothly trying to change the subject.

"Not when I was here. But I was out most of the time. Claire and I went to the Deja Vue Lounge to see a movie and then we went back to her room to study for our genetics test. Well - we studied a little."

Josh gave that big, dopey grin of his. It instantly made me feel better. That guy's got the world's goofiest grin. I swear to god, he's got the biggest mouth you've ever seen in your life. Not the lips. The lips are okay. But it's the size of the mouth - the width. Jesus! It stretches across his whole fucking face. When they say 'an ear-to-ear smile', that's Josh exactly. His grin is so big that it makes him look like a fucking circus clown. And you can see every single damn one of his teeth. It's amazing! It's like looking right into the keyboard of a grand piano. But I love it. It always makes me laugh. And he grins all the time.

But it didn't make me laugh today. I was trying hard to forget that he had mentioned Kyle's name.

Suddenly the hall door flew open and Reicher came strutting into the room.

"Jesus Christ - are you putting on a show!", he shouted at me with a booming laugh. "Why don't you put on some fucking clothes?"

"Why don't you fucking knock before you break into a room?", I replied with as much sarcasm as I could muster - which was quite a bit.

Reicher was this hulking guy who was one of the forwards on our soccer team. I was the captain, but he was about five inches taller and fifty pounds heavier than me, so I usually had to take a lot of shit from him off field. But he really wasn't a bad guy. Just loud and kind of obnoxious. And I don't think he was all that bright. Pretty stupid, actually. A great player. But, you know - kind of like a walking poster of the typical 'dumb jock'. But not really that bad of a guy.

"Hey - where the fuck were you yesterday afternoon?", he asked me with this kind of slack-jawed disbelief. "Why didn't ya go to the reception?" Why didn't ya go? Where did ya go off to after the service?"

"Which question do ya want me to answer first, Sherlock?", I snickered.

I've got a great snicker. I bet I'm one of the best snickerers on the planet.

"Everybody was asking me where ya were," Reicher continued. "Christ - you're the captain of the fucking team! You were Kyle's best friend. His mom came up to me three fucking times asking me where you fucking were. Three fucking times! I didn't know what to fucking tell her."

"How 'bout that you just didn't fucking know," I snickered again.

"Marco said that right after the service he saw you going out the side door by the bell tower. What happened? Why didn't ya fucking come with the rest of us out to the west lawn? Why didn't ya come out to the reception? Huh?"

I glanced over at Josh and gave him sort of this exaggerated pained expression. Then my mind raced really fast for a few seconds.

"I was sick," I lied with a smile.

"Sick?', both Reicher and Josh asked at the same time, like they were trying out for the men's chorus or something.

"Yeah. You know - not feeling well. Really shitty and crappy and all that. SICK."

"How could you be sick?", Josh asked, his eyes becoming almost as wide as his mouth. "You're never sick. I've never seen you sick even once."

I just shrugged and moved away toward the window and kept trying to think really fast.

"I had tacos for lunch at that Mexican place down the street and they tasted really shitty, and later on in the chapel I felt like I was gonna barf."

"Barf?", Reicher blinked.

"Yeah - heave - vomit - throw up. Get the picture?"

"So, what did ya do?", Josh asked really all interested-like.

"I came back up here to the room."

"Did ya?", Reicher really wanted to know.

"Did I what?"

"Barf?"

"Hell yeah - big time. Then I sacked out a little and must have fallen asleep."

"Bummer, dude," Josh kind of mumbled with this big sigh. "Everybody at the reception was asking where ya were. Kyle's folks looked really upset about it. And the coach had this crazy look in his eyes every time somebody mentioned your name."

"Oh, yeah!", Reicher gave this loud, excited snort. "Old coach was really pissed! He was in orbit! Shit, he kept chugging the wine, and when Dr. Delaney asked him where ya were, I thought he was gonna just blow all to shit right there in the middle of the thing. Fuck! He's gonna kill you at the meeting this morning!"

As he said that, I suddenly felt really sick to my stomach and dizzy. I moved closer to the window and stared at the pine trees.

"Later I went over there to the west lawn when I was feeling better," I tried to keep talking to steady myself, "but everybody was gone. Just a few of the student worker guys were there cleaning up the mess."

Fuck - I was turning into a championship liar!

It was like I couldn't stop lying. What the fuck was happening? What happened to my perfect day? Everything seemed like it was starting to get away from me.

"Well, you sure the hell missed a great spread," Reicher gushed with salvia almost dripping from his fat lips. "Turkey, roast beef, pizza, pastries, cake, and all that shit. It was a feast. I really fucking stuffed myself."

Reicher's detailed trip down the menu was making me sick to my stomach again.

"Yeah - I ate a ton of all that shit," Josh grinned. "I was so full that I didn't even have any dinner last night."

"Speaking of dinner," Reicher yelped with a big snorting laugh. "Beth came by the library last night and told Julie that fucking crazy thing you did at dinner down at the Marina."

"You went out to dinner last night?", Josh asked me with a look of this big surprise on his face - you know, that 'incredulous' type thing again. "I thought you were sick?"

"I was feeling a little better," I quietly answered, knowing what was coming.

"You should hear the fucking insane thing he did," Reicher excitedly went on. "It was so gross! I'm talking gross to the max!"

"Tell me - what did he do?", Josh asked him with this dumb, fascinated stare, like I wasn't even there in the room or something.

"Guess", Reicher commanded in this stupid shitty voice.

"Uh - he took a dump at the restaurant table?", Josh laughed with a huge grin, and that was some colossal grin, let me tell ya!

"That would have been a whole lot fucking better. You're not gonna believe what he did do."

"Tell me, What?"

"Beth said they were all sitting out on the patio porch, you know, down there at the Warehouse Restaurant in the Marina."

"Yeah?"

"And their table's right next to the railing, you know, right above the walkway down below. And it's Beth and her older sister and her husband -

you remember him? - that real snobby guy we met last May at Esther's wedding?"

"Yeah - that real GQ stuck-up guy. So - what happened?"

"So," Reicher paused for this really long second, trying to milk the shit out of his really big fucking moment, "this cruddy old homeless guy - this totally disgusting street person comes nosing along the walkway - and guess what?"

"What?", Josh excitedly gushed like a fool.

"Old Number Nine here looks over at this piece of human trash and says 'hi' and starts having a regular conversation with him like he's actually a real person."

Everybody calls me Number Nine. It's my number on the soccer team. It's right there big as life on my jersey, and I wear it around a lot, so everybody started calling me Number Nine. It's my nickname. It was kind of funny at first, and kind of neat. But that's all they call me now. That's even how my girlfriend Beth refers to me. Not when we're alone together. Then she calls me 'honey' and sweet stuff like that. But to other people she always calls me Number Nine. To tell the god's honest truth, it really got old a long time ago.

I haven't heard by real name said in so long that I can barely remember what it is. And I really like my real name. I really do. I hadn't realized how tired I was of hearing the 'Number Nine' bit until right now when Reicher said it in that shitty condescending nasal voice of his.

I wish they'd all stop doing it. I want my real name back. Not some number, like I'm an inmate in some prison or something.

"He's talking to this dirty bum right there at the table in this fancy place?", Josh was asking Reicher.

"Yeah - it was amazing. Number Nine is just sitting there at the table talking over the railing to this disgusting bum - and the bum walks over and stands there right next to them like he's a member of the party."

"Shit!", Josh roared. "I bet Beth's sister and brother-in-law went ballistic."

"Oh yeah - big time. Royally pissed. They couldn't believe it. Number Nine was trading names and life stories and the whole shit with this creepy homeless dude. Beth said he talked to him for more than ten minutes. Then guess what happened."

"What?"

"This bum has the fucking nerve to ask for a handout! And this is gonna kill ya! Old Number Nine here picks up the basket of bread at the table and he passes it over the railing and gives it to the dirty bum!"

Reicher and Josh howled with laughter and tried to speak, but they were so fucking choked up with themselves that they couldn't say a damn word. Nice.

"And that wasn't the worst of it," Reicher finally gasped after a few big gulps of air. "Nine then picks up his plate from the table and holds it over the railing and lets this gross old bum take his grimy fingers and help himself to anything he wants on his fucking plate - fries, pieces of steak - everything!"

The two of them were laughing so fucking hard at this that they almost fell down on the fucking floor. When he came up for air, Josh opened his mouth really wide - and shit! - let me tell ya - that was WIDE! - and he waved his hand all excited-like, sorta like me was trying to hail a taxi or something.

"Let me tell ya - let me tell ya," he kind of all exploded like he could hardly wait to say it, "he does that all the time. All the fucking time. Number Nine buys all this food in the Lair a couple of times a week and he has 'em put it in bags, and he takes it over to the Westchester Park down there on Manchester and he gives it to all these filthy, disgusting old homeless people that live down there in the bushes and stuff."

"No way!", Reicher went all slack-jawed.

"Way!", Josh excitedly continued, just really loving it. "We were driving down to the beach once, and he stops off there at the park with his bags of food, and all these gross old bums just swarmed all over us and followed us around like hungry animals. It was the most disgusting thing I've ever seen. And he knows all their names and they know his, and, I mean, I swear to god! - it's just so fucking ridiculous and insane!"

"Jesus Christ!", Reicher yelled with that amazed, how do you call it? Incredulous? Yeah - that incredulous kind of expression.

"What's wrong with that?", I calmly and very seriously asked these assholes as I turned away from the window and faced them.

"Well, if you don't fucking know, no one can fucking tell ya," Reicher shot back at me like I was some kind of retarded idiot or something.

I just gave a shrug.

I do that a lot. There's a whole lot of shit that I don't understand, and I don't think I ever will.

"Well, I'm gettin' dressed," Josh kind of self-consciously said, looking a little sorry for having gone off so much on me.

"Yeah, I gotta take off," Reicher announced with a yawn. "Team breakfast and meeting at 9:10 at the Training Center. I'll come by on my way up there and we can all go together."

"Fantastic," I said with this big, sarcastic smile, really happy to be finally getting rid of this fucking obnoxious guy.

I was standing there still all naked with my back to the window and the sunlight really felt good on my skin. Kind of comforting-like, if you know what I mean. Like everything might still be OK today, and everything was going to be fine after all.

Reicher had stomped over to the hall door and opened it, then all of a sudden-like he stopped, and he turned around and gave me this important look with his face all scrunched up all serious-like.

"Oh, Jeff wants to see ya. He wants ya down in our room ASAP. Pronto. Jeff said to come down right now. Sounds pretty important. He got in really late last night and he's in a real piss-ass mood. See ya."

When Reicher was saying this to me, I really didn't even hear the rest of his words after he mentioned Jeff's name. It was like he'd turned and sucker punched me in the gut - right in the bottom of my gut.

I couldn't breathe. As soon as I heard Jeff's name, I couldn't breath, and I couldn't even stand. I just sort of fell backwards down on my bed and sat there - all totally numb and cold. My head was spinning around inside and all my thoughts were crashing this way and that and seemed to be falling and smashing so fast that it was honest to god making me dizzy. I felt like I was just gonna keel over and die.

Reicher left with a bang of the door. That's about all I remember. I know Josh was talking and saying something after that, but I didn't hear the words. It just seemed like he got dressed really fast because a few minutes later he was gone and I was all alone.

I had only been thinking about Jeff.

Sitting there on the edge of my bed, I still was having trouble breathing, Then my whole body started shaking really bad, like I was sick or something. I lied down on the bed and kind of curled myself up into this little ball, my knees all bunched up against my chest.

I didn't help. I was still shaking.

Then all of a sudden I knew that I couldn't pretend anymore.

And I knew that it was real.

That it was true.

It hadn't been a dream.

8:27 am

I guess I must have fallen asleep. There was this really loud pounding on the hall door that suddenly woke me up, and I jumped out of bed and stood there with my heart racing like crazy. It was the weirdest feeling - like I had just run the marathon or something. I can't tell you how weird it felt.

I kind of stepped toward the door, my hands all kind of trembling the way they do in those horror movies.

The pounding stopped and the knob started turning, and then there was this kind of tugging and pushing sound against the door. Josh must have locked it when he left. He's always doing that. He grew up in Iowa and he thinks wherever he is in Los Angeles is Crime Central. He can't touch a fucking door without locking it.

But today I was sure the hell glad he had.

"Hey - Niner! Open up! I know you're there! Open up, Niner! It's Jeff! I gotta talk to you!"

FUCK!

I just stood there totally frozen - like I was a statue or something. I swear to god - I couldn't move and I couldn't even breathe.

"Niner! It's Jeff! Open up! We gotta talk NOW! Niner!"

That's my other nickname - 'Niner'. When they get tired of calling me Number Nine, they just shorten it to Niner. Get it? Really clever, huh?

"Open up!", Jeff's voice was getting louder and much angrier. "Niner! I know you're there! Open up or you'll be sorry! Open the fucking door!"

He started driving his fist really hard against the wood again.

15

I just kept doing my statue act.

There was no fucking way on the planet that I was gonna open that door, or even answer him.

He kept pounding for another two minutes. A whole fucking two minutes! Then he finally gave up with this really hard, mean kick to the bottom of the door that really scared me. I listened carefully and I could hear him as he went off swearing down the hall.

I waited for a couple minutes to make sure that he was really gone, then I went in and took a shower. I was thinking that I'd probably just stay in there under the warm water for like the whole damn day and sort of just let everything sort of just drift away until everything had just gone away. But there was only cold water left when I turned the shower on. Shit! Josh the fucking fish!

It was a pretty quick shower, and when I was done I put my soccer jersey on and my tennis shoes. Then I dropped to the floor and did another 50 pushups just to steady myself. There was more than 20 minutes or so until the Team Meeting, so I thought maybe I'd take a shave. But when I picked up my shaver and looked in the mirror I decided not to.

I shaved yesterday for Kyle's memorial service 'cause there was gonna be so many parents and faculty guys there. You know how it is. But usually I like to have this stubble thing going on my face - kind of this macho, unshaven look. So I only shave a couple of times a week. It's not that I don't have this really heavy beard. I really do. I mean, for a twenty year old guy, I've really got this manly beard. I really need to shave every day. But like I told you, I like people to be able to see how thick and rough my beard is. It kind of makes me feel good. You know - like a full-grown man or something.

I used to worry a lot about trying to have a mustache or a goatee or even a whole complete beard. I've tried them all, and they all looked really weird on me. Totally weird! No matter what I try to grow, I always end up looking like a total dork-face. So I gave up last summer and now I just go with the stubble thing.

And, plus - I kind of have this other problem. I've got this real delicate kind of face. You know - what they call fine, chiseled features and all that crap. I hate it! I think I must have got it from my mom. She's really beautiful. But I hate my face! I always have. People have always called me 'baby face' and 'pretty boy' and crap like that. Especially 'pretty boy' - I get that a lot. I really hate it. I swear to god I do!

Girls and these older women are always scoping in on me wherever I go. And even these certain kinds of guys. But I don't want to talk about that. I don't even want to think about that kind of shit. I don't know what the big deal is, but it's been going on ever since I was about fourteen or so. But it's no big problem for me anymore. Whenever these characters start doing that eye thing with me, I just plain stare right back at them like I'm looking through a clear glass window - like I'm just looking right plain through them like they're not even there. Works every time.

For some reason, when I was looking at myself in the mirror and deciding not to shave, I was thinking about that. I was thinking about that time at the airport a few months ago when I was coming back from home. There was this old lady who was following me all over the damn airport. All over the whole fucking airport. And she kept staring at me and giving me the eye. And I mean she was really old. Hell, I bet she must have been almost forty. A real cougar.

So anyway, this fancy cougar lady finally nailed me by the carousel in the baggage claim area and she tells me she's a producer at Fox, and she tells me I look a lot like Brad Pitt, and she says she can get me a screen test and she can make me a big fucking star or something. This cougar even has a card she gives me. A real legit-looking card with even the studio's name and everything. She told me to give her a call.

Shit! What a routine. All that phony stuff just to get a young guy in bed.

I mean, I know for damn sure I don't look like Brad Pitt. I mean, come on! He's this real old guy, and he sure the hell doesn't have fine features like I do. I'll bet you this entire dorm that nobody's ever called Brad Pitt 'pretty boy.' Come on!

But the funny thing is - I was standing there looking in the mirror and I started thinking, 'What if I had called that number on the card a few months ago, instead of throwing it in the gutter outside of the Baggage Claim? What if this cougar lady was really the real deal?'

I kept staring at myself in the mirror and wondering what my life could have been like today if I had called that fucking number. Where could I have been - this hour - this moment.

I was thinking that maybe none of this crap happening to me right now would ever have happened.

If only I had saved that damn card and called that fucking number.

Maybe right now my life would have been just beginning - instead of being almost totally over.

I'm glad Josh came back into the room right then. I really didn't want to think about that damn card anymore.

"Hey, you finally have clothes on," he said with a grin as he charged over to his dresser drawer. "Congratulations!"

"Thank you," I snickered.

"I saw Jeff down at the Lair when I was gettin' coffee. He said he's been looking for you. I told him you were up here, but he said he came by and nobody was here. Must have been in the shower, huh?"

"Yeah. Thanks for the cold water."

"You're fucking welcomed," he grinned again. "Anyway, the dude is actin' major strange. Shit, does he look pissed about something. He told me to tell you to get your ass down to his room right now, or else you're gonna be one fucking sorry hombre. What's up?"

"Fuck him!"

"No thanks," he said with a laugh. "But for real - what's going on with you two? What's the problem? He looks totally wasted - like one of those dudes from 'Dawn of the Dead."

"You tell me," I casually answered him, as if I had zero interest in the whole fucking thing.

"Maybe he's risen from the grave and wants to drink your blood," Josh said in this Dracula kind of voice which was really pretty lame.

I tried to smile and give a laugh, but I couldn't. I couldn't even begin. A chill was going down my spine and my whole fucking body was just sort of clenching the way that your teeth do when you're freezing cold.

Just then, there was this loud knock on the door and I felt like I was having a damn heart attack.

"Yeah?", Josh happily sung out. "It's open."

Marco and Will came strutting into the room. They lived in 327 down the hall and were also members of the soccer team.

Marco's a really good player and a pretty funny guy - you know, comical-like. It's just the way he is. The stuff he says always makes people laugh. He doesn't mean to be funny, least I don't think so. It's mainly just the way he says stuff - how he talks in kind of a funny way.

Will's a pretty good player too. But, Christ! Does he complain! All he does is bitch and moan and complain about every fucking thing! You could hand the guy a million dollars - tax free! - and all he'd do is look at it and complain about how the bills were too dirty and wrinkled. We all call him Will the Whiner.

When they came in the room everybody instantly started all that dumb ass whooping and 'hey, bro's and fist pumping. I hate that stuff! Fuck! Why don't they all just go and enroll at the local kindergarten or something. Give me a break!

"Hey, bro," Marco mumbled to me, "what's with the invisible act at the reception yesterday? Everybody was askin' what happened to ya."

"Yeah," Will jumped in with this really stupid all concerned look on his face, "you ruined the whole damned thing. God, you're the captain of the team and you were his best friend. Everybody on the team was there except you. Shit - it was fucking ridiculous! What the hell happened?"

Fuck me! Was I gonna have to go through all that shit again? Why can't everyone just give it a rest! You miss one dumb, stupid, phony fucking reception and everyone's all ready to nail you up on some cross or something. Shit!

"He was sick," Josh answered for me.

"Ready to go to the meeting?", I casually called out, trying to quickly change the subject.

"Yeah," Will said with a stifled yawn. "Tom and Nick are gonna meet us up there. Oh - I saw Beth in the Lair, Niner. She said she wanted to talk to ya. I told her you'd probably still be up here."

"Thanks."

"I think she's on her way up. I told her we had the meeting pretty soon. She didn't seem all that friendly. What's her problem?"

"No problem," I said with this really big fake smile.

"Yeah, Jeff was lookin' for ya too," Marco jumped in. "He was askin' everybody in the Lair where ya where."

"Thanks," I mumbled with a knot in my throat.

"Jeff seems really weird today," Marco continued. "Kind of all moody and sad-like - like his dog just died. Does he have a dog?"

"Probably not anymore, I guess," Josh cracked with a wicked grin.

I kind of dropped down on the edge of my bed and tried to get a grip on myself - I mean, you know - steady my nerves and everything.

Just then, Beth appeared in the open doorway and smiled and rushed in and sat down beside me. Running her hands up and down my right arm, she kissed me lightly on the cheek. She felt really good. And she looked really good. Really pretty. Her long, straight blond hair was flowing all over the place and her pale blue eyes were brightly shining.

"Happy Birthday," she said in this hot, whispery kind of soft purr.

She's always so sexy, I almost get a hard-on every time I hear her talk. Especially when she's right next to me like that.

"Not 'til tomorrow," I tried to smile.

"Then Happy 'almost' Birthday," she purred, kissing me again, but this time much closer to my mouth.

"Ready for the orgy tonight?", Marco asked me with this really dumb, comical leer on his face.

All of my friends were going to give me this big bash tonight in the Bird Nest - this funny looking clubhouse kind of small building on the bluff that kind of looks like a broken umbrella. You know - on the eve of my big 21st birthday and all that. Becoming legal and a man and all that crap.

Tomorrow my mom and step-dad are flying in and taking me up to Beverly Hills to some fancy ass place for dinner.

Actually - to be honest - the real reason my folks are coming tomorrow is because they're being dragged in by the Dean to watch me get the shit kicked out of me . Right now I have a 1.6 GPA, which means that unless I get straight A 's this semester, I'm gonna flunk out of here on my sorry butt. And my chances of getting A 's is about the same as me being able to fly to Mars and back every day. Pretty slim. But I don't want to talk about that right now. That's another story.

"They said we can only have the Nest 'til 11:30," Will was doing his whining routine. "What's with that? It'll ruin the whole fucking thing. Why can't we stay at least until after midnight? And they said we can't have any music. Who ever heard of a party without any music? It's stupid. Why didn't have the party at Kate's house or down at Tompkins? It's gonna ruin everything having at the Nest. Shit!"

Everybody just sort of ignored him - you know, took him in stride and everything. It didn't seem to bother him much. Will was pretty used to being ignored by most of the guys. I don't think he was too popular.

"I've been calling you all morning," Beth softy said to me as she ran her hand along the inside of my right thigh and made me have an instant hard-on.

With all these other guys in the room, I was feeling pretty self-conscious, so luckily I was able to put it in reverse before my cock started pushing its way out from under my shorts.

"Yeah, I called you a couple of times too," Marco said unhappily.

"Did you turn off the ringer on your phone?", Beth asked me, sort of annoyed and all.

"I guess I forgot to turn it on this morning when I got up," I answered in this really weak, stupid voice.

I reached up to the shelf above my bed and grabbed my phone and looked at it. Yep. 17 missed calls were showing. I quickly turned the ringer back on, but then, without really thinking about anything, I hesitated a moment or so, then all of a sudden just pressed the ringer button back off. For some reason, I didn't want my phone today. I didn't want to even touch it today. For some reason - I felt like I hated the fucking thing.

With this angry jerk of my hand, I tossed it back up on the shelf.

Josh had been texting on his phone while this had been going on, and Marco's phone rang and he answered it, and Will started calling somebody on his phone.

I put my arm around Beth and went to say something to her, but she had her phone in her hand and was calling somebody, so I just stared down at the floor and tried not to think of anything until a minute or two later when she was done talking to whoever she called and turned back to me with this warm, sexy smile.

"I gotta get to my theology class," she said, rising from the bed and gently taking me by the hand and pulling me up.

We walked out the door and stood there by the wall in the hallway. Beth sort of leaned against me like she always does and gave me one of her really hot looks.

"I didn't mean all that stuff I said last night when ya took me home after dinner," she said very softly.

"I know," I whispered, feeling pretty nervous and uncomfortable. "I understand. I just need more time to think, that's all."

Beth's face kind of changed into this sort of tight, hard expression.

"There isn't any more time. It's been too long already. You've been saying that since I told ya ten days ago. We've gotta decide today. We can't wait any longer. Today!"

"I know, I know," I whined, probably sounding just like Will.

"Look," she said with this big, emotional sigh, "I'm gonna be late for class. I gotta go all the way over to U Hall. And that priest is already looking at me like he knows what's going on. See ya later."

She stretched up on her toes and kissed me on the mouth and kind of pressed her body into me, and I could feel my cock start going all hard again. I watched her dance off down the hall in that sort of graceful way she has of walking, and as I looked at her I had this really crazy mixture of emotions. 'Paradoxical' is what my philosophy professor Dr. Blystone calls it. Like when you're experiencing two opposite things at once. Things so different that they just sort of cancel each other out. That's how I was feeling. Kind of paradoxical. Confused.

I hesitated for a couple of moments, then numbly went back into my room. Marco was spread out on my bed like some kind of Roman emperor or something. All that was missing were the grapes.

"Why don't ya make yourself at home," I told him with a nice dash of sarcasm.

He was texting on his phone and ignored me. Josh and Will were talking on their phones to god knows who, so I just sort of drifted over to the window and stared out at those pine trees. For some reason, they didn't loo so great anymore. I don't know why.

My thoughts started all crashing around again when Josh suddenly announced it was time to get going to the soccer meeting. We had less than ten minutes now, so he was right.

Josh reached in his dresser drawer and pulled out that fucking horrible black armband and slid it over his left shirt sleeve so that it tightly hugged his bicep. It made me sick to my stomach when I saw it. Then I noticed that Will and Marco were wearing theirs too.

Fuck! I never realized before how much I hated that black armband. Right then, I hated it more than anything else in the world. It even had Kyle's initials on it - a big KM - and in this really creepy silvery lettering. Fuck! It was so stupid. Like it meant anything or something! Like it was gonna bring him back from the dead or something. Jesus - how I hated that goddamned armband right now. Jesus!

"Hey, Niner - put your band on and let's get going," Josh called over to me.

I just ignored him and stayed by the window.

Everybody was sort of scrambling toward the hall door, and Josh repeated what he'd said to me, and then Will and Marco all excitedly took it up.

"Come on, we'll be late. Get your armband and let's go!"

I followed after them, but I didn't get my goddamned armband. Josh turned and looked at me all puzzled-like.

"Where's your armband?", he asked me kind of funny-like.

"I don't know," I lied. "I must of lost it somewhere."

"Sure it's not over there in the right drawer where ya always keep it?"

"Naw - I looked/"

"I saw you toss it in there yesterday," the fucking guy kept insisting. "It's gotta be in there somewhere."

Then the jerk went over and opened the drawer and yanked out the fucking armband and gave this triumphant grin like he had just landed on the moon or something.

"Here ya go," he said all happy-like, charging toward me and dangling the black armband out in front of him like a victory flag.

The whole thing just totally creeped me out. It was like he was trying to hand me a fucking rattlesnake or something. All I remember is that I just spun backwards away from him and sort of crouched down on my bed.

"NO," I heard myself say.

"What?"

Everybody was staring at me like they thought I had just gone nuts or something.

"What did you say?", Will asked me with this totally amazed look.

"I'm not gonna wear it," I said without even taking a breath - just real calm and firm without even thinking about it.

"What'a'ya mean?", Marco sputtered. "Ya gotta wear it - you're the captain - we're all wearing 'em."

"Not me."

"WHY?", Josh loudly asked me.

"Because I don't want to."

They all just sort of stared at me, kind of like they couldn't believe what they were hearing.

"But ya gotta!", Josh insisted.

"No I don't."

"But ya gotta - we all decided - we all agreed - the whole team - ya gotta," they were really excitedly all saying at once, sort of like in a panic or something. It was quite a fucking sight.

"Not me. I didn't agree. I didn't decide. And I'm not wearing it."

Reicher came through the open hallway door just then and couldn't help but notice how tense the vibes were in the room. He kind of curiously looked at our hard stone faces.

"Come on - we're gonna late for the meeting," he kind of barked at us. "What's goin' on? What's wrong?"

"Niner says he won't wear the armband," Will announced in this really shitty cold voice.

Reicher seemed like he was almost stunned. He took his hand and made this really fast inventory of his fat face.

"Are you fucking crazy!," he shouted. "What's the hell wrong with you! You gotta wear it! Why won't you?"

I just stood there feeling all numb and everything, staring calmly straight ahead but not really focusing on anybody.

"He says he doesn't want to," Marco stammered like a child.

"Are you fucking crazy!", Reicher exploded again. "You fucking idiot asshole! What'a'ya mean you don't want to! Ya have to! Put it on!"

"No," I said in almost a whisper.

Reicher looked at me like he was gonna pick me up any second and heave me through the plate glass window. But for some weird reason I didn't care. I couldn't have cared less if he had. I don't know why.

"FUCK!", he screamed at me. "Do whatever ya want! We're gonna be late! Fuck, just do whatever ya want! The coach is just gonna cream your sorry ass! Christ - I just wanna be there when ya tell him! Jesus - this is gonna be fucking priceless! Holy shit!"

At the end of Reicher's moronic screaming marathon, everybody just kind of moved quietly over to the open door and started slowly filing out into the hallway - you know, with these really lame looks on their faces, all kind of confused and disappointed and upset and all that crap like that.

It almost made me feel kind of all guilty and everything.

But it didn't.

Not really.

I slowly started to follow after them when suddenly my heart froze and I nearly dropped dead right there on the spot.

Jeff was standing just outside the doorway.

I swear to god - I thought I was gonna die of a heart attack!

Everybody else had filed out of the room by then, so I hesitated for a minute and tried to think. But I couldn't. I just wanted to get away - to get out of there as quick as I could. So I just started following after them and kept my head down and stared at that stupid dirty gray carpet.

Moving into the doorway and trying to slip past Jeff, I thought I had almost made it. But suddenly Jeff grabbed me as I passed him.

I was so surprised I really didn't even know what had happened. Jeff just took me really hard by my arms and pushed me back into the room and crashed me up against the open door. It really hurt.

The other guys were already starting down the hallway and I don't think they even noticed what had happened. They were making these loud jokes about me and laughing and all that crap.

Actually, I was really amazed that old Jeff could plaster me up against the wooden door like that and pin me the way he did. He's almost my height, but he only weighs about 150 pounds. I mean, he's like this fucking walking skeleton or something. And he's playing tough like this with me. But I guess maybe I kind of let him do it because I was feeling so scared about last night.

Scared as shit!

I mean, to tell you the truth - I was never so scared in my whole fucking life.

I had no idea what Jeff was gonna do. Or what crazy thing he might have buzzing around in his head.

Jeff pressed his face right up against mine so that our noses were almost touching. It really freaked the hell out of me. It was like me was gonna kiss me or something. Then he burned his eyeballs down into mine and he said in this insane, crazy, totally flipped out mad whisper:

"You shit head! You've been giving me the finger all morning!"

I fought to get some air in my throat and make sound kind of decent voice.

"Last night - we agreed," I said in this really pathetic shaking, choked squeak, "remember - we promised - you promised - we'd never talk about it - never - we said we'd forget it - never talk about it again."

"That was last night," he said in this really angry shitty voice that really frightened me.

"What'a'ya mean?", I gasped. "What's the matter with you?"

He relaxed his grip on me and smiled this bitter kind of smile that frightened me more than anything else.

"Didn't you hear the news on TV this morning?", he asked me in this kind of cold, dead tone.

"No," I gasped with a totally confused shake of my head.

Jeff stood there just staring into the centers of my eyeballs.

"They've arrested somebody else."

I was totally wrecked by his words.

"Huh? What?"

"The police caught some poor, dumb bastard and they're charging him with what you did," Jeff said very slowly and coldly. "We don't have a choice anymore."

"What'a'ya mean?", I was so scared and shocked that I could barely speak. "We swore last night - you promised that . . "

"We don't have any choice now," he said really emotionally, letting go of my arms and backing away from me a little.

"No! You promised!"

"But they're pinning the thing on somebody else, you shit head. Don't ya understand? Now we HAVE to tell. We have to go to the police."

"No!"

Jeff pulled back a little more and stood there looking at me with the hardest, shittiest look anybody's ever given me in my life.

"If you don't go with me to the police, then I'll go by myself."

"You can't, Jeff!", I really pathetically pleaded with him.

"We have to!"

"NO!"

He suddenly grabbed the front of my soccer jersey and pushed me against that damned wooden door again.

"Listen to me carefully, you crazy asshole," Jeff angrily whispered to me in this really icy, threatening tone. "You can go to your big fucking birthday party tonight. But you've only got 'til midnight."

"Midnight?"

"Right after midnight you meet up with me and we'll go to the police together. Right after your fucking party."

"Or?", I was sorry I asked as soon as I said the word.

"Or - you can sit in a fucking prison cell for the rest of your fucking goddamned life!"

Jeff let go of my shirt and he gave me this really odd little smile that made a sharp chill go through my whole damn body.

Then, he hurried off down the dark hallway and joined the other guys in their stupid, loud laughter.

I just stood there in the doorway for a very long moment and watched them all disappear into the descending stairwell.

I was late for the soccer meeting. The seven minute walk to the Lions Training Center took me twice as long this morning. I kept stopping along the way and looking at stuff like I was seeing it for the first time. The Sunken Garden, the bell tower, the construction site for the new science building, the Burns Rec Center. I kind of wondered in the back of my head if maybe I'd never see them again after today. It was a funny feeling. I mean, not the kind that makes you laugh or anything - but strange. Really strange, and unpleasant, and upsetting and everything.

I was still scared.

Scared shitless, to tell ya the truth.

I let Jeff and the other guys get quickly way ahead of me until I couldn't see them anymore. I didn't want to see Jeff ever again in my whole fucking life. But he was on the soccer team and one of the better players, so he'd be there front and center at the meeting and naturally at the big game this afternoon. In fact, he'd probably be glued right next to me for the whole goddamned game. Fuck!

As I slowly walked along, dozens of people I knew kept giving me these stupid phony friendly greetings and talking to me. I had this big fake smile plastered on my face and really didn't hear a word they were saying, as if it mattered at all. It was only a bunch of bullshit anyway. You know - you're captain of a sports team and everybody is automatically your best friend. That really started bothering me for some reason today.

When I finally arrived at the Training Center, I went in the wide open side door and walked through the weight room. The crew team was having one of their workout sessions and about twenty guys were spread all over the equipment pushing and pulling all these heavy iron weights and looking like a bunch of fucking galley slaves.

I stopped for a minute and watched them.

I love it! These clowns were working harder than those jerks on a prison chain gang - you know, like they had in those dumb-ass old movies, always breaking those big rocks and digging ditches. But it's not just these idiot jocks. Everywhere ya go, everybody is busting their butts all day in all these gyms everywhere. Fuck, in this city and in my hometown there's a fucking gym on every corner. And everybody's beating their brains out on all these machines, almost dropping dead from all that slaving away. The world right now seems so easy - you can do anything with your mind and a few tiny flicks of your fingers. I mean, you can control everything from here to Mars in a few seconds if ya want to. So what do these clowns do? They all decide to workout like dumb animals all day and all night in these gyms - like it was a thousand years ago and they were living in caves and having to lug around those huge stones to build those pyramids and every-thing. How dumb-ass stupid can ya be! Fuck! I love it!

After a minute or so, I moved on and went up the stairs to the big conference room on the second floor where all the athletic team meetings take place. Today all the tables were moved together at the far end of the room and everybody was sitting around them and eating breakfast. That was coach's cute idea. I guess it was part of all that team spirit crap. You know, like 'the team that eats together, wins together,' or something like that. The guys on the team could pretty much eat all they wanted, and there was quite a spread. But you weren't supposed to touch another bite of anything for the rest of the day until after the game.

I kind of tried to quietly sneak in behind a whole bunch of chairs, but before I got halfway to the tables, everybody noticed me. A few of them kind of chanted my nickname - you know - Number Nine - Niner. But most of the others were acting really weird and just looked at me and then stared at my naked left bicep. I assumed that Reicher and Josh and Will and Marco had all done a pretty good job of telling everybody there what I had said up in my room about refusing to wear the armband.

Maybe it was just my imagination, but I felt like everybody was staring at me with these really pissed off attitudes as I kind of slowly moved between the chairs and took one of the empty seats at the end of the table. Coach Bonner, our soccer team coach, was standing at the front of the tables and blathering away like he always does about how great our team was and how we were gonna cream UCLA that afternoon out on Sullivan Field. Fuck, yeah! In his dreams! We've never beaten UCLA. They have the best team in the division. If we beat them today, it'd be some fucking kind of miracle. But I guess it could happen. Ya gotta think positive and all that kind of crap, I guess.

When old Bonner was winding down and getting his breath back after almost jumping up and down with this really phony cheerleading bit, he bowed his head real dramatic-like and launched into this really lame and corny tribute to Kyle. Shit! It almost made me barf! And I hadn't even touched any of the cafeteria junk yet that everybody else was cramming down their throats by the bucket full.

"He was a player who exemplified everything that was the best in young manhood," I remember Bonner sickeningly shoveling it. "He will live in our hearts forever, and his spirit will illuminate and guide this great team to achieve greatness in the years to come. We dedicate this game today to Kyle Martinsen. May his strength and kindness and great loyalty lead us to victory on the field. Let your memorial armbands show the world that we remember our beloved player and that we are showing our love for our late teammate and using this treasured armband to make us invincible. Let us win this game today for Kyle - and let us proceed all the way to the victorious glory of the West Coast Division and the National trophy."

God! It really did make me sick! Shit! Just let the fucking guy rest in his grave, why don't ya! Bonner was really one screwed up son-of-a bitch to wave Kyle's corpse around like a flag or something. Shit!

Why do they have to keep talking about him? Kyle's gone. He's dead. End of story. Shit!

When the coach was finally done slathering all his dumb words, he sat down and dug into the huge pile of shit on his plate. While he quickly starting woofing it down, he eyed the tables in front of him, and I noticed how his face changed color to this kind of bright shade of purple when he glanced over at me. I looked the other way.

Coach Bonner was pretty typical of most of the college athletic coaches that I'd seen over the years. Really overweight and out of shape. Fat, you'd have to say. Just plain fat and flabby. I saw him in the pool once and it turned my stomach. Really pathetic. Probably almost 300 pounds if he was an ounce. Shit! He was once a championship soccer player. Trophies to burn - a whole shitload of them. But like all these coaches, they just start expanding like the National Debt for some reason after they stop playing their sport and become a great big fucking authority on it.

And like all the other coaches, he wanted to be your best buddy, but at the same time he wanted to control you like something he'd captured in a nice glass jar - something to keep and play with and do what he wanted to with. It's hard to explain. All the coaches are like that. It's really weird. I don't know what the deal is. I don't know what they want or what they get out of it. All us guys on the team are kind of like their pets. It's like they own us, the way people own dogs and cats and stuff.

I always kind of had a feeling that what almost all these coach guys would really like to do is to capture some small little country - you know, like one of those places down in South America - and take this fucking little place over and make it their own private little kingdom and rule it with the old iron fist. Yeah - these guys really seem like 'iron fist' kind of guys who would really get off on being a total dictator somewhere.

I always got along with Bonner pretty well. He could be a pretty OK guy if things were going OK. But ya didn't want to hang around him much if we were on a losing streak. So far this season, we'd done pretty good. Really good, in fact. We have a pretty good shot at the Conference title right now. But, of course, after Kyle died, we lost the next game we played against Pepperdine. That was last week. But nobody really felt like playing that day. It was too soon. Kyle had probably been the best player on the team and everybody liked him so much.

But I don't wanna talk about Kyle. Forget it.

I started eating the breakfast they were serving. It was supposedly this really healthy stuff, so naturally it didn't taste that hot. And I wasn't very hungry anyway. I actually wasn't hungry at all. But I ate a little. I was feeling all dizzy and weak from being so scared and all. I thought some food would make me feel better. Or at least stronger.

As I picked at my fruit salad, I glanced across the table and noticed that Jeff was sitting a little bit to the left. I tried not to look at him, but the more I tried, the more I couldn't help but keep looking over at the damn fucking guy.

Jeff wasn't exactly staring at me. He just had this real steady gaze in my direction, and every time our eyes met, Jeff would lock right in with this really cold, dead-like expression. It made my heart race like crazy, and my head felt like it was gonna fucking explode or something.

I never really hated anybody before like I now hated Jeff.

I guess there had never been anyone before in my whole entire life who had had the power to totally fucking destroy me.

And Jeff had that power now.

And he was going to destroy me.

Thinking about it, I couldn't eat anymore. I just kind of sat back in my chair and pretended to listen to whatever Dave Patton, the team goalie who was sitting to my right, was saying.

Why did Jeff have to be such a fucking boy scout about everything? I always knew what he was like. I'd met his dad and saw them together at a half dozen games. His dad was a boy scout too. I knew that. All perfect and proper and fucking honorable and shit like that. Really heavy into the father and son routine. You know - Mr. Perfect and son. I knew that. Jeff was the campus ideal. He was president of his frat. He helped out in Campus Ministry and he even took up the goddamned collection plate at mass. And he was the president of Crimson Circle, the top men's service club on campus with the best scholars and the biggest shots who all dress up in these horrible dull red sweaters and go marching around the place all the time like a bunch of happy robot clowns.

What had I been thinking last night when I asked him to go with me? What the fuck was I thinking! We'd never been out alone together before.

I guess he'd been so bummed out by the memorial service for Kyle yesterday afternoon and all that corny shit that everybody was saying - he just wanted to forget it, and that's why he let me talk him into it.

Jeff didn't drink as much as I did last night, so he must have known what was coming. Why the fuck didn't he do anything! He could have stopped it. Why didn't he? He could have kept the whole fucking goddamned thing from happening! I know he could have. He must have known what was going to happen. Or, at least, what could have happened.

And now he's gonna ruin my whole fucking life.

I hate him!

Keeping my head down, I just tried to ignore Jeff as much as I could, concentrating all my attention on my scrambled eggs and bacon. Pretty soon the Director of Athletics, Dan Petrie, stood up and started carrying on about Kyle. He was this old guy with white hair who just stayed in his office all the time doing all the paperwork and crap for the department. Nobody really ever saw him at all, so every once in awhile when he did make these big phony public appearances, nobody really knew who the hell he was. He was going on and on about Kyle - you know - shoveling it on even thicker than old Bonner had. Fuck! It was sickening! His old voice was kind of choking and all, and I think there were even tears in his eyes. They looked all moist and everything. And that made some of the guys at the table start sniffing and wiping their eyes with their napkins. Fuck me! It was the worst crap you've ever seen.

I've never cried in my life. Not one fucking time! Never.

You should have seen all these guys two weeks ago when the coach got up in front of all of us in the weight room downstairs and told us about

Kyle. That he was dead. That he'd been hit by a car the night before. Shit! Everybody was screaming and crying and carrying on like the world had come to a fucking end. It was the most pathetic thing I've ever seen in my life. It actually turned my stomach. Even the coach was crying. Shit! Give me a break. What was the use? What good did all that crap do? Ya gotta move on. All these guys are so whipped. Ya gotta just get a grip and go on. What's the use of falling all apart? Ya gotta just go on.

When Petrie was all done and collapsed down into his chair, some guy that I'd never even seen before got up and made a speech about the power of teamwork and positive thinking and all that shit. Jesus Christ! He must have been dragged over from the Psychology Department or something.

Everybody was sort of finishing up eating and getting up and moving around, so I slowly went over and poured myself a glass of orange juice. Todd Andrews, the assistant coach of the soccer team, was standing close by and talking to this really old man.

Todd was a pretty good guy. He'd been a big star player on our team about five years ago, then he'd played pro on some German team in Europe for a couple of years, and now he was back here again working for Bonner. He still kind of looked and acted like a college guy - you know, in really good shape and all happy and friendly all the time. I guess that coach thing - that fat and flabby dictator thing - must not kick in until a few more years when they move up to the top spot and get all that power and ego stuff. But, so far, Todd was OK.

I sort of hung around for a minute waiting to talk to Todd. I thought it might make me feel better - maybe a little better. He was a pretty caring kind of guy and you could feel it when you talked to him. All the guys on the team usually took their problems to Todd, and they always said how much help he was. I never had, but somehow I just wanted to hang with him for a little bit this morning. You know - the armband bit and everything. I thought he might understand.

Pushing a little closer, I could hear what Todd was saying to this old guy who seemed to be some kind of reporter or something from a local newspaper.

"Kyle Martinsen was 21, a senior English major from Seattle," Todd was telling the guy. "He was an only child, so it's been extra rough on the parents. They'll be here this afternoon watching the game. It's dedicated in his honor."

The reporter guy was writing all this down and then asked Todd what kind of person Kyle was.

"He was a very rare kind of kid," Todd said in this calm, soft voice. "He was tall and blond and well-built and exceptionally handsome. A real manly kind of boy with a very kind and gentlemanly manner. He was sensitive to life and to other people. He always wanted everybody around him to be happy and to feel good. Girls loved him. You'd never see him without a girl hanging on him. Sometimes two or three. He was the kind of guy that girls adore. He'd always be riding around campus on his bicycle and you'd never see him without some girl riding on the handlebars. Everybody loved Kyle. He was just that kind of very gentle, very modest, tender-hearted kind of guy that everyone always loves."

Todd glanced to his left and noticed me standing there.

"Well - here's his best and closest friend," he said with a big smile as he motioned towards me with a nod of his head. "He can tell you a lot more about Kyle - about who he really was."

40

I felt my throat tighten and my face burn really hot.

"Naw - you said it all," I heard myself say in this weird kind of high voice.

I quickly moved away from them.

Christ! Saint Kyle. Can't everybody just get over him. They don't even know what the fuck they're talking about!

I went to the opposite side of the room where Coach Bonner had been sitting. He wasn't there now, so I felt pretty safe and relaxed. But all of a sudden I felt this huge hand come crashing down on my shoulder from behind me. I spun around and there was the fucking coach glaring down at me about a foot away from my face. He looked at me like I had just shot his mother.

"What happened yesterday?", he asked with this really mean growl.

"Huh?", was all I could think of saying, kind of biting down on my tongue and stiffening my back and bracing myself for when this human time bomb was gonna fucking go off.

"Where the hell were you! Why weren't you at the reception!"

I took this really big gulp of air and eyed the ceiling for what seemed like an hour, but was probably only a few seconds or so.

"I got sick," I sort of squeaked nervously.

"Sick! Bullshit! You weren't sick! What'a'ya mean you were sick! Since when were you ever sick!"

"It was my stomach," I weakly tried to explain, continuing on with the taco story and the barfing and all that fake shit.

But he wasn't buying it. Not a bit of it. And he kept getting more and more pissed the more I tried to explain. And no wonder. I wasn't even believing this phony crap myself. Fuck!

"I want you to know that you let every single member of the team down," Bonner announced in this really emotional tone, pretending like he was really hurt or something. "And you let me down. And you let the whole university community down. And especially Kyle's parents. You really let Mr. and Mrs. Martinsen down."

Shit! The world had caved in and everybody under the sun had had their damn hearts ripped out all on account of me - just because I didn't show up at some phony fucking slobber fest out on the cold, windy lawn.

"Yeah - well . . ", I nervously started to say.

"And where's your armband?", he kind of barked at me, glancing down at my naked left bicep.

"Uh . . "

"Where is it!"

"I don't have it," I mumbled, looking down at the floor.

"Why!"

"I didn't wear it."

"Why not! You have to wear it! Why aren't you?"

I didn't answer. I just kept staring down at the floor.

"Answer me!", Bonner shouted angrily, really getting so pissed that his face was turning this kind of bright red - you know, like this huge split open watermelon without the seeds. "Put it on right now! Right now!"

"I don't have it," I quickly replied, half holding my breath and getting ready for a nuclear explosion.

"Then go to the office right now and get another one!"

I don't know why I did it or what I was thinking, but I looked up from the floor and stared really calm-like straight into his tiny bloodshot eyes and I actually gave him this big, happy smile. He looked a little confused, but I'm sure he was expecting me to do exactly what he had commanded. After all, these tyrant types are always pretty used to calling all the shots and getting their own way.

"No," I said in a soft, quiet breath.

At first, the coach looked like he didn't understand what I had said. His forehead just sort of squashed into a hundred deep wrinkles and his jaw dropped to the side. I guess 'incredulous' - that's the word to describe him. He was totally incredulous. Then - mad as hell.

"No?," he sort of spit it out. "What'a'ya mean? That's an order! Go in and get one of those black armbands we made for Kyle and put it on! Right now, mister!"

"No," I calmly repeated, staring at him now like he was the enemy.

I honest to god thought that the fucking guy was either going to keel over dead or just dive right at my throat and rip my fucking head off with one twist. He was upset.

"Why?", he finally managed to gasp as if he were choking on something. "Why? Why won't you?"

That was a good sign. He was still alive and he still hadn't killed me. I was feeling stronger now. You know - more full of courage and all that bullshit. And my knees had even stopped shaking.

"I don't want to," I answered in this slow, firm voice. "I know all of you took this really big vote and you all decided to do it and that's OK for you if that's what you all want to do. But I don't want to. I don't want to anymore. I'm not going to. That's it. And don't keep asking me 'why'."

Bonner just kind of trembled and raised his right hand towards my face. I was dead sure he was about to punch me out. I think I must have frozen or something because I felt my body kind of pounding all over from

43

my hair to my toes. But he didn't hit me. He just gave me another one of his dead mother looks. This time with a pretty heavy dash of pure hatred.

"I could gut you out right here and now, kid - but I'm not going to. I'm not going to spoil this whole goddamned event here because of one ass- hole prick. Get back to your seat and just keep out of the way if you know what's good for you. I was gonna have you get up and give a little confi- dence speech before we started the film, but you can forget about all that now. You're a fucking disgrace to the team! I don't even want you in any- one's goddamned sight without that armband! So go sit the fuck down and keep the fuck quiet til everything's all over! And just a word to the wise, Pretty Boy! You wear that fucking armband at the game this afternoon, or you won't be playing! I won't even allow your ass on the field! You got that, asshole! No armband, no fucking game for you!"

"Fuck you!"

I don't which one of us was more amazed by my instant reply - him or me. I think it must have been him.

Bonner just stood there with an open mouth staring at me like he'd suddenly found out I was really a zombie. I walked back to my chair at the long table and sat down. I guess I should have felt all victorious and everything, but I didn't. I was actually feeling shittier than ever. I just wanted everything to be over. I guess there was no way it actually could have been, but all I wanted was for everything to just be finally over and ended and gone. It was getting harder and harder to go on.

All the guys at the table were talking about the game and a bunch of other lame crap. Nobody mentioned my missing armband until Chad Christoff called to me across the table. I tried to ignore him. But he was pretty impossible to ignore. He was one of these real campus big shots.

All the right friends, all the right clubs, good grades, the prettiest girlfriends. He wasn't really all that handsome, to tell you the truth. I mean, you could call him good looking, but in sort of the rough kind of way guys are often described. You know, really strong features and dark hair and all that. But what Chad did have was what every guy admired - this incredible body. Right off Muscle Beach, this guy. He could probably win a contest. But I mean, who couldn't - if they spent four hours a day in the weight room every fucking day of the week like Chad did. I mean, Fuck! Who wouldn't look like Mr. Universe spending half your fucking life pumping iron all the time.

"You miss the reception yesterday and now you're not even wearing the armband anymore?", Chad loudly called to me. "I thought you and Kyle were best buddies. Blood brothers and all that stuff. What gives? Was all that just an act? Just for team spirit?"

I didn't say anything.

"Niner didn't even cry two weeks ago when they told us Kyle was dead, that he'd been run over by that car," Marco butted into the thing with that real dumb-ass voice of his. "Niner didn't even cry. He didn't cry once. He was the only one who didn't. Everybody else cried."

"Big deal," I kind of snickered. "So what? So I didn't cry. I never cry. I've never cried once in my whole entire fucking life. I don't cry. My mom says I never even cried when I was a baby. My grandma died last year and I didn't cry. I just don't cry. End of fucking story!"

"Niner's a real poet," Jeff laughed sarcastically from down the table. "A real deep feeling guy. Real emotional type. Ask his girlfriends. Nothing bothers this guy. He can love 'em and leave 'em like nobody ya ever saw. Kyle was just another member of the team, far as Niner was concerned.

You're all making this huge fucking thing out of the fact that they just hung out together a lot. Kyle and Niner weren't that close at all. They probably didn't even like each other all that much."

"That's Number Nine," Josh added with a grin, "the Escape Artist. That's what we all call him. He always gets away with it. He always gets away. Nobody can hold him for long. Ask the girls. Even Beth. She'll probably get her walking papers pretty soon now. Good old Niner - the world's best damn escape artist."

I glared at him and he got the message and quit talking.

"Niner was probably jealous of Kyle," Reicher bellowed like an idiot. "Kyle was the only guy on campus who was even prettier than old pretty boy here. I bet Number Nine was kind of pissed about that

Everybody around me laughed and hooted.

"You guys are so full of shit!", I said all hot and upset. "And stop calling me that fucking nickname! It's old. It's over. I hate it now. No more 'Number Nine' or 'Niner'. I want to hear my own name. Nobody's called me by my real name in fucking ages. I want to hear my name again. Got it! Just only call me by my real name from now on!"

"Sure thing, Hortense," Reicher said all loud and serious-like.

"Yeah - anything ya say, Mortimer," Will laughed.

"You're the boss, Percival," Tom chimed in.

"Whatever ya want, Ambrose," Josh giggled.

"You're the man, Siegfried," Dave announced, slapping me on the shoulder with a real phony sincere look.

Then a chorus of these really weird, stupid names were shouted towards me from every direction. All I heard for the next minute or two was one dumb fucking bogus name after another -   Clyde, Sebastian,

Bartholomew, Ethelred, Jedediah, Methuselah. The best one was probably Marco's late entry - Rumplestiltskin. That was the one everybody laughed at the most and really latched onto.

Fuck! Why did I have to open my mouth! I never learn. I should have gone the opposite way and told them I loved my nicknames and begged them not to ever call me by my real name again. Then they would have called me by my real name from then on. You know how these fucking morons are. Anything to really pull your chain where it really gets ya good. They see a soft spot and they always go for the jugular. Fucking guys! I should have known.

"Hey, Rumplestiltskin," Christoff called across to me all happy-like. "I don't know why ya don't like hearing 'Niner' anymore. I'd think you'd be proud about it. Linda Johnson told me that all the girls know how ya got the name - and it has nothin' to do with the number on your soccer uniform, if ya know what I mean. All the girls you've been with traded notes and they all agreed that it was the perfect nickname for you."

Everybody cracked up and made these really gross sounds, whistling and hooting and stuff. What a bunch of jerks.

"Yeah - I heard the same thing from your old girlfriend Joan Perez," Will said in this really snarky superior tone. "I'd think you'd be all happy about it. Ya know what they say - 'It pays to advertise.' "

Cute! No comment.

There were some more catcalls and hoots, and then the lights went down, and the screen on the far wall lit up and Coach Bonner started loudly honking about the fantastic soccer film we were about to see. He did this dumb thing every time we had an important game. He showed his collection of DVD's of the best college soccer matches in the history of the world. One boring game after another. Today it was Stanford versus Berkeley from like twenty-five years ago. Jesus! Why not sit back and study the maps from the Battle of Gettysburg or something? Ancient history. Who gives a shit!

As the game started playing out on the soiled, torn screen, Bonner stood to the side and began pointing all excited-like and commenting on every move, criticizing all the mistakes and bad plays, kind of like he was a tall, fat Napoleon or something.

I wasn't really watching the video. I was noticing Jeff across the table. He wasn't watching either. He was looking at me. Staring at me.

I couldn't really see the expression in Jeff's eyes. It was pretty dark in the room. But I could feel it. I could feel what Jeff was thinking and what he was feeling. It made my stomach knot up and my heart race like shit.

And he kept staring at me.

Leaning all nervous-like back in my chair, I could tell that nobody was really paying much attention to Bonner's excited little lecture. And only a few guys were even looking at the screen. Ted Ainsley, who was sitting on the other side of Dave, started talking to him in this really loud whisper and I could hear every word he was saying.

"Kyle's dad was talking to President Hawkins yesterday at the reception," Ted was saying all-important-like. "He was talking about the accident. How it happened. What the truck driver said."

"Yeah?", Dave was all ears.

"The guy said that Kyle was jogging right there in the street. Not even near the sidewalk. He was right out there in the street. Two other cars almost hit him before the truck driver guy ran over him. He said Kyle just ran right into the front of his truck. The guy couldn't understand it. Kyle just ran right out there in front of his truck, all of a sudden-like."

I closed my eyes and bit down on my tongue. I didn't want to hear this. I didn't want to hear any of this shit. But they kept talking and I couldn't help hearing them.

"That's crazy," Dave said, so loud that the guys at the front of the table all looked back towards us. "He NEVER jogged in the street before. I ran to his place in the Marina and back with him dozens of times. It was our favorite run. Ask anybody. We always ran on the sidewalk. He never ran in the street. Shit! Lincoln Boulevard! At rush hour! Who the hell would jog out there in the street? You'd have to want to kill yourself to do a crazy thing like that. Jogging in the traffic on Lincoln at rush hour. That would be suicide. Suicide!"

"Shut the fuck up!", I yelled, jumping up from my chair and angrily balling my right hand. "Just shut the fuck up!"

The room went totally silent.

I took this long, trembling breath and just went storming off out of the room, slamming the door really loud as I left.

10:43 am

I quickly walked back to my room to get all my books and stuff. Sitting down on my bed, I looked at the pine trees outside the window for almost twenty minutes. Then I hurried off to my American History class at eleven in Seaver Hall. There was a big test today that I never got around to studying for. I was still telling myself that somehow I was going to get through it OK.

I was crossing the quad next to the Desmond dorm when I noticed Megan McCarthy coming out the door of Whelan Hall.

Megan was in my history class and was like the best student in the whole fucking school. I knew her just a little. Mainly from hanging around in the Lair and from a philosophy class I had with her last year.   A real brainiac.   She was a film major and wanted to make documentaries or something like that. A real quiet girl. A junior, I think. You know the type - they're all alike. Decent looking enough, but kind of plain and all prim and proper. The tight ass kind. Never go to parties. Never have fun. Just study, study, study. But nice. A really nice person. And I was hoping she could help me with the history test, so I put it in overdrive and sprinted up to her.

"Hey, Megan - can I walk ya to class?", I asked her with this real big, fake smile.

"Sure," she answered, all sort of surprised-like.

"Ready for the test?", I cranked up the sex appeal stuff to the max.

"Yes," she said a little uneasily as she glanced up into my eyes. "I've been studying for days. I think I'm ready. I hope so."

My god!, I thought to myself. How was it possible for anybody to study for days! Get a life, why don't ya! Shit!

"That's great," I said. "But I didn't get a chance to. You know, with soccer practice and all that. I hope it's all stuff I already know."

"I think she's going to ask us mostly about the Reynolds book and the essays by Stevenson."

"Reynolds? Stevenson?"

Shit! I didn't even bother to buy them, let alone read them.

"Yes," Megan said kind of shyly, looking up at me with this warm, soft expression. "I read them twice and took notes on every page. I don't think it will be a very difficult test. But it does count for a third of our grade."

I didn't say anything. I just kept walking with her and trying to smile. She was still looking at me with that kind of goofy look. That's the way a lot of girls look at me. I'm kind of use to it by now. But usually they toss a bit of sex into it - you know, some hot energy into the thing. Their eyes usually have a kind of invitation in them, whether they know it or not. It's just all part of the chemistry thing.

But Megan was so shy and reserved and up-tight that there wasn't anything hot or sexy in the way she looked at me. Not at all. She just kind of looked at me the way my mom does sometimes - like on her birthday when I give her a present. The more we walked and I kept looking down at her, the more she looked OK. I mean, the prettier she looked. Not beautiful. Don't get me wrong. She wasn't a beauty. Not in the least. But she was kind of pretty. Hardly any make-up. Just real fresh and clean and all sort of natural looking. I was beginning to like her.

We'd gone down the steps and were walking along the path in the Sunken Garden. It was a really beautiful morning. The wind had been blowing kind of gently from the east for the past day or so. They called it the Santa Ana wind, and it was this really warm, dry breeze that made the air so clear that the mountains looked like you could reach out and touch them. I always loved it. Every time it blew in from the desert, I felt really

51

great - all full of energy and just aching to have an orgasm every time I took a deep breath of that dry air. I wondered right then if Megan felt like that too. I kind of doubted it.

"Have you decided if you're going to go on to law school?", she asked me a bit awkwardly, like she was a little anxious or something.

"Naw. I don't think it's gonna happen. I gave up that dream a long time ago. The grades kind of killed all that."

"Oh - that's too bad," she said with this real genuine concern that kind of surprised me.

"How did you know I planned to be a lawyer? I haven't bullshitted about that since I was a sophomore."

"I heard you telling Alexandra Walker once in the Lair about how you wanted to go to Harvard Law like your stepfather did. You were sitting at the table next to me. You had your hair cut real short then because it was just after you started working as a lifeguard at the pool."

Fuck! What was this chick doing? Having the FBI following me around and making special goddamned files on me or something?

"Well," I said with one hell of a snickering laugh, "I've got about as much chance of going to Harvard Law now as I do flying to Mars and back. There's just no fucking way."

As soon as I said it, I felt really shitty. Most of the girls I know and hang out with say 'fuck' all the time. Well, maybe not all the time, but some of the time. A lot of the time. And they damn well expect to hear it from you and the other guys all the time. Even Beth says it whenever she's excited or mad. It's no big deal. But there are some girls and women that you don't say it around. You just don't swear around them. You know - it's kind of like the same way you don't swear around your mom. I don't know why. That's just how it is. And Megan kind of reminded me of my mom, so I was feeling all guilty and everything that I had just said 'fucking' to her.

"I'm sorry," I apologized. "That just slipped out."

"That's OK," she said very shyly and quietly. "Almost everybody talks like that. You should hear how the girls in my apartment talk. I just don't say those words because I don't like to. It just seems like it's a lot nicer if I don't. I like it better. The bad words really don't mean anything. It's just mainly how they sound and why they're being used. The reason behind them. That's what's not so nice sometimes. But they're really only words. Sounds, really. Unpleasant sounds."

Wow. That was the most I'd ever heard her talk. She was totally off on a tare. I was really surprised. But it was kind of neat. Really neat.

"Yeah, you're right," I was all excited-like. "That's exactly what I always thought. It's just noise - just sound. That's all. It's not even words. Not words that mean anything. At least not the way they're always being used and all. Everybody's going around all the time saying fuck, fuck, fuck, fuck, fuck. Every goddamned sentence is 'I fucking did the fuck this last fucking night at this fucking party where these fuckers were having a great fucking time at this fucking great house.' I hate it! I really hate hearing the word 'fuck' all the time. I wish they'd all stop it. I really fucking do!"

Megan had stopped walking for a moment and was looking at me with this almost stunned-like expression. It was pretty funny. She looked like she was completely confused and didn't know what was happening. I guess I'd over-done it with dropping the F-bomb so many times in a row. I was only trying to give her a good example of how some of these morons on the soccer team talk. But I guess maybe I did over-do it a bit. She really looked stunned.

"Uh - so you get what I'm sayin'?", I kind of quietly added, feeling a bit like a jerk. "Everybody says it way too much. It doesn't mean anything anymore when you hear it - you know, that word I was talking about - the 'F" word. You see what I mean?"

"Yes, of course," she sort of breathlessly replied. "I understand completely. The excessive and redundant usage of that word is very unpleasant and unintelligent. I agree with you."

Megan had this really pale, kind of Irish-like complexion, and I could tell she was blushing. Embarrassed, I guess. Couldn't blame her. I'm always doing stupid stuff like this. Talking before I think. My mom is always telling me that I'm impulsive. It drives her nuts. Always has.

Starting to walk again, we came to the other end of the Sunken Garden and began climbing the steps of Regents Terrace. People I knew kept walking by us and giving me some kind of greeting. Some of them shot me this real questioning kind of look, like 'What the hell are you doing with her? or "Why are you walking the dog?" I didn't care, but Megan noticed a couple of their weird expressions when they gave me the secret eye, and I think it must have hurt her feelings. And it kind of really made me feel uncomfortable and a little bad, because she's a nice girl and I don't like nice people to feel hurt. Not nice ones like Megan.

"They probably wonder why you're walking with me and not with Beth," she said in almost a whisper, looking sort of all sensitive and everything.

"Oh, I don't walk with Beth all the time. I walk with lots of different girls."

"Yeah - I see you walking with them. They're usually the prettiest girls on campus. Not ones like me."

"What'a'ya mean? You're pretty. You're really pretty. You should see the way the sun is shining on your red hair."

Megan kind of froze still, then glanced up at me with this look that I really can't describe. I think maybe you might call it 'electric' - like she was suddenly lit up all inside, because she was really happy and feeling all this other hopeful stuff. I don't know. But it kind of made me nervous when I first saw it. Very uneasy and guarded.

Then, I got this flash of an idea.

It seemed my only chance, and I wasn't sure if it would work or not, so I suggest we sit down for a couple of minutes on the recessed stone bench in the center of the terrace and I tried really fast to think how I could get things to work out.

I didn't say anything for a few moments and just stared straight ahead across the wide lawn of the Sunken Garden at the Sacred Heart Chapel directly across the way and the clock on its tall bell tower. It was almost eleven, so I didn't have much time for a lot of salesmanship.

But I pretty much had the basic idea, so I ran with it.

I turned and looked right into Megan's light blue eyes, and what I saw convinced me that my idea was gonna be a winner. Her eyes were fastened onto mine like glue, and if you were walking by and happened to give her face a quick once-over, you would've been convinced she had just won the lottery. Tax free!

"I sure am worried about that history test," I began, fixing her with my very best seductive smile. "Like I said, I didn't have a chance to study. I'm sure I'm gonna flunk it. And if I flunk it, I'm gonna flunk the whole damn class. I just don't know what I'm gonna do. If only there was some way someone could help me. I really need help."

Megan seemed really taken in, I mean - deeply concerned by what I'd said. She thought for several seconds, actually wrinkling her brow and doing all that serious expression kind of facial stuff.

"Maybe you could talk to Dr. Thompson and explain your dilemma and maybe she could . . . "

"Naw," I gave a really good snicker. "That'd never work. No way. She hates me. She'd never help me."

"Why do you say she hates you?", Megan asked all innocent-like. "Why would she hate you? I don't know anybody that hates you."

That winning-lottery-ticket-look was back in her eyes again. It really stoked up my confidence. I knew I was gonna be able to pull it off.

"I think she must be a lesbian," I matter-of-factly explained. "I could tell the first day of class by how she looked at me. You know - glaring at me when I smiled at her and refusing to look at me when I wore my soccer shorts to class. Stuff like that."

"But she's married. I'm pretty sure she's married."

"To a man?"

"Yes. I think she said he was an engineer."

"Uh," I tried to quickly change gears, "well, then, maybe she's in love with me, then. Maybe that's it. It's something weird - you can bet on that. She hates me, though. I can feel it. I'm a pretty sensitive guy. I can tell."

"But if you talked to her and explained . . "

"Won't work," I interrupted her real firm and all. "Not in a million years. You're the one. You're the only one, Megan. You're the only one who can help me. Save me."

Wow! Those words were like magic. She was totally hooked.

I had tossed in my hottest smile - a smile that had always gotten me almost anything I'd ever wanted in life. I mean, I have to tell the truth. It's the best smile you'll probably ever see in your life. Girls have always told me it's irresistible. They say I have these gorgeous lips and beautiful, perfect white teeth that sort of almost glow when I give a big smile. I have to confess, I look at it in the mirror all the time and I can really see what they're all talking about. It's pretty overwhelming. When I talk to myself in the mirror, even I would be willing to do anything for that guy I see in there looking and smiling back at me.

"But . . . what can I do?", Megan said kind of really all uneasy-like. "I don't think Dr. Thompson will listen to me. I don't know her that well. I mean, we're not friends. Did you want me to try to talk to her anyway?"

"Naw - that wouldn't help. Like I told ya, she hates me. You can't reason with somebody like that."

"Then . . what can I do?", she asked all worried-like. "I could have helped you study. But it's too late for that now. The test is in ten minutes."

I took a deep, silent breath and prepared to give one of the best performances of all time. I made my eyes fill up with this really sad, helpless, lost expression. And I strained my eyes to moisten them up a little and, honest to god, a drop of water magically spilled out of my left eye and slowly sort of slid down my cheek. If I'd been playing some tragic scene in some dopey chick-flick movie, I couldn't have done it any better.

"You can save me," I said in this tender, almost begging voice. "You're the only one that can, Megan. The only one. I'm in your hands now, Megan. Just this one time, and never again - if you could just let me see your paper during the exam. You know this stuff backwards and forwards. You'll probably be done with the test in half the time. If you could just somehow pass me your essay and let me copy your answers."

She looked really shocked. I mean, sincerely - not phony or anything. Just truly shocked by what I'd asked.

"You're kidding," she said in this kind of scared, shaking little whimper. "You're joking, aren't you? You can't be serious."

"I'm afraid I am. It's the only way. If I flunk this exam, I'll flunk the course. And tomorrow my folks are coming to talk to the Dean with me, and I already have one foot out the door of this place. Flunking the test today will guarantee the permanent disappearance of old Number Nine from this campus forever."

"But you're a senior. You graduate in May. They couldn't kick you out now. Not now. And what about the soccer team? You're the best player. Surely they'll consider that."

"Nope. It's Aloha on a steel guitar for little Niner if I flunk this history test. Adios muchacho. So long, farewell. End of story. That's all he wrote. Bon Voyage, to me."

Megan stared at me with this really completely helpless, crushed expression. The old 'your dog has just died' look, as Marco always calls it.

"I want to help you," she said in this funny kind of tortured tone. "I really do. More than anything. But that would be cheating. Dishonest."

"Yeah, I know," I replied in this even more tortured sounding groan, burying my face in my hands. "Don't you think it's tearing me apart to even consider doing such a bad thing? It's cheating. That's what it is. And I never in my whole life thought I'd ever cheat on a test. But, now. This is different. I have no choice. It's sink or swim. My whole survival depends on this. I want to survive, Megan. I don't want to sink and drown. I don't want to have the plug pulled on my whole life. Megan - won't you help me? Won't you help me survive and live on? Please, Megan. You're the only one who can help me. Please save me, Megan."

Jesus! I was really pouring it on thick. I kind of even surprised myself. When I was a freshman I kind of thought for awhile that I wanted to be an actor. I even changed my major in the second semester to Theater Arts. But my stepdad sort of talked me out of that. He thought my talent for seducing and conning people would be put to better use if I became a lawyer like him. But now I was really wondering if I had made the right choice. I really did seem to have quite a knack for this acting thing. I think the job I was doing right here could have easily won me an Oscar, had somebody from Hollywood been hanging around here with a movie camera.

Megan was just sort of staring into space. It looked like her mind was totally blown away. Jesus! I didn't mean to really shock her or anything. I was beginning to worry that I had wiped out one of her circuits or something. Girls can be really silly and all sensitive sometimes. You really have to watch out. I think I really hit a nerve.

The chimes in the bell tower across the way started ringing. It was eleven o'clock. I stood up kind of slowly and gazed at the top of the tower. I always do that when I can. I love those chimes. I think I like them more than anything else at the university. I forget what they call them, but some priest told me that they played the same melody that Big Ben plays. You know Big Ben - that huge clock over there on that big church in England somewhere. Really beautiful to listen to. Of course, here on campus there aren't really bells or chimes up there in the tower. It's some kind of record or tape that some guy puts on and plays, and if you get close to the base of the tower, you can look up and see all the loud speakers they have up there sticking out at the top. Pretty phony. But it sounds pretty much the same as that church in England, I suppose. Least it's always sounded great to me. I love it. I always stop what I'm doing if I can, and I just stand there looking at the clock when it chimes the hour and the quarters.

Megan was still sitting on the bench and kind of looking like she was in a daze. I wasn't sure if I'd won or lost. I was hoping that after a little time had passed she might be able to wrap her mind around the idea of helping me cheat.

"We better get to class," I very quietly told her.

She got up without a word and we began walking up the four steps to the second level of Regents Terrace.

"I don't know what to say," she finally said in this real timid and nervous voice.

I instantly decided that I'd have to move in for the kill.

"I'm sorry," I painfully stammered, looking all disappointed and full of shame. "I apologize. I shouldn't have asked you. I mean, it's not like you're Beth or anybody. It's not like you really like me or anything. You see, just because I really like you, I . . I just was kind of hoping that you liked me. I don't know why. I don't know why you should like me a lot. I mean, I'm not nearly as smart as you or anything. Why should you?"

I was watching her out of the corner of my eye.

Bulls eye!

Jackpot!

It hit the mark exactly!

"But I do like you," she said very softly. "I like you a lot. And I want to help you. I really do. But this? Uh - let me think about it for a few minutes."

"We don't have much time," I anxiously reminded her.

"Let me think. Let's just walk on to class and I'll think about it."

"OK. I trust you, Megan. I know you'll help me all ya can."

Picking up our pace a little, we continued walking across the terrace and off into the Alumni Mall, pushing past a pretty heavy crowd of kids hurrying this way and that. Dozens of people were tossing me greetings, but almost everybody was on their cellphones or iPods and no one was really up for stopping and talking to us.

"You don't have a cellphone or anything?", Megan turned and curiously asked me. "You're the first person I've walked with in a long time who didn't have a ringing phone or didn't check their messages."

"I left it back in my room. Where's your phone and stuff?'

"I don't have one, " she said kind of embarrassed-like.

"No cellphone? Really?

"No. I don't like them."

"iPod? Nothing?"

"I have a laptop in my backpack," she smiled shyly. "That's all. It's enough. I don't like the feeling of machines completely controlling my life. I like to feel free. That must sound kind of weird to you."

"Yeah," I said with surprise. "I mean, NO - not at all. That's neat."

"Really?"

"Yeah. I kind of feel that way too a lot of the time. I feel like I'm a slave to all this electronic crap. I mean, it never lets up. All the time. Your brain just melts like a chunk of ice cream. It never lets ya rest. I swear to god, I think it can really drive you crazy - all the time like that. But every-body else has everything they make - so you kind of gotta. Or you're total-ly out of it - a real loser. Oh - sorry - you're not a loser. I didn't mean to say that. It must take a ton of courage not to do it - to not go along with it like that. I really admire you, Megan. I really do."

And I really meant it. I did admire her. She was kind of out of it on campus, but sometimes I wished that I could be out of it too. Being cool and all hip didn't make me as happy as I always thought it would. I don't know why. It seemed like some kind of fast race I had entered when I was in high school back home, and I had always been ahead and winning the race. But now that I was thinking about it, I don't think it had ever made me feel happy. In fact, just the opposite. What was I winning? What? I really started thinking about it as we walked past the Foley Pond and headed toward Seaver Hall.

We stopped for a moment to let the crowd of student headed into Seaver pass by. All of a sudden I felt a hand take hold of my left arm. I spun around and was face to face with Jeff.

FUCK!

He was just standing there freezing me with this horrible, evil stare.

Christ! I remember my freshman theology class when Fr. O'Connor had described how god was present everywhere at once. He said that god was 'ubiquitous' - meaning that god was always present front and center wherever you went, wherever you were. That's what I was thinking right now. That Jeff was ubiquitous. Just like god. An evil kind of god. A god who was out to get me - to destroy me. To completely destroy me.

I sort of felt like I had jumped out of my skin. In fact, I half expected to find a big bunch of my hide piled behind me like a stack of dirty laundry.

I was that shocked and afraid when I suddenly saw him like that. But then he turned and gave this really nice, warm smile at Megan, and, for some reason, I felt a little better. You know, kind of protected-like by her.

"Hi Jeff," she said, returning his very friendly smile. "How are you?"

"I couldn't be better," he happily replied, shifting his focus back to me with a really cold, threatening glare. "Today's going to be a very important day. Maybe a historic day."

I took a really hard swallow and looked away from him toward the pond. A big Mallard duck was swimming near the center of the water.

"Oh, you mean the soccer game," Megan said brightly. "It is an important game, isn't it. For the league championship or something?"

Jeff gave this huge weird grin that I noticed out of the corner of my eye.

"Or something," he repeated with this creepy, hard tone. "Yeah. It's going to be a very important day."

"Good luck this afternoon with the game," Megan sort of cheerfully added, not really knowing what else to say. Kind of awkward-like.

"Thanks," Jeff casually replied, beginning to move on, but reaching out and taking me really hard by my forearm and fixing me with this deadly gaze. "See you tonight, Pretty Boy. See you at midnight."

I couldn't breath for several seconds.

He walked off whistling a happy little tune that sounded like something out of a Disney movie.

"What did he mean by that?", Megan asked me with a bit of curiosity. "Tonight? At midnight?"

"Oh, my friends are throwing me a party tonight at the Bird Nest. Tomorrow's my 21st birthday. You know - big deal and all. I'll be legal."

"Oh, well, Happy Birthday."

"Thanks. Uh - I didn't know you knew Jeff."

"We had a film class together last year. He's a really good student.
We had a study group together. He's a very nice boy."

"Yeah," I kind of acidly agreed, bitting down on my tongue. "He's a
real prince."

"Both he and Kyle Martinsen were in the class, " she very sensitively
added. "I meant to tell you how sorry I was about Kyle. That was so tragic. I know you two were best friends. I'm so sorry. It must have been so
awful for you.   I was going to go to the memorial service yesterday, but
they said . . . "

"Yeah," I said sharply, cutting her off. "We better get going to class.
We're gonna be late."

We went up the steps of Seaver and into the building. Room 100
was right next to the entrance door. It was kind of an auditorium-like classroom with these wooden theater-like seats that spread back on a gentle
incline. It was usually used for science classes, but there were so many
kids taking this required American History class, I think around sixty, that it
had been scheduled here.

I hesitated by the side of the door and looked lovingly at Megan.

"Well?", I whispered with as much emotion as I could muster.

Megan looked like a wounded deer. She dropped her head and bit
down on her lip.

"What . . do you want me to do?", she whispered almost painfully.

"Write your answers as quick as you can, then wait until I give you
the signal, then just reach down really low and pass your paper to me.

We'll sit next to each other. I'll go in first and find a good place in the back, and then you come in and sit next to me. Got it?"

"Yes," she said with this awful look on her face, kind of like she was about to walk to the electric chair.

It made me feel really bad when I saw her reaction. Really bad. I almost said 'forget it', but I couldn't.

I tried to give her one of my best smiles, but I think it must have been a little weak, because I was nervous and not feeling very good about myself right then. I didn't like myself very much when I glanced over at Megan and she didn't return my smile.

Streams of kids were filing into the auditorium, so I just gave Megan a very appreciative nod of my head and walked off into the large room. I took a seat as far back as I could. It was three seats in from the left aisle, and I sat down and pulled up the arm of the swinging desk top, and I just sort of waited there feeling like an idiot.

Fuck! I felt like a total asshole. Why did I ask Megan to help me cheat? What did it matter? A stupid history grade? What was the point? Compared to what I was facing with Jeff and Beth, a grade in a class couldn't have mattered less. I mean, come on! Who cares what the fuck I got in American History 220 when I'm sitting there in prison for the rest of my life, or slaving night and day in some dark salt mine to support a kid I don't want. Fuck! Give me a break! This all felt just so insane.

I looked towards the right entrance door and saw Megan entering the room. She glanced around until she finally saw me, then started hiking up the incline of the sloping floor to where I was staked out. For every test, Dr. Thompson had us sit one seat apart from each other so that nobody could copy anybody else's answers. Jesus Christ! A real trusting soul that

Dr. Thompson. A true believer in the honesty and the goodness of her fellow man.

When Megan slowly approached me, she almost looked like she was gonna cry or something. Really upset inside. I tried not to show that I noticed her, so I kind of stared straight ahead at the huge blackboard on the front wall of the auditorium. But I made a really dumb mistake. As Megan sat down in the seat one down from me, I automatically reached over and helped her take off her heavy backpack and place it on the floor. I couldn't help myself. That's just how I am. I think the word for it is 'gallant'. You know, like those old knights who were always doing all that polite crap for women. It's just how I was raised, I guess.

But Thompson was glaring right up at us when I did it. She was watching. And she seemed really suspicious. I could see it on her face. Her hard, pointy witch's face that made her look like a wooden puppet. It might have been my guilty conscience that made me think she knew what was up, but I don't think so. She always seemed to know the score. She wasn't a dope. And she hated me. No matter how much I tried to sweet talk her during the semester and flash her my sexiest smiles, the bitch never once let me get away with any shit. She was impossible! It was just all so unfair.

Marching up to the blackboard, Dr. Thompson loudly called the class to order and instructed two students to pass a stack of test papers down each row. I took a copy and passed one over to Megan. As the professor announced that we had fifty minutes to complete our two essays, I started reading the first question. Jesus Christ! It said, "Write 500 words describing how the philosophy of 'Manifest Destiny' influenced the 19th Century physical metamorphosis of the United States."

Jesus Christ! What the hell! 'The philosophy'? This wasn't a god-damned philosophy class! It's a history class! What the fuck was this lesbian doing asking me about some fucking philosophy stuff? Christ!

I stared at the question and kept repeating it to myself again and again. I just couldn't even begin to make any sense out of it. Peeking up at Megan and the other kids around me, I noticed that everyone was furiously writing away. Jesus!

I was ready to just throw in the towel and try to wait for a chance to copy the information in Megan's essay, but Thompson was standing up there and gazing all crazy-like at us like she was trying to spot a fire or something.   If she kept doing that, then I'd never have a chance to get ahold of Megan's paper and cheat. Life can be so unfair!

The word 'philosophy' did kind of help me a little. It made me think of the class in Ethics I had last year with Dr. Blystone. He was a word nut. That guy loved words - especially the origins of them - where words came from. I remember him saying that you could kind of study and take apart any word and know what it meant by seeing the parts of other words that were in it.

Uh - yeah - I know - it's really confusing. But if you do it slowly, it kind of makes sense. You know - just take the word 'woman'. It's 'wo' put together with 'man'. So - if you didn't know what a 'woman' was, all you had to do was study the two parts of the word. So, what'a'ya get? A 'woman' is a 'man' with a 'wo', which is short for 'womb'. So - a woman is actually just a man with a womb. That's the origin of the word, and if you break it down like that you can really understand what the word 'woman' means. A man with a womb.

Thinking about that made me think I could figure out what these words 'Manifest Destiny' meant. I already knew what 'destiny' meant. You know, it's like fate or what's meant to be. Karma, and all that stuff. So I was already half way there. It really encouraged me. And 'manifest', that wasn't so hard. There was 'man' and 'fest'. It was simple. I know, of course, what a man is, and I know what a 'fest' is. So - it means that guys like me are having some kind of fest, or festival. It was as easy as that. I thought about it a little and figured the whole thing out in no time.

'Manifest Destiny' - a bunch of guys just hanging around having this festival, like that thing they have in Germany every year where they drink all that beer. Something just like that. A tradition. It was the tradition here in America for all the guys to just always sit around and drink and celebrate and stuff, and that was their destiny - what was meant to be.

Yeah. Manifest Destiny - what the good old USA was always meant to be - just a bunch of guys sitting around drinking beer and watching football games on TV and just hanging and enjoying themselves. That was 'Manifest Destiny'. The pioneers probably thought it all up and just passed it on down the line til that's what eventually made our country great.

I quickly started writing my essay.

I'd written a whole paragraph before I glanced up again and saw Thompson kind of pick up her purse and straighten her spine. And that was quite a sight. She already always looked like she had a whole broomstick crammed up her ass, so when she really stiffened up, it was a pretty awesome thing to see.

Hesitating for a moment, she suddenly made a dash out the front left door. Ah - it had all the signs of an uncontrollable bathroom break. Nature called, Thompson couldn't say no, and now lucky Number Nine was sitting there as free as the air and ready to be handed Megan's essay totally sight unseen. Nobody there to witness the deed. Perfect!

I cleared my throat and stretched out my right arm and looked over at Megan. She glanced up at me with this weird kind of fearful look, then noticed Thompson was gone from the room and took a hard, sort of trembling swallow and lowered her paper down beneath her desk and very smoothly handed it over to me.

Quickly and firmly taking it, I slid it up to the top of my desk and began copying all of the facts that she had written down. Megan's handwriting was really clear and really neat and precise, so it was really easy to read it real fast and write down all her ideas.

I have to say, I was really surprised and disappointed when I read her first answer. I thought maybe Megan had kind of goofed up. Her idea of what 'Manifest Destiny' meant was nothing like what I had come up with. Nothing. I wondered if she had really understood the question. She was totally off on this crazy tangent about this and that, and about what people way back when believed the geographical size of the United States was meant to eventually be. I mean, crazy, confused crap like that.

But I had to put my money on Megan. She was the brainiac. She was in the Honors Society. She had straight 'A's. I wasn't gonna argue with all that. So I crossed out my essay and began trying to write it again just like Megan's - with all her weird ideas and strange facts.

I was really breezing away and feeling all happy and pleased when suddenly I felt really uneasy - like something was moving close to me.

I jerked my head around, and there standing in the aisle right behind me and Megan was Dr. Thompson. She had this evil look on her ugly face.

I instantly stopped writing, and I nervously put my pen down.

Before I could even think about what was happening, Thompson clutched out her hand like a claw and yanked up the two papers on my desk.

She stared very carefully at the two essays for several seconds, then held them tightly to her side and kind of crumpled them up in her big, meaty paw. She just kept looking down at us with these sad, kind of evil eyes.

"F", she said very sharply as she glared down at Megan. "And I'm very disappointed in you."

Then she fixed me with an even nastier look.

"F", she repeated with almost a streak of disgust in her voice. "And I'm NOT disappointed in you."

What the hell did she mean by that!

Thompson took a deep, painful breath and began walking away from us, our papers tightly in her grip. Then she turned back.

"Please leave the room," she said firmly and kind of angry-like. "Now. Both of you."

Megan picked up her backpack and I gathered up all my crap and we slowly walked down the aisle and out the door. I could feel my face burning and a hard lump in my throat, and Megan looked like she was gonna cry.

This was all I needed today. Everything seemed to be turning to shit. Everything!

As I walked out of the classroom with Megan, I could feel everyone's eyes on us. It was awful. I thought Megan was really gonna break down crying. She had tears running down her face, and she was taking these huge gulps of air. We both were moving as fast as we could. We just wanted to get the hell out of there.

I guess I really didn't mind flunking that much. I really didn't give a fuck about the whole fucking world right now. To tell you the truth, I was almost glad I was failing American History 220. Fuck it! I can graduate without it. My step-dad always fixes everything. He's got a lot of pull around here. He has two good friends on the Board of Regents here at the university. All he has to do is make a few calls. It always works like a charm.

The only really bad part of it is that I have to get all this shit from him and my mom and the Dean. They yell and threaten and make me feel like something that slithered in under the door. Like I'm just some totally hope-less fuck-up. But I always just sit there and take it and try to think of some-thing else - like being in Hawaii at the beach or fucking my girlfriend up in her apartment. And it usually works pretty good. I don't really mind all their angry threats and insults and put-downs. Not really that much. Not too much, I guess.

Exiting the door of Seaver Hall, Megan and I slowed down as we walked down the steps and headed over to the Alumni Mall. It was a little warmer now and the sun was hot and bright and it was more beautiful than ever outside there in the open. I think they call that 'irony.'

When we silently crossed to the other side of the mall, i decided it was time to say something to her. I was hoping she had gotten a grip and wouldn't start throwing a crying fit or anything, now that a few minutes had passed and we were sort of standing out there in the sunshine next to the flowers and everything. I was sure trying to figure out what to say to her. I really liked Megan. She was a really neat girl. She'd really tried to help me. And, now, thanks to me, she flunked the exam too and was called a cheater in front of the whole world. I hated myself for having done that to her. I really felt like a total piece of shit for what I had done. More than anything, I wish I could have taken the whole crazy thing back.

It was like I had some kind of poison inside of me. I was poison to people. First Kyle, then Beth, then that guy last night, and now Megan, who probably never did anything wrong in her life.

"Megan," I kind of nervously said in this real gentle tone, "I feel so crappy about this. It was all my fault. I never should have asked you to do it. You didn't want to, but I almost forced you to. I'll talk to Dr. Thompson and tell her it was all my fault. I'll just tell her that I grabbed your paper and you couldn't do anything about it without making a racket. I'm really sorry, Megan. Can you ever forgive me?"

She was looking down. After about a minute or so, she took the back of her hand and sort of wiped her eyes and her face. Then she gave this choking kind of cough and drew in a long, trembling breath of air.

"Yes - I forgive you," she said kind of real casual-like.

It sort of amazed me. I never thought she would. Oh, maybe some day she would. Good people like that usually always do forgive you sooner or later, but I never expected that Megan would forgive me right now - only a few minutes after she'd been crushed like that because of me.

Holy shit!

I sat down on the brick bench in the middle of the mall and just looked up at her. Her red hair was really shining now in the strong sunlight and she really did look pretty. Almost beautiful, in fact.

She seemed like she didn't know what to do - whether she should just walk off and leave me there or stick around for awhile. I got the feeling she wanted to stay, but wasn't sure if I wanted her to. So I kind of nodded at the space next to me on the bench, and she sort of slowly lowered herself down, about two feet away from me.

I didn't know what the hell we were going to fucking talk about. I mean, how many times can I say I'm sorry, and I was still feeling so bad for what I had done to her that I was almost too ashamed to look her in the eyes. I felt like the prize asshole of all time, even tough she has forgiven me and everything.

"Thompson must have gone around and come in the back door," I said sort of bitterly. "I forgot Seaver 100 had that damned back door there on the left. It's usually locked. She must have a key. How sneaky can ya get! Talk about dishonesty and cheating. Pretending to go to the bathroom and then circling around for an ambush. She loves going in for the kill. I told ya she hates me. Talk about unfair!"

"Is this going to hurt your chances on the soccer team?", she asked me real quiet-like, seeming all concerned about it. "Will you be able to stay on the team? Sometimes some of the sports teams take these things very seriously. I remember last spring Dave Kenney was caught cheating in one of his classes and they kicked him off the baseball team."

I gave this bitter little smile.

"Dave was just a so-so player," I sort of numbly explained. "They really didn't need him anyway. He wasn't the captain of the team or the best player like I am. They need me. They won't do anything."

"Do you really like playing soccer that much?", Megan asked me, like she couldn't believe anyone could possibly like it.

It was really strange. Unexpected and all that.

"Of course I like it. It's almost my whole life."

"Does it make you happy?", she kind of shyly went on asking.

I was really confused by her question.

"Make me happy? That's a funny question."

"Why?"

"Well - I mean - make me happy? How do I know a thing like that? I never think about it. You just do stuff, that's all. You don't think about if stuff will make you happy or not."

"Why not?", she asked, giving me this really serious look.

"Because - ya just don't. How the hell do you know when you're happy or not? You just never think about it that much. Sometimes you're happy, and sometimes you're not. Who knows why you feel happy or not."

"How is it that you started playing soccer? Did you play it in high school back east?"

"Yeah - in high school I was the star of the team," I said kind all proud and everything. "I was rated the fifty-sixth best player in the whole damn country. That's how I got a full scholarship here. I've been playing soccer ever since I was about three or four - before I even went to kindergarten. It's just something I've always been really good at. I guess the only thing, really. Kind of funny, huh?'

74

"Funny?"

"Not funny to laugh about. Just kind of weird. You just start doing something you're good at and you just keep doing it and doing it and you don't ever think that you could ever just stop doing it. Understand?"

"Yes - I think I do," she said softly. "Sort of. I really don't know much about the game of soccer. I've never played it. I've seen a few of the games, but it just looks like everybody's running all around trying to kick the ball wherever they can. Is it just kicking at the ball? Is that what you do so well? Is that how you win the game - kicking it across the goal line more than the other team does?"

Wow - what a dumb question! This girl wasn't as smart as I thought she was. Not nearly. Christ! I thought she was kidding me. Come on!

"That's just a small part of how you play it - what I do," I began explaining in this really serious and excited voice. "My position on the team is the Defensive Midfielder. It may not be a kind of glamorous job - I usually don't get to score very much and I'm not noticed by the fans all that much - not in the 'limelight', as the coach calls it. I guess I'm mainly there on the field to help all the other players on the team - you know, assisting them in making goals and defending them from the other team. They all really depend on me. The whole game. If I lose my concentration just once, everything falls apart - the other guys get disconnected and they fall out of their proper positions. I have a really hard job out there. I have to cover a lot of ground and I'm putting myself on the line for the team all the time. It's just one battle after another. I'm the Enforcer. When they hit us, I have to hit them back twice as hard. That's how we win."

I was almost out of breath when I finished explaining it to her. I couldn't remember the last time I talked so much to anybody. I was really carrying on. But I really believed every word I was saying. And it kind of surprised me that I could express it so well like that. I guess Megan just sort of brought it all out of me. I don't know why.

When I finally stopped talking, I felt a little embarrassed and kind of gave this quick smile and looked away for a couple of seconds.

Megan had this expression on her face that reminded me of how a lot of people look in church when they're supposed to be praying. I don't know how you'd call it. Just kind of a happy, peaceful look.

"Being a soccer player," she said in this really gentle, understanding voice, "is who you are. It's your life."

"Yeah - well, yeah - it's a big part of it. I guess - it is who I am. I can't remember when I didn't do it."

She slowly glanced up at me with a kind of concerned expression.

"This is your last season on the team," she said in sort of this very meaningful way. "What happens then? Are you going to become a professional player?"

"No way," I laughed. "I'm not nearly good enough."

"So then what? Won't you miss playing? Won't you miss being the Enforcer and winning?"

That was a pretty funny thing to ask me. I mean, really, it wasn't very funny at all. And I hesitated and didn't know how to answer.

"There's other stuff in life besides soccer," I heard myself saying, almost amazed that those words actually came out of my mouth.

I stood up because I suddenly felt kind of all restless and uncomfortable, and Megan followed my lead, gracefully rising up.

"I imagine you probably have a lot of other dreams," she said kind of dreamy-like.

"Megan," I interrupted her on purpose, "will you come to my birthday party in the Bird Nest tonight? It's at 9:30. I'd like you to come if you can."

She looked kind of shocked, like she couldn't believe it.

"You want me to come? But all your friends are seniors. They're all on the sports teams and in the fraternities and sororities and everything. Why would you want me there? I don't think I'd fit in. I wouldn't know anybody."

"You'd know me. And it's my party and I'd like you to come."

She stood there kind of just gazing up at me like she was seeing me for the first time in her life. It made me feel a little creepy, but I tried to ignore it. I just thought about how nice she was and how much I liked her.

"Well, I have a film class until ten tonight, but I guess I could come by afterwards. Would that be OK?

"That'd be great," I said all happy-like.

We started walking down the mall together and headed toward the Lair.

"But you didn't tell me about your other dream?", Megan said to me in almost a playful kind of way. "What's your other dream besides soccer?"

"To be a movie star," I laughed.

"And what if that doesn't work out? And then what?"

I gave this sort of goofy shrug and a sharp little laugh.

"And then - nothing."

That suddenly made me think of Jeff and last night, and I felt sick to my stomach.

 Sick with this awful, cold fear.

11:53 am

Megan ran into two of her friends from the Classic Cinema Club outside the Lair and they went inside for lunch. I couldn't eat anything until
after the game. It was the coach's rule. That's why they'd stuffed us like

pigs at the team breakfast. We'd been fueled like prized animals for our performance later in the day.

So, instead of going into the Lair to chow down again, I drifted off back toward my room.

I was in a really bad mood.

Thoughts kept coming into my head that I didn't want to think about. I tried to just think about the game. That usually was pretty easy. But today - it was like I couldn't think about it at all. It was like I didn't even care about it anymore. I don't know why. I just didn't seem to care.

What kept coming into my head was what had happened last night with Jeff. And the more I tried not to think about it, the more it was filling my brain from the top to the bottom. I even started to remember what it looked like last night. All that horrible blood and everything. I could see it all there again right before my eyes as I was walking down the sidewalk back to my apartment. Fuck! And I could hear Jeff's crying voice again just like it was in the car all the way home last night - asking me over and over again why I did it. Why did I do it. And saying it was all my fault. All my fucking fault! Christ! I couldn't get that terrified, choking voice of his out of my head. And now he was practically blackmailing me! Fuck!

Three girls I met at a frat party last weekend came walking toward me and giggled and stopped to talk. Thank god. I needed something mindless right then, and this exactly did the trick. All of them were talking on their cellphones, but they still talked to me and asked about the game and what was up this Friday night. We shot the shit for a few minutes until I saw my old girlfriend Chelsea across the way and I kind of put a lid on it and made a bee-line for her.

Chelsea and I hooked up last spring after a dance in the Gersten Pavillion. I was really drinking that night and she took me back to her dorm room and took my clothes off and fucked me only about fifteen minutes after I met her. She was on the swim team and had this great body and a great tan. She really turned me on, and I turned her on. In fact, she was even more turned on than I was. She was kind of aggressive and domineering like my mom, and I didn't like that too much. But the sex was great, and we kept hooking up every weekend after that, and for awhile we only had sex with each other until she met this guy on the USC football team and started fucking him.

I don't know why, but that was kind of a bummer for me, so I stopped calling her and just hooked up with any available girl for the rest of the school year. I guess I slept with about a hundred girls until I met Beth last August at a soccer party. That's when I kind of settled down. Beth was fun and she was nice, and I actually liked her. And I thought I could trust her. But I guess I was pretty dumb about things. I hadn't counted on her falling in love with me so much and going all ball and chain on me and tricking me into that baby trap thing. Shit! What a mess. But that's another story. I didn't want to think about it right now.

Chelsea seemed really glad to see me when I came jogging up.

"Hi cowboy," she sort of sung out in that real sexy way that she always had.

She always used to call me Cowboy. I don't know why. I don't think I ever heard her say my real name. And for some reason she didn't like the nicknames everyone else called me - Number Nine or Niner. So she called me Cowboy. She even bought me this neat cowboy hat that I wore for awhile. I don't know - maybe she had this thing for cowboys.

"Hi," I smiled. "What's up? How's it going?"

"Fine. Couldn't be better. Where's Beautiful Beth? Does she know you're out loose like this? You could get into trouble."

"I wish," I laughed. "Got any ideas?"

She stood back a little and fixed me with this incredibly hot look.

"I've got plenty of ideas," she said kind of like a cat that was purring.

"Yeah - I bet you do. You always have."

"Too bad you can't share them with me anymore. As I recall, you used to really like my ideas. Almost as much as I liked yours."

"So - what's up with Mr. Football from SC?", I said kind of sarcastically. "Isn't he enjoying your ideas that much anymore?"

"Oh, Rick?", she sniffed like she couldn't have cared less. "Rick is history. He has been since last summer. It was good riddance. He was a jerk - and one of the worst fucks I've ever had."

I raised my eyebrows.

"That's saying quite a bit," I couldn't resist saying, still a little pissed at the way she dumped me last spring.

"And you're one of the best fucks," she sort of whispered all sultry-like, leaning into me and stroking my cheek with the back of her hand.

Shit! I got an instantaneous hard-on.

"Yeah," I managed to say. "I remember."

She took my arm and lightly squeezed my bicep.

"Still as hot as ever, I see. Walk me to my room?"

"Uh . . "

"Beth won't mind, will she? Or, do you need to ask her? To get her permission? I don't want to upset any apple carts."

"Sure - I'll walk ya," I said with a big smile. "Are ya still in Whelan?

"Rosecrans this year. I wanted the apartments, but I lost the lottery."

"Tough."

We started walking slowly off towards Rosecrans. It was only about a hundred feet away, just right past Huesman Hall.

"Are ya positive Beth isn't gonna mind, Cowboy?", she kept teasing me with this kind of wicked half-smile. "I don't wanna get ya in any trouble. I know how she keeps you on a pretty short leash these days."

"You're pretty funny," I snickered. "A real comic. Nice that some things never change. If you're so concerned, why don't you call her?"

She squeezed my bicep again and leaned against my side as we walked. My hard-on was almost at full-mast, and it was becoming a little difficult to walk. Twisted to the left, my cock was all caught up under the bottom of my jockey shorts. I wanted to reach down into my soccer shorts and straighten it out, but it would have been a pretty gross thing to have done with Chelsea right there next to me on the sidewalk.

When we came to the front entrance door of Rosecrans Hall, I sort of stopped there and curiously looked down at Chelsea and wondered what was next. Where it was all going. I knew as soon as I looked her in the eyes. She was already on fire. But I really couldn't make up my mind. I was kind of worrying that sex right now might later affect my soccer game.

"So - here we are," I brilliantly announced in this kind of edgy voice.

"So we are, " Chelsea laughed. "Why don't ya come in. I've got some Scotch. Still your favorite drink?"

"Yeah - I guess so."

She hugged me and pressed her crotch tightly against mine and solidly felt my stiff cock right up against her.

"Let's do something about that," she purred in this incredibly sexy voice, glancing down at my shorts. "The room's empty. Cindy has a class til 12:30. Come on, Cowboy."

She took my hand and off we went to her room, Rosecrans 136.

By the time we got inside the door, we were both so turned on that we really didn't have anything else to say to each other. I slid out of my T-shirt and my shorts in record time while she pulled off this green sort of tube-like dress she had been packed into. She wasn't wearing a bra, so that just left her panties which I yanked off in a flash.

To hell with foreplay. We just sort of collapsed together onto her bed and I was deep inside her before we barely hit the sheets. And she was ready for me. I think she'd been ready ever since she'd felt my bicep back on the sidewalk.

"I don't have a condom," I said a little bit too late, already thrusting away pretty good into her.

"I know," she kind of excitedly whispered in my ear. "I saw. But it's OK. You've been exclusive with Beth for the past few months, haven't you? You haven't hooked up with anybody else lately, have you?"

"No," I breathlessly replied as I really started amping up the pumping, "I haven't been hooking up since I met Beth last August."

"So - you're OK? Right? You don't wear a condom with her, do ya?"

"Naw. We're both healthy. And we trust each other."

Shit! I'd been feeling so great. I'd been 100% into this whole scene. Nothing else had been in my brain. But as soon as I mentioned that shit about Beth and me trusting each other, the whole thing just sort of collapsed. Like, literally. I could feel my cock start losing a little fuel and my mind falling into these worried thoughts about what I was doing. This

83

wasn't right. Beth trusted me. And what if Chelsea wasn't being careful either. All I needed now was ANOTHER kid on the way. Christ!

"What's the matter?", Chelsea asked me like she was one of my professors ready to give me a B- instead of an A+ on my current performance.

"Nothing," I said kind of defensively. "What's the matter with you? Let's do the Cowgirl Rodeo bit. I've gotta a big soccer game later on, and I don't wanna put too much strain on my back."

We automatically flip-flopped and I rolled over on my back across her narrow bed and she knelt across me and straddled my cock and slid it into her. This had always been Chelsea's favorite position. Naturally. She was on top and probably felt totally in charge. I always went along with it in the past. It gave me kind of a rest while she did most of the work, bouncing up and down on top of me. It was OK. But it didn't turn me on as much as the three or four other positions we always fucked in.

Chelsea called this position the Cowgirl Rodeo. She liked to pretend she was this cowgirl who's captured a handsome cowboy and was roughly breaking him in like a wild stallion. Yeah - I know. Don't tell me. Really dumb! Yeah - I guess. But when she had ahold of the cowboy hat she bought me and was waving it wildly in the air and screaming and yelling and massaging my chest and bending down to my face and kissing me. Shit! You can't believe how totally hot and turned on I got. Fuck! For more than a month last spring we'd fuck like this about twice a day. Sometimes three - if I didn't have a tough soccer practice that day. Shit!

I suppose that's why she liked to call me Cowboy. You know, fantasy stuff. It can be pretty exciting.

But today, it really wasn't that hot. I just wanted to get my rocks off and she seemed in kind of a hurry and sort of bored by the whole thing. I

84

guess it would've been a whole lot better if I had had my cowboy hat with me so Chelsea could do her routine. Without it, the thing kind of fell flat. Not my cock. It was hard as ever and getting closer and closer to launch time. But the whole thing just wasn't that exciting. Kind of 'been there, done that' territory - if ya know what I mean. It just didn't feel like it used to. It sort of didn't feel right. I started thinking of Beth. I tried not to, but I still thought about her as Chelsea was jacking and whaling around on top of my cock. I kind of wondered what Chelsea was thinking about, 'cause she never looked at me once as she pumped away. I kind of wondered if she might be thinking about that football player from USC and maybe pretending that he was below her and not me.

I continued just lying there and trying to make my mind go blank. Usually that was pretty easy for me. But, now, I kept kind of having these really strange, odd kind of feelings. Maybe it was what some people sometimes refer to as a conscience. You know - sort of feeling bad about doing something you're not supposed to be doing when you're doing it. Sort of like that, maybe.

Beth and I had agreed not to have sex with anyone else about three months ago when we decided to be a couple and start a serious relationship. It was sort of her idea, but I went along with it. I was so tired of hooking up almost every night with some new girl that I didn't even know and feeling really shitty and pissed about it the next day, and then doing the same fucking thing the next night and the next and the next. Hell! It was nice to finally feel like I belonged to somebody - somebody that really cared about me. Somebody nice and sweet and all that crap.

I did kind of cheat, I guess, during the last three months. It took awhile to get used to being exclusive with somebody. So the first month was rough on me. I guess I fucked maybe four or five other girls during that month. You know, the groupie type who follow you around and kind of try to corner you and get you all hot and stuff. That usually happened when the guys on the team and I went out drinking on Thursday nights when Beth had her Philosophy class in St. Robert's Hall. I'd almost always get drunk and some skanky girl would scoop in on me and we'd go out to her car or to her place.

But the last two months I'd been pretty faithful to Beth. I only strayed once, and that only happened when I was on the road up in San Francisco playing a soccer game against USF. I got nailed after the game by this really hot chick that took me back to her apartment on Nob Hill. A really ritzy place. She must have been almost 25 or 26, but she was really hot and had all this cocaine, and we got really high and had this fantastic sex. But that was the only time, so I figured it really didn't count. Just that one time. It wasn't like I'd planned it or anything.

This last month Beth had been kind of weirded out by everything, so things weren't the same. It took her awhile to tell me about the kid. That was almost two weeks ago, just after Kyle died. It really hit me hard. Like a ton of bricks! Just completely wiped me out. We hadn't had sex too much after that. Actually, the last time was ten days ago. Fuck!

I was really on fire. We'd only been fucking for eight minutes or so, but I felt like I was gonna cum any second now. Just all set to explode. My legs tensed really hard and began trembling. At that moment, Chelsea suddenly pulled away and swung her body up and off of me and sat down on the side of the bed.

"Hey," I called out all surprised-like, "I'm gonna cum any minute. What'a'ya doing? What's the matter?"

She looked over at me with this really snarky smile and sort of tossed her hair back real bitch-like. Old Chelsea! Always in control.

"What's the matter?", I anxiously repeated, grabbing onto my cock and jerking it to keep it hard.

"I just don't wanna end up like Beth," she said very cooly.

I was kind of shocked.

"How did ya know about that?"

"Good new travels fast," she answered in kind of a nasty voice.

I couldn't believe it. Chelsea knew all the time? What the hell was she doing? What was the point? I didn't get it.

"I'm all ready to cum", I said excitedly. "I won't cum inside you. Just another couple minutes. Then I'll pull out of you just before. Can't you - ?"

"No," she said really firmly. "That's it. Just keep jerking yourself off if ya wanna cum so badly. Fuck! Grow up."

I hesitated and considered her advice for a moment, then quickly decided against it. There was no way I was gonna give this bitch the satisfaction of seeing me having to jerk off in front of her. So I kind of flexed my body a little and relaxed until I lost my hard-on, then quickly put my shorts and shirt back on and headed out the door without saying a word to her.

"See ya at the party tonight," she sort of fake-happy called to me as I left the room.

I didn't say anything.

I just kind of stumbled down the dark hallway of Rosecrans and headed out the entrance door. It felt a little weird to be out in the bright sunlight after having just spent the last ten minutes fucking away in a dark room. I was feeling a bit weak and dizzy. And incredibly frustrated. I was so close to shooting my wad. I hate when that happens. What do they call it? Coitus interruptus? You've all been there. It's the pits. I don't know how it is for a woman, but for us guys it's totally wrecked. You know - you're sure you're sliding into home base, and then, suddenly, you're all alone out in the cold with no place to take your business. I really do hate that. I really do.   It's so unfair.

If only life were more fair.

12:16 pm

I decided to go back to my room and jerk off. I didn't want to run into Jeff, so I went up the stairwell at the far end of the building.

Josh was there when I got to the room, so I knew I wasn't gonna get my rocks off any time soon. He was going in and out of the bathroom and really hogging the whole scene. I just sat on my bed for a few minutes, and then decided that what I really needed right now was a little pot to smoke. That always did the trick. No matter how shitty I was feeling, pot never failed to lift me right up to the sky and make me feel like I was on top of the world. For me, it's almost impossible to worry about anything when I'm high on pot.

I thought I had a little pot left from last weekend, but when I checked out my secret stash hiding place at the bottom of my sock drawer - SHIT! - it was empty. Not even a shred. Then I remembered that I had meant to buy some more on Monday, but I was short of funds and couldn't talk Cutter into any credit. Nobody could. With Cutter, it was cash up front, or no weed.

Cutter was this sophomore who lived down the hall. I think his real name was Jim - Jim Drayton, or Drake, or something like that. But everybody called him Cutter. Get it? He cut all the weed and put it in little packages for all of us. He was the cutter. Clever, huh? He was the main supplier of pot for most of the sports teams and for half the dorms and apartments on campus. He had a pretty big clientele, and god knows where he got all the pot that he sold, but it had to come from somewhere. Reicher was one of his best customers, and he said that Cutter got all the junk from one of his mom's real estate business partners who was married to a professional drug dealer who worked out of the Valley.

I noticed that Cutter would disappear for a whole day every week and when he came back there would always be this huge swarm of kids down by his door at the end of the hall. It looked like the line for a Friday night movie down there. And nobody ever said a thing. The priest who was the apartments' resident supervisor just totally ignored it. I guess maybe he was one of Cutter's customers too.

Whatever the setup was, it was pretty sweet, let me tell ya. Cutter drove a brand new Porsche and spent every summer in Hawaii, and took break trips to Europe and Tahiti. Pretty sweet. And guys said that he even paid his own $50,000 a year tuition. They also said he had this apartment down in Manhattan Beach and this girlfriend who was a lingerie model that lived there. Pretty sweet.

I picked up the last twenty dollar bill I had in my desk and rushed out the door and down the hall to Cutter's room. There was no response to my knock. I knocked louder. The door finally opened a little bit, kind of really cautious-like, and Cutter edged his face through the crack. When he saw me his uptight expression instantly relaxed and he swung the door open and told me to come in. He was a really skinny guy with this bright red hair and almost chalk white skin. Kind of funny looking. It always made me wonder why he'd want to have a place down at the beach. He looked like he'd never been out in the sun in his whole life. Kind of weird.

"Got the cash?", he sort of bluntly asked me. "I told ya last time I wasn't no credit bank. Cash only. Forty bucks."

"Forty!", I said with a whole lot of surprise. "I don't want that much. Just a little. Give me half that for twenty."

"No can do, amigo. Forty's the rock bottom price from now on. I don't do sales for any less than that. It's forty or nada. Take it or leave it."

I held the twenty dollar bill in my hand and stood there all kind of confused and trying to think of another suggestion.

"All I need is a quick smoke," I said all soft and smiley, something that I could immediately see was totally wasted on Cutter. "I'll give ya this twenty just for one joint. Just give it to me and I'll smoke it here right now."

"No way, Niner. You're not smoking that fucking thing here. All customers have to take their purchases elsewhere. You think I want pot vapors coming out of my room and filling the hall and flagging down some Boy Scout that might be hanging around. No way. I don't wanna get busted, ya know. I don't wanna get caught doing anything illegal."

"OK," I sort of stuttered all anxious-like, "I'll just take it down to my room or someplace else - out on the bluff or somewhere. I won't smoke it here. Just give me one little joint and I'll hit the road."

Cutter thought for a moment, then reached under his bed and took out this padlocked brown box. With one of the keys on his belt, he opened the lock and then lifted the lid of the box. There must have been ten pounds of pot and hash and all sorts of things in hundreds of little plastic bags inside there. Fumbling around, he took out this tiny, really crappy looking little cigarette from a small white paper bag. He held it out to me with his right hand and quickly snatched the twenty dollar bill out of my fingers with his left hand. Pretty smooth.

I thanked him and left the room. Out in the hall, I took a better look at the small, two inch joint. Twenty bucks, my ass!

Walking back to my room, I noticed that Josh was in the doorway talking to somebody across the hall. When I got closer I could tell that it was Einstein. He was standing in his door and it sounded like they were having some sort of discussion about economics.

Einstein was probably about the smartest guy at the university. Probably the smartest guy anywhere. Really a brain. Even smarter than

Megan. And the funny thing was - he really didn't have to study all that much. He was just this walking, talking giant brain. I couldn't believe it when I first met him last year. He was only a sophomore then, but he knew more about everything than anybody. He was in my philosophy class and he even knew more than the fucking professor! It was incredible!

His real name really wasn't Einstein. That was just what everybody called him because he was so smart. His real name was Paul Epstein. So, since Epstein was kind of close to Einstein, and Einstein was this major genius of all-time, everybody just sort of gave him that as a nickname and it really stuck - like Number Nine for me. Shit! I wondered if he hated his nickname as much as I now hated mine. I wondered.

Anyway, Paul Epstein, or I guess, Einstein, was this super-brain from New York City who lived right across the hall from Josh and me. Some of the guys said he was Jewish, but I don't know. We never talked about religion. But he could have been. Seems kind of funny that some Jewish guy would want to come and study at a Catholic university. I don't know. I guess knowledge is knowledge. It doesn't really have a religion. I never thought that much about religion, to tell you the truth.

"Hey, Number Nine," Einstein said happily to me as I approached. "What's up? Big game today?"

"Yeah - the biggest," I smiled. "League championship."

I really liked Einstein. A lot of the guys didn't. I think he really intimidated a lot of people. I think he kind of made them feel dumb. Not that he tried to do that or anything. But a lot of people just don't like to be around really smart genius types. It never bothered me, though. I guess I was so far behind Einstein's level that there wasn't even any competition. He was a brain, and I wasn't. I mean, come on. He knew it and I knew it. I didn't

92

feel threatened at all.   In fact, I liked learning new stuff from him.   He always had this really neat take on everything and kind of a really smart way
of looking at crap and understanding it.   He was always helping me on my
papers and stuff, and when I was having problems with my folks, he always would listen real sincere-like and say things that really made me feel
a lot better.   My folks were really hard to understand.

And Einstein seemed to really like me.   I think he admired all my
sports stuff and the fact that I was so popular and had all these girls all the
time and everything.   He seemed to be pretty fascinated by all that.   He
had a couple of good friends in the Honor Society, but other than that, he
kept to himself a lot and seemed to be reading all the time.   He almost
lived in the library.   I guess if you have a brain like that, ya just have to feed
it all the time with facts and thoughts and ideas and stuff.   Really weird.
Interesting, but weird.   I was kind of glad I wasn't like that.   But I still really
liked him, and I guess I even admired him a little.

"See you guys later," Josh said as he took off down the hall, leaving
Einstein and me standing there in doorway.

"Everything OK?", Einstein said in a sort of sensitive voice, looking at
me kind of all probing-like - you know, like the the way the doctor always
first looks at you when you come in and sit on the table.

"Yeah - just - you know - the same old shit.   Just everything."

"Classes OK?"

"Ahhh - next subject," I gave this lame little laugh.

"Beth OK?"

"Ahhh - next subject," I repeated - this time without a laugh.

While we were talking I had put the marijuana joint in my shorts'
pocket.   I didn't really know what Einstein thought about this kind of stuff -

you know, taking drugs and all that - but I imagined he was too smart to think that it was cool or anything like that, so I didn't want him to know that I smoked pot all the time. I didn't want him to like me any less because of it. But who was I kidding. Einstein always seemed to know more about everybody than they even knew about themselves. His brain just seemed to have this way of understanding what nobody else seemed able to understand. Kind of weird and strange. But also kind of neat. Kind of cool, if you know what I mean.

"We're running out of subjects," he said gently with this serious kind of smile. "What's the problem?"

"Nothin'," I casually shrugged.

"Really?", he softly replied with this doubting expression on his face. "Seems to me like it's almost everything. Anything you want to talk about? Something's really bothering you today. Was it the service for Kyle Martinsen they had yesterday? That must have been hard. I know how close you two were."

"Naw - that was OK. It was kind of boring. You know, all that phony shit that people say at those things. But it was OK. He was a pretty good friend and I'm gonna miss him, but life goes on, ya know. No big deal"

Einstein sort of narrowed his small, dark eyes until you could barely see them in his face, and then gave me this long, deep look.

"No big deal," he very softly repeated after me with a really strange toss of his head and this kind of weird, sad smile.

Out of the corner of my eye, I noticed that this guy down the hall named Fred was coming our way. I sort of braced myself and instantly felt this really annoyed, kind of pissed-off and hostile thing suddenly burst from the inside of me.

I barely knew Fred. He was a young skinny guy, probably a fresh-man or maybe a sophomore - just this real wimpy-looking kind of guy that was really quiet and delicate-acting. All the guys on the floor called him Freddy the Faggot - behind his back, of course. I guess I did too. I really never thought about it - I just did it 'cause everyone else did it. It was just a nickname they gave him. Freddy the Faggot.

But what really pissed me off was the totally weird way that this Fred character always sort of stared at me and followed me around campus. I tried saying "hi" to him whenever I'd pass by him in the hall. But he'd just turn all red and put his face down and not say anything. Then, he'd always stop walking and just hang around staring at me the way a dog does when you're holding out its dinner dish.

Shit! What'a'ya do with a guy like that? I mean, I kind of felt sorry for him at first. None of the other guys wanted anything to do with him, so I felt sorry for him. But then they gave him that nickname and he kept hang-ing around me and staring at me all the time, and, shit! All the other guys started making this joke that Freddy the Faggot was in love with me and that he'd probably end up marrying me. Then these frat guys at the other end of the hall started referring to him as my 'wife'. Fuck! I ignored all that shit and pretended I didn't care. But, fuck! I hated it! And him!

I just didn't want him near me. I felt like smashing him in the face.

Approaching Einstein and me, Fred bent his head down and started his old routine. I could already see how red and tense his face was when he began hurrying by us.

"I saw your painting over at the gallery showing last week," Einstein said in this really sensitive tone. "I liked it very much. The deep blues and the purples - and the way you did the water. It reminded me of Monet. Was his "Water Lillies" your inspiration, Fred?"

The guy totally yanked himself together and forced himself not to look at me, and, instead, focused all happy-like on Einstein, giving him this huge, shining smile.

"Yes," Fred said in this high, sort of girly voice that kind of creeped me out a little. "That's it exactly. It's my favorite Monet. I used his colors. I tried to put the deep blue and the bright purple in the patterns that he used. You're the only one who noticed. Thanks."

Christ! It just dawned on me. This was the first time I had ever heard Fred speak. And, god! His voice! Shit! It really made the whole thing a lot worse. The total visual thing was way bad enough. But his voice and the way he spoke! Shit! No wonder all the guys called him Freddy the Faggot. I mean, come on! It made you wanna puke.

"You know good old Number Nine here, don't you, Fred?", Einstein casually asked him, putting his hand on my shoulder and giving a nice, warm, friendly smile.

Fred looked over at me for the first time and I kind of thought he was going to faint or something. His eyes looked really terrified. Like he had seen some kind of monster or something. Then, they kind of melted all of a sudden into that dog-waiting-for-his-dinner look. But even more than that. Like he was falling into my eyes, the way girls always do.

Fuck! It really freaked me out . It really did.

"You know, Fred - don't ya, Niner?", Einstein sort of took up the slack a little when the weirdo just kept standing there like a statue and staring at me without making a sound.

"Yeah, sure," I replied with about zero enthusiasm. "I've seen him around. Hi, Fred."

"Hi," he sort of croaked in this incredibly nervous, high voice.

"Number Nine is turning twenty-one tomorrow," Einstein announced in this real friendly voice, like he was trying to play matchmaker or something. "He's celebrating with a big bash at the Nest tonight. Aren't you, Niner? All your friends coming? Probably almost everybody you know. Right?"

"Yeah, I guess," I shrugged, wanting to make a pretty quick exit. "You're coming too, aren't ya, Einstein?"

"Of course. Wouldn't miss it. I imagine almost all the guys on the floor here are going to be attending. Right?"

Einstein then gave me this sort of really hard look - a look that was meant to tell me something, and then he smiled kind of all gentle-like and motioned with his head toward Fred.

Shit! So that was it! No fucking way! For such a bright guy, Einstein really needed a reality check on this one. Fuck!

"Gotta go," I kind of cheerfully called out. "Gotta give a speech in my philosophy class in an hour. Later."

I flashed this phony smile and turned around and dove into my room and firmly slammed the door behind me.

Close call. That asshole Einstein! What the fuck was he thinking? Yeah! Right! Ask Freddy the Faggot to come to my party! Jesus Christ!

I stretched out on my bed and put my hand down my shorts. Now that Josh was gone, I thought it'd be a good time to finally jerk off. I really needed to release some tension. That whole thing with Chelsea had really cranked me up like you wouldn't believe. Shit! I'd already forgotten about the marijuana joint in my pocket. I just wanted to get my rocks off. So - I went right at it and started whacking away at Big Niner - the name Beth gave my cock the first night we ever fucked. I think it was on our second or third date. She wanted to act all proper and everything. Make me think that she was special and all that. I guess it worked pretty good. I did think she was pretty special when she held out a little like that.

Within a minute or two I was really stroking away and getting totally back in the game. All hot and turned on. I was thinking of this girl in my English class that had this incredibly hot body and wore these short-short jean shorts all the time. If I hadn't been exclusive with Beth, and if this girl, Laura something or other, hadn't had this boyfriend on the crew team who was about twice my size, I really would have hit on her and tried to hook up with her for some of that great ass. But this was the next best thing - just trying to imagine what she looked like naked lying there next to me in the bed as I was jerking off.

Things were proceeding all on schedule for blast-off when there was a knock on the door.

Christ! The first thing that came into my mind was Jeff. That son-of-a-bitch had come back again. I sort of froze there with my cock in my hand and didn't even breathe for several seconds. And my cock started deflating like a flat tire. Shit!

"Niner - it's Einstein," his voice called from the other side of the door. "Can I talk to you for a minute or two? It's important."

Christ! What did he want now? Is the whole fucking world trying to keep me from getting my rocks off today? Fuck! What's the story?

I tucked myself back in my shorts and got up and opened the door. Einstein was standing there all serious-like and just sort of stepped into my room and shut the door behind him. I kind of wondered what was up. I really didn't want to deal with anyone else's problems today. Not at all.

"What's up?", I asked him, drifting back from near-orgasm land and trying to focus my eyes.

"I wanted to ask you a favor," Einstein said very softly.

Studying him for a moment, I couldn't imagine what it could be. He never asked me for a favor before. Never. He was an odd guy. Much more like a full-grown adult than a kid like me. He even looked like an adult. He was my height, but weighed a lot more than me. He wasn't fat. He just had this soft look about him. You couldn't see any muscle. It was funny. I don't have an ounce of fat on me, and Einstein looked like he didn't have an ounce of muscle. Even his face was all smooth and full and kind of flabby looking. He reminded me of my uncle. And his hair was this dull black color that almost looked gray. He just didn't really look at all like one of us kids - like the guys on the team or anything. But I still liked him a lot. He was somebody that you instantly respected as soon as you met him. A smart guy. A really nice guy. I was glad he was my friend.

"Yeah?", I said kind of cautiously.

"I'd like you to invite Fred to your party tonight," he said very simply.

"What?" I couldn't believe it. "Are you crazy?"

"Not at all. Fred needs some help. He's a different kind of guy and he really needs friends. He needs to make friends here in the Hall and on campus. Friends who will accept him - make him feel good about himself."

"He's got friends," I argued, getting all pissed about the whole thing.

"Yeah - a few. And they feel just as isolated and unhappy as Fred does. They're outsiders just like him. We need to reach out to Fred and make him feel appreciated and understood. This will really increase his

99

self-confidence and self-esteem. I've already done it, and it works. But I'm not the one he wants to please. You're the one he likes most."

"Look, Einstein," I said angrily, "you don't have to tell me how much he likes me. I know how he fucking feels about me! It's a bunch of shit! You're full of shit, Einstein! Haven't you heard all the jokes! Why do you think they call him Freddy the Faggot. I tried being nice to him once, but he just took it and used it to fall all in love with me. The asshole follows me around and is always staring at me.   Haven't you heard all that crappy bullshit the guys down the hall are saying? Calling Fred my 'wife'. All that shitty crap! I hate it! I don't want anything to do with that weirdo!"

Einstein looked unhappy.   Then, he hesitated and gave this calm smile and took a long, deep breath.

"You're right. I think Fred is in love with you. Oh, I'm not sure he knows what love is yet. He's too young. But he certainly has a crush on you. You're his fantasy dream. It's a certain kind of love. But just as real and as strong as a more mature love. Maybe even stronger."

"Yeah - well, you see," I said all victorious-like.   "The guy's gay. Everybody knows it. And he's trying to put all that shit on me. I don't want anything to do with a gay guy. I mean - shit! Come on!"

"You're afraid?"

"What!"

"Are you afraid of him?", Einstein quietly asked me.

"What the fuck do you mean?", I was really pissed.

"I mean - does the fact that Fred is a homosexual make you feel threatened in some way? Does it make you feel things and think about things that disturb you? That make you feel uncomfortable? If it does, that's OK. That's human nature. Things we're not used to - things we don't have any experience with or things that we don't have any understanding of - these things always make us feel uneasy and threatened and a little afraid. That's just how human beings are made. That's all."

"Well, then," I said kind of nervously, "that's how we all feel, I guess. Yeah - so what's wrong with that?   Maybe I do feel that way. I just don't want any part of it, that's all. So what's wrong with that? Like you said - everybody feels that way. How else should I feel?"

Einstein thought deeply for several moments.

"But it's not how we're supposed to behave. We all feel things that we have to learn to control and overcome. We feel basic things like greed and anger and hatred and fear. But that's what growing up is all about. It's about learning how to deal with these bad impulses in all of us. How to control and overcome them. So that we can all help each other and share life with each other, instead of killing each other and always being at war."

What he said really struck me. I'd never heard anybody state it so plainly and simply before. He had talked very slowly and I had followed every single word he said. I started thinking a lot. I wasn't used to thinking in this kind of way.   It kind of overwhelmed me and made me feel really strange and a little frightened, to tell you the truth. But my mind kept coming back to just one thing, and I couldn't shake it.

"But the guy's gay," I complained. "Fred's gay and he loves me."

"So what?," Einstein happily shrugged. "So what?"

"Are you kidding?'

"No - I'm not. So he's gay. Some people are gay, some people aren't. What's the big deal? Does being kind to a gay guy make you any different than who you've always been? Does making friends with a gay guy make you gay? The whole thing about being friends with someone is to expand your experience - to join with someone who might be totally different from you - different background, different ethic group, different religion, different way of thinking. These kind of friends open you up and give you a new way of seeing life - they make you richer and deeper and more fully human, Niner."

"Maybe," I cautiously agreed.

"And because Fred has such a crush on you, thinking that he truly loves you - you're in a special position to become his friend and make him feel good about himself. Niner - you're the only one who can make Fred feel like a valuable person and feel appreciated and genuinely liked for who he is. And even though you don't love him that same way in return, by showing him that you respect his feelings and value who he is as a person, you can make him grow and accept himself and feel like he can join with the rest of us to share and learn from each other."

"I don't know," I mumbled, feeling really all confused and everything.

"Niner," Einstein said in this gentle, very emotional and firm voice, "Fred's a very unhappy guy. He's miserable here. All the other guys laugh at him and ignore him. I think he's about to drop out of school. You can change all that, Niner. Make a friend of him. You're good at that. I've seen you. You're better at it than anybody. Take the lead. Set the tone of the friendship. You're an only child, aren't you? Well - pretend he's your little brother. Help him. Be super friendly and steer his crush into a nice comfortable friendship. And then all the other guys will follow your lead."

Shit! What was I supposed to say? Einstein made a lot of sense. I didn't want to do it, but how could I refuse? I immediately began seeing Fred in a totally different way. Like he was some little guy in trouble that only I could save. Like we we're hiking someplace and he got lost and only I could find him. Something like that. I wasn't that pissed off at Fred anymore. In fact, I didn't hate Fred anymore at all. I was feeling sorry for him again.

"Uh - OK, what should I do?", I asked in this kind of defeated voice.

Einstein gave this huge smile.

"To begin with, ask him to your birthday party tonight."

I think I winced. It didn't make sense to me. I just couldn't see Fred fitting in with all my friends. It seemed insane. But maybe it might be OK. I didn't know. Einstein was always right, so I didn't feel like arguing with him. He must know something that I didn't. He always did.

"OK - he can come," I agreed. "You can tell him he's invited. How's that? Is that OK?"

"That's fine. But you have to be the one to invite him. You have to go down to his room and make contact - be friendly and shake his hand and tell him you'd like him to come."

"What!"

"Tell him that you hope you two can be good friends. And invite him to watch you play in the game this afternoon. He knows you have a steady girlfriend, so you can talk about Beth a lot and make him fully aware that this isn't a sexual thing between you. He'll realize that even though he has these feelings for you, it's OK, and you respect him and value him as a friend, and that it doesn't matter. He'll be a changed man, Niner."

I thought really hard for what seemed like a long time.

"Alright," I finally said with a deep sigh. "You win. I'll go ask him. What's his room number again?"

"317."

"OK."

Einstein never looked happier. He gave me this nice pat on the shoulder and opened the door and left the room. I kind of began running things through my mind that I was gonna say to Fred. It sure as hell wasn't gonna be easy. I decided I'd just treat him like the guys on the soccer team. I'd just ignore that weird way he looked at me like I always did with all those older guys who were always scoping in on me. No problem, I thought. It'd be like I was a coach trying to buck up and toughen and encourage a new player on the team. Yeah. No problem.

Just to make it a bit less awkward, I took off my soccer shorts and put on my jeans and a flannel shirt. I had to sort of dress up a little for my speech in my philosophy class, so I just thought I'd get ready a little earlier. Then I stretched a little and did a few pushups and headed down the hallway to room 317.

Waiting outside the door for more than a minute, I glanced back and forth up and down the dark hallway. It really wasn't Fred I was so worried about. It was the other guys. This could really be murder if they saw me. The last thing I wanted today was to go through that whole half-assed routine of Freddy the Faggot being my 'wife'. Shit! I really was fucking hoping I could quickly do this whole fucking thing without any of those fucking fraternity assholes coming by and going ape-shit about it.

Fuck!

I quickly knocked - kind of quiet-like.

The door slowly opened and old Fred was standing there. If I had been pointing a gun at him, he would have reacted exactly the same.

"Hey, Freddy - I mean, Fred," I called out to him all gung-ho like. "What's up? How are they hangin'.?"

Poor guy. His eyes were half-falling out of his face and his mouth was all wide-open and just flapping there in the air like a freshly caught sea bass. He looked just like those guys you see in those old movies who are suddenly cornered and about to be rubbed out by the Mob.

"Uh - uh - yeah - OK," he managed to stutter.

"When we were shooting the shit down the hall about my party tonight and saying how all my friends around here were coming - well - I was just assuming you'd be coming too. I mean - I didn't know if you knew you were invited too. I mean - you're a great guy and - well - we've never been good buddies or anything - I mean - we do different stuff and have different interests and shit and all that - but you're a great guy and one of my friends and all that, and I like you as a friend, and I'd really like you to come to my party tonight."

Shit! I was just rambling on like a moron. It was so awkward trying to talk to a guy that was looking at you like a lovesick girl. I mean - come on! You just can't really focus and you find yourself jabbering away like an idiot. Shit!

"You - want - me - to - come - to your party?", old Fred stammered with this kind of stunned expression of total disbelief.

It was a perfect example again of that word 'incredulous.'

His pale blue eyes seemed to spread to almost three times their size, sort of like what happens when you drop an egg in a frying pan.

"Sure thing, buddy," I said with a big smile, all jock-like and everything. "You're gonna be one of my buddies one of these days and, well - who knows - you might even wind up on the soccer team next year."

"Huh?", he sort of gasped.

"It could happen, I guess," I said with all this phony cheerful energy and stuff. "You play soccer, don't ya?"

He looked at me like I'd asked him if he could walk on water.

"No."

"Oh. Well - you can always learn. It ain't hard. You're a smart guy. You could learn it easy. No problem. Maybe I can teach ya. Be good for ya. Great way to make new friends. Be one of the guys. And it's a great way to meet girls."

"Girls?", he asked kind of all uneasy-like.

"Yeah. Girls love soccer players. You'd be a natural. You're a little light right now, but a few months in the weight room and you could be in pretty good shape. I bet you're even a pretty coordinated guy. You might be a good forward - or a goalie. You should give it a try. I'll help ya."

Christ! There I was yammering on again. He was giving me that dreamy, lovesick look, and it really made me so uncomfortable and nervous that my mind felt like it was melting into jello.

"You'd - help - me, Niner?", he was all incredulous again.

"Sure - why not. And you can come to the party tonight and you can meet the other guys on the team and get to know them. OK?"

I held out my hand. Fred very slowly reached out and took it like he was in some kind of dream. Awkwardly latching onto it, I gave it an extra hard and firm shake - just like I would out on the field - just so Fred wouldn't have any misunderstanding about it. His hand was all soft and mushy, and he just held it there and didn't squeeze back at all.

"OK," he said in this really tiny, girlie voice.

"OK, buddy," I kind of happily bellowed in my deepest voice.

"Thanks - Niner," he said, almost choked with emotion. "Thanks a lot."

"The party starts at 9:30. It's in the Bird Nest. See ya there, buddy. Take care."

With that, I marched off up the hall in the most masculine, macho walk I could muster. Again - making sure old Fred got the right message.

When I got back to my room Josh was there. So that was the official end of my quest for an orgasm that day. He was working on his laptop and I just quietly gazed out at those pine trees outside the window for a couple of minutes.

For the first time in a long while, I felt kind of good. I guess I'd forgotten about everything when I was trying so hard to deal with Fred. It made me forget about last night and about Kyle and Beth and the history test and Megan and my grades and the game and Jeff and my parents and the Dean tomorrow. Everything had been out of my thoughts when I was down the hall there talking to Fred. It kind of gave me this good feeling.

But, now, everything started floating back into my head. I could feel my whole body tensing up again and my heart kind of racing again. And when I thought of Jeff, my hands tightened up into these rock-hard fists and I started to angrily beat them against the sides of my legs. Even Josh noticed what I was doing.

"What's the matter?" he asked me with this look of concern.

"Nothin'. I gotta get to class. Later."

I picked up my philosophy junk and stuffed it in my backpack and walked out of the room.

In the hallway, I noticed Einstein's door was wide open and he was sitting there at his desk inside his room.

"How'd it go with Fred?", he asked me with this hopeful smile.

"OK," I casually replied. "I invited him. I think he's gonna come. He doesn't really seem all that bad. Just a little mixed up, that's all. He's OK."

"Yeah - he is OK. Good job, Number Nine. I'm proud of you."

Shit! Who was he to be proud of me! I mean - come on! Like he owns me or something! I can't even recall the last time anybody ever told me that they were fucking proud of me. It sounded so stupid. It really did. And it really pissed me off. At least - that's how I felt when I first heard Einstein say it. But really fast-like, I suddenly wasn't that pissed off anymore. I mean, I wasn't pissed off at all.

In fact, it actually made me feel kind of good after Einstein said he was proud of me. The more I thought about it, the better it made me feel. In fact, in just another few seconds or so, I felt great about it. And I guess I must have smiled, 'cause Einstein gave this huge smile back at me.

12:58 pm

I had about ten minutes to get to my philosophy class in St. Robert's Hall right across the way on the other side of the Sunken Garden, so I sort of took my time and didn't hurry at all. Almost everybody I passed along the way gave me a high-five or a fist pump, but they were all on their cell phones or iPods talking and texting, so it was kind of like I really didn't exist to them.

It pissed me off a little. I mean - it just all seemed so stupid and phony. Like nobody can stand to have an empty moment in their day. They all have to be plugged into something every second of their fucking phony lives. Shit! It's so fucking ridiculous!

Funny I never noticed it before. But I sure as shit did right now.

And it made me feel really weird - like I was all alone and like I really didn't exist or anything. I was right here, but I didn't really exist for them. The only thing that existed and was real for all these guys were the people who were on the other side of this fucking electronic crap.

Jesus Christ! How weird can stuff get!

When I started up the steps of Regents Terrace I noticed that my old psychology professor, Dr. Shepherd, was coming out of St. Robert's Hall across the way. He saw me and gave this big wave and began coming over in my direction. I was really happy to see him.

Dr. Shepherd was probably about my dad's age, I guess - but he looked really young. I mean, not like all the other old guys. He had this dark hair that didn't have any grey in it yet, and he had a good tan all the time. And he was a pretty handsome guy with this great smile with a hundred white teeth - you know, like those guys on TV that are always trying to sell you something. I think he must have exercised a lot, cause he was pretty well-built and looked like an athlete. As I recall, he told me once that he rowed on the crew team when he was at Georgetown. I guess a guy can stay in shape if he wants to. Dr. Shepherd sure did. The coaches in the gym should have looked more like him, instead of being such big fat slobs.

I could see Shepherd's smile before he even got close to me. I really liked him. I had him for Psych 120. It was a pretty interesting class. And Shepherd took a real interest in me, and I have to say, I encouraged it.

I always try to make good friends with all the adults I come across. You never know what you can get out of them, or when they can do something to help you. I kind of consider them 'fans'. They're my fans. And the more fans you can have, the better. They're easy to use - you know, to get what you want. If you really make them like you, you can use them a lot to get stuff and to get away with stuff. And adults always seem to really like me a lot - in one way or another - so I've always gotten away with a lot of shit. And I've gotten a lot of neat stuff out of them too.

Nothing like having fans!

And I'd made a pretty good one out of Dr. Shepherd. I even got an 'A' in his class last year, when I really should have gotten a 'C'.

That's what having fans can do for you!

"Here's the handsome scholar," Shepherd kind of radiated that smile of his as he warmly shook my hand. "How's school going? How's life?"

"Uh - it's been better," I kind of confessed with a a sigh.

He sort of narrowed his eyes and looked at me more carefully.

"Problems?", he asked quietly as his smile disappeared.

"Yeah."

"Big ones?"

I hesitated, then looked down at the brown, cracked concrete of the Terrace. I wasn't sure how much I should tell him. I trusted him and all that - but, I mean - hell - what good would it do?

"Too big to talk about?", Shepherd gently asked again.

I was still thinking and looking down. More than anything, I wanted to talk to somebody - somebody who would understand and help me. But, I mean - what could he do? Could he bring Kyle back? Could he make Beth less pregnant? Could he make them keep me in school? And how could I ever tell him about Jeff and what I did last night? How could I ever tell him about that?

How could I tell cheerful, smiling Dr. Shepherd that I murdered somebody last night!

"Uh - I don't know," I said real glum and hopeless-like. "It's a pretty big mess. You don't wanna go there."

"I do - if you do," he replied in this kind of slow, really warm and sincere voice that made me want to tell him everything right then and there.

"I don't know," I shook my head, barely able to say it. "I don't know."

"Feel like talking? Walk with me. I'm on my way to a meeting."

"I've got philosophy right now," I shrugged, trying to smile, but I couldn't. "I'm giving a presentation today."

"Oh," he gently smiled. "What's the topic?"

"St. Augustine's Philosophy of Evil," I said in almost a whisper.

"That's cool," he gave a slight chuckle - I think trying to lift my spirits a little bit. "I didn't know he had one. What made you choose that?"

"I didn't. It was assigned."

"Perfect. Well - good luck."

"Thanks."

"And let me know if you want to talk," he said, lowering his voice and giving me this really intense and serious look. "I have a seven o'clock class tonight, but I'll be doing paperwork in my office between six and seven. You can come by then, or you can meet me after ten. Your choice. OK?"

He reached up and gave me a firm, reassuring pat on the shoulder. I managed to give a smile. I didn't feel like smiling, but I did. But I don't think my eyes were smiling. Not at all.

"OK," I weakly mumbled. "Maybe at six - after the game. Thanks, Dr. Shepherd. I gotta get to class now."

I nodded my head and started walking away.

"Try to make it," he called out to me. "OK?"

I waved back at him and headed toward the east entrance door of St. Robert's. Just as I was approaching the open doorway, I moved out of the heavy flowing stream of students and glanced up at the Sacred Heart bell tower. It must have chimed the hour several minutes ago. But I didn't even hear it. And it seemed kind of strange.

That was the first time, I think, that I didn't even notice the chimes.

1:14 pm

There were more than forty students in the second floor classroom of my philosophy class. I was probably the last one to arrive, so I took a seat at the back while Dr. Delaney was explaining the assignment and talking a little about St. Augustine's place in Western thought.

It was incredibly boring, but I felt pretty good about my essay that I was going to stand up and present to the class.

I'm a really good public speaker. I love getting up and taking center stage and talking about this and that. Whatever group I've ever belonged to, people have always immediately seen that I'm the best fucking one to get up and talk. I'm this really smooth talker and can think really quickly and know all what to say and everything. I love talking to a big audience of people. I've been told how I have this whole bunch of charisma going for me. You know - this magnetic quality that makes people want to look at me and listen to me. They usually really get off on that. Star Quality, I think it's called. So it never bothers me at all when I have to give a speech or shoot the shit about anything in front of a bunch people.

I was the first one up. I was all pumped and raring to go - just like out on the soccer field right before a game.

After five more boring minutes of shitting away about Augustine's early life, Delaney - this really tall and skinny and soldier-like looking old man - announced my topic and motioned to me with his hand as he sat down in a chair at the front of the classroom.

I got up real confident-like and took my time strutting down the aisle to the head of the class. I'd memorized my speech - it was always easy for me - so I really didn't need any notes or papers or stuff.

Standing there at the front of the classroom, I gave everyone a big smile and began making my presentation, talking in this real piss-ass kind of voice - you know, like I was some big professor authority figure or something. Like I was an expert on what I was saying. It was pretty easy. What

I'm actually an expert on is making people believe that I really know what I'm talking about. Snowing people is one of my biggest talents. It never fails.

So here I am, shitting away all this useless crap about this old guy named St. Augustine. I think he was the guy that they named that city in Florida after. It would make sense, I guess.

"Evil does not exist in itself," I announced all dramatic-like, making this big meaningful pause, "but rather it is a corruption of goodness. The cause of evil is simply humanity's abuse of their power of free will. This was the basis of St. Augustine's philosophy concerning the existence and nature of evil. We are going to examine the metamorphosis of Augustine's conception of evil and how it influenced the great thinkers of his time."

Shit! This junk was sounding fantastic. I copied most of it out of a book last Sunday, and Beth kind of helped me string it all together so it sounded OK. In fact, to be honest - she wrote almost the whole thing. I had a soccer meeting and then the guys went to the beach and out drinking later on, so naturally I didn't have time to do all the basic crap. But I memorized the whole thing myself, so I guess it was OK because they were sort of my words - you know, I was saying them and they were coming out of my mouth - so it was really my own work. Right?

"St. Augustine believed that God is all-perfect, all-good, and all-loving," I pretty impressively continued, glancing across the students near the windows. "He believed that God created a perfect world out of nothing, and that evil entered this perfect world through the imperfection of human beings - that God's gift of free will to humans resulted in the occurrence of original sin - and all sin which followed. The introduction of evil in the world was the punishment for . . . the . . uh . . . it was the punishment . . . punishment . . for . . . uh . . . the . . . uh . . uh . . the . . . sins . . . of our . . our sins . . . evil is the punishment . . . I mean, we . . uh . . . because we're evil . . . we . . . do bad things . . . uh . . . we do really bad things . . . and God punishes us . . . and he . . . uh . . . uh . . . "

I had glanced down to my left and noticed for the first time that Jeff was sitting right below me in the center of the first row - just four feet away.

And he was staring up at me with these burning, angry eyes. Accusing eyes.

Condemning eyes.

My mind just went blank. Maybe not really blank - but all scrambled and confused and afraid. I just felt so afraid. Like someone had just stepped up and was holding a fucking knife against my throat. Shit!

I couldn't think. Honest to God - I couldn't think!

"Evil is the punishment," I stammered, "the punishment for human sin. For . . our sins. For all the evil things we do. God wants to punish us because we do such bad . . things. We do . . . such . . bad . . things."

I'd suddenly forgotten my whole speech. It was gone. Completely gone from my head. I didn't even know what I was saying.

What the fuck was Jeff doing here! He wasn't even a member of the fucking class!

What the fuck was he doing here sitting all front row and center like he owned the whole fucking place or something!

I turned and looked at Dr. Delaney. I guess I must have had a funny expression on my face. Maybe a kind of begging and helpless look. Least that's how I was feeling.

Delaney was staring at me with this really concerned and curious gaze, sort of twisting his neck back and sideways like a duck when you get too close to it and it doesn't know what the hell to make of what you're try-ing to do.

I glanced back at Jeff.

His eyes were burning right through me.

I started feeling weak and sort of dizzy.

"The evil in the world," I tried to go on talking in this strained, totally pathetic voice, "the evil continues, it always continues because of all the bad stuff we do. When guys do bad stuff - when they sin. They do evil . . . and . . and it's not God's fault. God didn't make them do it. God is perfect. That's what St. Augustine said. So it's us guys who are evil. We're the ones who have to . . . who have to suffer . . . 'cause we made it happen. It's our fault. We made it happen. It's . . . our fault . . . "

I couldn't go on.

Putting my hand up to my forehead, I closed my eyes for a moment, then felt this violent shiver go through my whole fucking body.

Dr. Delaney had stood up and was slowly walking toward me.

I gave this hard shake of my head and just ran out the front door of the classroom and down the hall to the stone staircase at the end. I don't think I said anything to anybody. I just ran. And I ran down the stairs and didn't stop until I was outside and almost all the way across Regents Ter-race.

Shit! I really lost it!

A tall palm tree kind of caught my attention as I stopped running and sort of slowed down to a walk.

It was hotter than ever now. Probably almost 90 degrees. The sun felt really good. But my brain still seemed pretty racked. I wish I had brought that marijuana joint with me. I could have really used it right now.

I stopped walking and looked up at the palm tree. It was one of those kinds that were thick and chunky, sort of just like a huge pineapple. For some reason, it made me feel good to stand there and stare up at it. Maybe I was pretending I was someplace else. I don't know.

All I could think about was that fucking Jeff. I felt like I could have killed him. He knew I'd be presenting my paper this afternoon in Delaney's class - I'd told him all about it early last night, before everything started falling apart and I committed that murder.

Shit! Jeff was really out to get me. I couldn't get away from the fucking guy! Why couldn't he leave me alone!

I swear - right at that moment - I wanted to kill him. I honest to God wanted to kill him and get rid of him for good.

Pacing all anxious and excited-like back and forth beneath that palm tree, I was still struggling to unscramble my brain and figure out what to do next. What I really needed was to calm down so I wouldn't explode into a million little pieces.

That marijuana joint from Cutter that I left in my shorts' pocket back in my room would quickly do the trick. I spun around and took off across the Regents Terrace toward the Sunken Garden.

Joanne Lawson was on the pathway below heading right towards me like a missile closing in on it's target. She must have been about 300 feet away from me and moving fast. Fuck! Joanne has had this super-huge crush on me for almost a year now, but I never could stand her. She talked a mile a minute and had this high, nasal voice that drove you crazy. Just talk, talk, talk. And about nothing. I think she must have been a little nuts. Probably certifiable. I mean, a real walking nut case. Christ! I think all she really needed was a good fuck. That was my professional opinion. But I sure the hell wasn't gonna be the one to give it to her. No thanks!

I knew she'd be all hugging and pawing me to death and clinging on to me like glue if she managed to intercept me, and there was no way in hell I could deal with that today. No way! So I quickly spun around and took off like a rocket up the steps next to Malone and headed toward the safety of the Campus Ministry Center. I figured I'd zig a fast zag through the Center's hallways and lose that wacko chick when I came out the other end at the Malone elevator. I'd be almost home free after that.

The only problem was that I flew in through the doorway of the Campus Ministry building with so much speed that I couldn't slow down in enough time to avoid running over Mike Davis, one of the Center's spiritual counselors, and about as tiny a human being as any adult could possibly ever be.

1:32 pm

Mike Davis must have weighed less than 70 pounds. He probably wasn't even 5 feet tall. Christ! Almost a full-fledged dwarf or something. I really creamed him when I came flying in that door. I honestly felt kind of bad about it as I started scraping him up off the floor, being careful not to do any more damage than I'd already done.

He took a couple of deep breaths and made this funny little whining sound, then straightened his yellow bow tie and pulled his tiny little jacket back up around his bird-like shoulders. I think he was OK. He managed to smile at me and make kind of this dumb joke about the whole thing - you know, some fancy crap like "when man hastens forth unto destiny, so shall destiny conquer man," or something really stupid like that.

I smiled back at him all fake-like impressed because I was sorry I had creamed him so badly.

Davis was kind of surprised to see me. I never really came near the place if I could help it. I mean - come on. How depressing can you get! Campus Ministry? Fuck! Just give me a handful of sleeping pills instead.

I only really knew Davis because he was one of my counselors last year when I was having so much trouble with my drinking and partying and everything. The school was gonna kick me out when I showed up drunk in my theology class two times in a row. My step-dad talked them into putting me in this therapy program and I talked to this priest in the center who was a pretty well-known shrink. I think he even had an office up near Beverly Hills and had a whole bunch of movie stars that he was always trying to cure.

Anyway - part of this torture routine they set for me was that I also had to talk twice a week to a pastoral minister of my own religion, and since I wasn't a Catholic, I was assigned to Mike Davis.

I can't really say that he helped me all that much. In fact, I don't think he helped me at all. Not one bit. But I think he was sort of a nice guy. Not crazy like the priest was. And Davis was really sincere and all

119

eager and enthusiastic - kind of like some dopey little kid that still believes in Santa Claus.

He studied me pretty closely once he made sure that he wasn't dead or anything. Asking me how I was and if everything was OK with me lately, he barely waited for me to answer him. One look told him everything. So I figured - what's the use? - this guy was fully equipped with some kind of radar or something. He could always tell if something was wrong with you. He may not have been able to ever fix it, but he knew it was broken.

So big fucking deal! I already knew it was broken. I didn't need anybody to tell me that. But he insisted on talking to me, so we went down the hall and into his small, closet-like office.

"Can you verbalize your feelings?", Davis gently asked me as he sat down behind his super-cluttered desk and motioned me to sit in the chair opposite him.

"Uh - you mean talk about stuff?"

"Yes - to put it in the vernacular - precisely. What's happening in your life right now? What particular stresses are impacting your daily schedule, both implicitly as well as explicitly? What special conflicts and traumas have recently touched upon your spiritual well-being?

Shit! Give me a break! What a bunch of horse shit! The same old horse shit he was always shoveling last year! Christ! I might as well be sitting in church. It was just the same old ten dollar words and bible stuff all balled together to make a good show. What did all this crap mean anyway? Fuck! Who knows!

I just sat there and looked at him like he was something under a microscope, and I didn't say a word.

"I fully realize that these concerns must be exceeding difficult to articulate," Davis kind of nervously continued, clearing his throat and eyeballing the wall behind me. "Perhaps if we went directly to scripture and read the words of St. Paul. This would most likely instantly solve all of your problems. How would that be?"

"Great," I quickly replied, thinking some miracle was just about to rain down on me and magically make all the crap go away.

"Very well," Mike Davis said all excited-like, his big green eyes kind of all happily dancing and spinning around like frisbees. "Are you ready to commence and hear the divine solution to your dilemma?"

"Sure," I eagerly smiled. "Shoot."

He gave me this kind of surprised little double-take, then relaxed and assumed a sort of trance-like expression as he opened this thick book and fumbled around until he found what he was looking for.

"The Second Letter of St. Paul to the Corinthians," he began reading in this really corny and phony voice, all loud and important and really precise - pronouncing almost every letter of every word. "Blessed be the God and the Father of our Lord Jesus Christ, the merciful Father and the God who gives every possible encouragement. He supports us in every hardship, so that we are able to come to the support of others, in every hardship of theirs because of the encouragement that we ourselves receive from God. For just as the sufferings of Christ overflows into our lives, so too does the encouragement we receive through Christ. So if we have hardships to undergo, this will contribute to your encouragement and your salvation. If we receive encouragement, this is to gain for you the encouragement which enables you to bear with perseverance the same sufferings as we do. So our hope for you is secure in the knowledge that you share the encouragement we receive, no less than the suffering we bear."

Holy shit!

What the fuck did all that mean!

Davis gently closed the book and looked up at me sort of like somebody who had just won a Gold Medal in the Olympics.

"Could anything more be possibly said?", he very softly announced with the same kind of smile I always get on my face after I have an orgasm and cum all over the place.

"Huh?"

"It's all right here," Davis very proudly stated, pointing to the book in his hand. "You'll never find better advice. Just follow these words exactly - they will lead you to the solution of all of your problems."

What the fuck!

That holy stuff was nothing but a bunch of double-talk! I couldn't understand a word of this shit! I was more confused than ever.

"So - any questions?", Mike Davis asked me with this big, phony smile on his narrow little face.

"No," I mumbled, looking down at all the junk on his desk.

"Then, go forth and seek God's word," he kind of joyfully gushed.

I stood up and shook his tiny little hand when he offered it to me. I gave it an extra hard squeeze and felt a little better when I saw his face painfully scrunch up like a sponge. It sort of made me feel good. Shit! Some help this dude was. Same old shit. Always the same old shit. Just a bunch of empty words and crap.

"You're lucky that your problems aren't serious," Davis said happily as I started going out the door. "Some day - when you're an adult and far from here, you'll know what real problems are. So just remember how lucky you are right now that these small things can be so easily solved."

Right! I was so tempted to just stop right there in the doorway as I looked at his stupid smiling face and just smile back at him and casually tell him about last night - about how I had murdered somebody.

Fix that with your magic words, you jackass!

But I didn't say a word. I just turned and left.

And I slowly walked back to my room and took off my jeans and shirt and put on my soccer uniform. That made me feel a little better. It was getting hotter and hotter outside, plus - I loved wearing my uniform. The big number Nine on the front of it. I looked more like who I really was when I was wearing my soccer uniform. I guess it was who I was. It was me. When I was in my other clothes I always felt kind of funny. Like I didn't really know who I was. But I always knew who I was when I had my uniform on. It made me feel good. Almost kind of calm and confident.

I went over to the bluff behind Sacred Heart Chapel and sat down on a bench. Taking the marijuana joint out of the pocket of my shorts, I lit up and began puffing away.

1:59 pm

As always, the pot worked like a charm. I was relaxed and kind of carefree for the first time today. There was a bottle of scotch in my lower dresser drawer back in my room. It had hardly been touched yet. It al-

123

ways did the trick too. But I needed about three or four good shots 'til I got mellow enough to feel like I was floating on top of everything. Pot was much better. It didn't knock you out like booze did. It actually made you feel all better and everything. Like you could do anything.

Anyway, the big championship game was a little later, and there was no way I could get myself buzzed on a bottle of scotch. I would have been staggering all over the fucking field!

The bells in the tower right next to me began chiming two o'clock. I stood up and stared through the trees at the loud speakers at the top where the recording was coming from. I loved the sound of those bells so much that I always sort of pretended that I didn't really know that it was just a recording - a tape or a CD or something. I really wanted to believe that it was real. That there were really bells up there. It made me feel good to pretend they were real.

Feeling kind of sleepy, I walked along the bluff pathway back toward the apartments. I thought I'd go back to my room again and take a little nap until I had to go to the Training Center at 2:45.

I was following the dirt pathway and sort of looking through the pine trees at the edge of the bluff at the awesome view of the whole fucking world that you could see from there, and as I walked past this huge memorial sculpture that was off to the side and kind of all hidden-like in the shadow of the tall bell tower, I suddenly just sort of hesitated and stopped. Then I very slowly stepped over close to it and stood there.

It was strange. I never had gone over to it before. It always gave me the creeps. It just weirded me out. It was a memorial to all of the students who had died while they were studying here at the university. It was huge, and made out of this real heavy-looking metal - bronze, or some-

thing like that, I suppose. And it had all these life-size figures of people -
about a dozen or so of them - and all draped in these dress-like gowns.
Maybe they were supposed to be the graduation gowns that guys wear at
the commencement ceremony. I don't know. They kind of looked like it.
And all these people were divided into two groups. One group on the right
kind of were sort of all holding back together, and the other group on the
left were kind of marching up a couple of steps, like they were waiting for a
taxi or something. And all of them looked totally sad - like they were crying
or something. I hate anybody that cries, so I never went too close to this
creepy memorial thing. I looked at it once when I was a sophomore, but I
never went back. It was just so gross and dumb. It didn't make me feel
good.

But today, for some reason, I went over to it again and took a really
good look. Now, today, it didn't seem as weird as I remembered it. In fact,
it was actually kind of nice. A real work of art. Sort of what they might
have over there in Europe and places like that. The guy that made it must
have been a pretty talented dude.

Looking at it more closely, I could see that it was supposed to be a
scene where the living students are saying goodbye to the departing students - the dead guys. I really checked it out. But it was hard to tell which
group was which. I mean, everybody in the damn thing was so fucking
sad-looking that you couldn't tell who had died and who was still living. I
couldn't tell the living from the dead.

I looked down at the large cement base of the memorial and noticed
that on all four sides there were these tiny little plaques with names written
on them. And dates. There were probably almost a hundred of them. I

bent down and started reading a few.   All of these guys here were only teenagers or so.   Really young guys.

Just like Kyle and me.

I suddenly felt really funny.   Not funny exactly.   Just kind of creeped out and maybe a little afraid and sad and upset and everything.   I turned and started jogging back down the pathway.   I wanted to get the hell out of there.

Running through the pine trees and across the grass lawn, I kept thinking that Kyle's name would probably be there pretty soon on that weird memorial.   They were probably making his little plague right now, and then they'd come out here and glue it right into the empty space I'd just seen at the far end of that ugly cement base.

Kyle's name.   And his birth date, and his . . . the other date.   That day two weeks ago.

I kept jogging and crossed the faculty parking lot on the east side of Sacred Heart Chapel and began heading back to my room.   To my right, I saw Mr. Kirkland, my English teacher, getting out of his car.   It was this really old VW that had they really odd shape - like half a donut.   It was kind of crappy and beat up and looked like it should've been sitting in a museum somewhere.   You know - a real relic.   Probably of some big historical interest.   But who'd want to drive around in a piece of shit like that?   I mean - come on!

Mr. Kirkland was kind of a young guy. He was still in school - I think at UCLA - studying for his doctorate.   He had this really long hair and glasses and kind of a pointy face.   You know the type - real arty-like. Some of my friends said he was a writer and a poet. I'd believe it. Don't know what he was doing here. But he was an OK teacher.

I had him for an American Literature class this semester. In fact, the class was at 2:10 - so it was gonna begin in only a few minutes over in St. Roberts. But I was blowing it off today. Whenever we had a afternoon soccer game, we all had to be at the Training Center at 2:45 to give us plenty of time before the game began. Kirkland knew it and he never complained, but I always got the feeling that he didn't like it very much that I and Chad and another guy on the team were always cutting his class once almost every week.

Kirkland gave me this kind of suffering look and walked quickly toward me, so I slowed down and sort of prepared to apologize for missing his class again today. But I thought maybe I'd be a nice guy about it and pretend that I really wanted to come and hear one of his excruciatingly boring lectures on Mark Twain or Hemingway or some guy like that. You always wanna make these nut case teachers think that you really wanna hear all their shit. That's how you get a good grade. And I also wanted to keep him as a fan. A guy like me can never have too many fans.

For some reason the English Department seemed to have a lot of gay guys in it. The professors, I mean. At least they all sure seemed gay. And they usually really came across like these really phony actors or something. The way they talked and moved and the clothes they wore. They all seemed like they thought they were always on some fucking theater stage or something. It was kind of funny really. The phoniest guys on campus were these fags in the English Department. And the queers in Theater Arts Department, of course. Christ! Give me a break!

I could kind of tell they were gay because every time I had to go and talk to one of them, they always kept their eyes down and never looked at me once. And they seemed all nervous around me and dropping stuff when we'd be talking. One guy that taught my freshman English course - I forget his name - used to totally freak out every time I'd come up and talk to him after class. I mean totally freak out! Once I walked with him to his car in the Leavy lot and he was so fucking mental about the whole thing that he slammed his car door on part of his jacket and couldn't get it open again, and then he locked his keys in his car and had to run off and call somebody. Probably his boyfriend. I thought I was gonna flunk his class, but when I went up to him at the end of the semester and started trying to sweet-talk him into a passing grade, he couldn't deal with it and just went ahead and gave me a 'B+'.

I'm pretty sure that Kirkland wasn't gay. He seemed pretty normal to me. I mean, every time I tried sweet-talking him into getting a better grade, he'd just narrow his eyes at me in that kind of piss-ass way that my step-dad always does. Kirkland seemed always ahead of me, just like that bitch Thompson in my history class. I never could get an extra inch out of either of them. Shit! I guess it was my fault - my own fucking fault. I should have been more carefully when I was selecting what classes to take at the beginning of the semester. I should have chosen the teachers that I knew I could have made fans out of, so that I could really get around them all easy-like and not have to do any work. You know - make them like all the other 'fans' in my fan club. Like all those other teachers that always cave right in and totally fall for my routine - my melting smile and my eyes and my voice and all that seductive crap.

But it was my own fault, I guess. I should have checked them out and made fans of them before I signed up for their stupid classes.

But, at least now I had learned a valuable lesson, and, after all, isn't that what education is really all about? Isn't it? Right.

Kirkland came up behind me and punched me in the shoulder - all friendly-like. But it was really kind of a hard punch. He was always sort of putting me on the defensive. Challenging me and stuff like that. Always arguing with what I thought and said. Sometimes it was OK - not really that bad. But most of the time it was kind of annoying and upsetting. You know - saying stuff that really made me think and have all these questions and doubts. I didn't like it so much when it did that. It wasn't fun.

I made my phony apology to him about being forced to miss his class. He walked with me as we talked.

"Well, Number Nine - first things first," Kirkland announced in this really serious and sincere voice. "After all, this is a sporting event and sports must always come first. At least, at the university they must. Learning isn't all that important. It's sports! Getting out there and hitting and kicking that ball around. That's really what counts. What goes on in the classroom is nothing compared to the glory of winning that old game and packing those seats in the stadium and making the alumni proud and happy. Those are the values that make life worth living. Mastering hitting that ball and winning that game. Win - win - win! Always remember that. It's all that time you spend perfecting the skill of kicking your foot at a ball that will ultimately bring you joy and success in life. Forget about putting useless information in your brain. What possible use can that ever be? Where can it possibly ever get you? Nobody's ever going to applaud you for getting an 'A' for learning things in a classroom. Isn't that true from your own experience? Am I right, or am I right?"

I really wasn't quite sure what to say. Sometimes I got the sense that he might be kind of kidding me. You know - sort of putting me on.

"Uh . . yeah," I sort of mumbled, a little confused. "I guess so."

"Of course I'm right," he said very forcefully, turning around with this huge hard smile and slapping me on the shoulder again. "Sports rule. The team. The ball. The football, the baseball, the basketball, the volleyball, the soccer ball. All bow to the almighty ball! Nothing else in life matters except the all-powerful ball! Good luck, sport! Win! Win! Win!"

Kirkland pumped his fist in the air and let out this loud, whooping sound and marched off toward St. Robert's Hall to his English class.

I watched him as he descended into the Sunken Garden and quickly made his way between the lawns.

Some birds were singing in the trees in front of me. I just sort of stood there and listening to them.

Then I started thinking.

I hate it when that happens. When something makes me start thinking. But I couldn't help myself. My mind just kind of started collapsing onto this one thought and it wouldn't let go of it.

What was Kirkland really saying to me? Was everything he'd been saying to me just one big joke? Had he been totally goofing on me - just punking me along?

If he had been punching me - then that meant he thought I was just some kind of a joke. It meant that Kirkland really thought I was just some dumb, stupid joke.

What the hell did he have against sports, anyway!

Shit!

Sports are everything!

I mean - what's more important than sports?

Than soccer?

It's my whole fucking life!

Why was he saying all that shit, anyway?

Come to think of it - he was really making fun of the whole fucking thing and putting it down like some worthless asshole.

And putting me down!

All just because I had to cut his fucking worthless class today because of the game!

Fuck!

Maybe that was the real reason why he'd been giving me all those fucking D minuses.

Shit! Who needed his half-assed fucking literature class anyway!

Fuck him!

What makes that asshole think he's better than me, just because he's read all these really boring old books and can recite every fucking word on every fucking page of them! Shit! Give me a break! Big deal! What the hell did that ever get anybody! Some shitty little job in a nut factory like this crummy university? Big fucking deal!

The more I thought about it, the madder I got.

And I couldn't stop thinking about it.

But I wasn't just mad at Kirkland - I was mad at Jeff and Beth and Chelsea and Dr. Thompson and my mom and step-dad and my real dad and the coach and that guy last night and nearly everybody who had ever come near me. It sounds stupid to say. But I was mad at everybody right now. And, most of all, I was mad at Kyle.

I don't know why. But I was really mad at Kyle right now.

Moving really slowly along the sidewalk by the parking lot, I came to the entrance to the quad and I looked across and saw Beth going in the front door of the apartments. I knew instantly that she was on her way up to my room. She knew I'd be there 'til I left for the Training Center at 2:40.

Shit! She was swooping down for another shot at me. Probably tears and all - just like last night. Pushing and pulling and hammering at me again. Trying to guilt me all out about it.

Fuck! Like it wasn't her fault too! How the fuck was I supposed to know she was gonna get knocked up! She told me it was OK - that I didn't need to wear a condom! That it was OK to cum inside her all the time. How the fucking hell was I supposed to know she didn't know from shit about it! Like I'm supposed to fucking know what's going on inside her whole fucking body! I can barely keep track of my own goddamned body without having to worry and be all expert on anybody else's. Especially some dopey girl who can't even keep track of her own cycles.

Shit! I was really pissed.   And I was getting more and more pissed as I stood there thinking about all this shit.

There was no way I was gonna go back up to my room right now. Not with her up there. And I didn't want to go up to the Training Center yet.

I was really feeling so angry that it was making me all sort of con-fused and kind of lost-like.

Wandering through the quad and out behind the apartments, I glanced over and saw my truck parked across the way. Without even thinking, I went over to it and climbed in and drove off. Really fast.

It felt so good to finally have some control over something today. To have some complete power over something. Fuck! It felt so good.

I really slammed it going around the curve of Ignatian Circle and by the time I passed Hilton and the Von der Ahe Center, I was doing almost fifty. I know it was sort of dangerous and all that - but I really loved it.

Suddenly these three guys and a girl came out from nowhere and flew into the crosswalk, and I had to go up on the opposite sidewalk to avoid making road-kill out of them. It was a pretty close call. And it kind of shook me up a whole bunch. I came an inch close to just creaming all four of them. Jesus Christ! Was it close!

That's all I needed. Four more dead bodies on my hands. The one last night was more than enough, thank you.

I really slowed down after that. And it was a good thing that I did. There was a campus cop car just beyond the stop sign, kind of lurking behind a high hedge of red-flowered bushes. You know - sort of that chicken-shit way those cops always have of hanging around like that trying to nail some poor helpless guy like me who's just driving a little fast and only trying to have some innocent and harmless fun.

Picking up speed again when I blasted out through the university's front gates and turned left on Lincoln, I didn't have a clue where I was going until I came to Manchester and turned right and headed west toward the beach.

2:37 pm

It was a great day to be at the beach in Playa del Rey. I'd been there a lot in the past. When the hot wind blows it makes it so clear you can see islands all over the place way off on the horizon. Sometimes when you think they're islands, they're only just clouds or fog or a reflection of the ocean in the misty sky. But today was so bright and clear that I knew for sure they were islands.

I'd parked my truck up on Vista del Mar Street and walked down the steep, crumbling asphalt pathway that led to the sand. The beach was humungus - nearly half a mile wide. You've never seen so much sand in your life. And nobody was hardly ever there. It always looked funny to see this giant sandy beach and only a few people stretched out on it, all far apart from each other.

The sand was boiling. I tried taking my tennis shoes off, but I quickly put 'em back on. Holy shit! You'd have to be a fire walker or something to walk on the sand barefoot on a day like this.

I walked all the way to the shore and took off my soccer T-shirt and sat on it to make sure I didn't fry my butt when I squatted down on a sandy ledge right above where the waves were breaking and sloshing in almost all the way up to my feet.

It was so great just sitting there all by myself and watching the blue-green wall of waves, one right after another, come smashing and crashing down on top of each other and flooding in and out toward my feet with this really neat sort of white, bubbly foam.

I just sat there staring at them and watching how the sunlight kind of lit them up like a glowing turquoise window every time each one of them arched its back high up just before it came booming and smashing down.

Pretty soon the waves began getting bigger and bigger. I think the wind suddenly had started blowing sort of strong from the north and the west. It was kind of a cooler wind and not nearly so dry as before.

Shit! Those waves were really breaking like maniacs now. Just thundering all down and smashing each other to shit. Fuck! You should have seen it. It was so awesome.

I closed my eyes and just kind of drifted - listening to the lapping of the water and the constant booming explosions of the surf. The air was so fresh and sharp that I could actually feel the salt in it when I took a deep breath. It made my nose kind of tickle and burn a little. I really liked that. It really felt great.

Before I was even conscious of it, I was thinking about Kyle.

I'm not really sure what I was exactly thinking about him. But I know I was. It's like when sometimes you just sort of feel a thought and don't really think it. You know what I mean? It's like the feeling just comes to you and you don't even have a chance to know it's even there yet. You just feel it. You feel it really strong.

That's how it was. I was feeling Kyle more than I was thinking anything in particular about him. It was like he was with me - sitting right there next to me on the sand, the way we always used to on hot days when we'd come here in the afternoon after soccer practice and sit and talk and swim in the ocean.

With my eyes all shut and everything, I really could almost feel him sitting there right next to me. It kind of overwhelmed me.

My brain was just sort of all frozen-like. Everything inside me just seem to shut down. It was so weird. I felt like I was just being sucked backwards in time - like it wasn't now, but it was back then.

I was floating away like that when this loud, deep voice suddenly called down from right above me.

"Sorry, son - the water's closed this afternoon. No swimming is allowed."

Really startled, I opened my eyes and glanced up and saw this guy standing next to me. I could tell me was a lifeguard. He had on those dopey bright red shorts and a white T-shirt that said 'LIFEGUARD' across the front of it. And he even had one of those bogus-looking whistles on a chain around his neck. So - chances were pretty good that this guy was the real deal - an official lifeguard.

"OK," I mumbled. "I wasn't gonna swim, anyway."

"Surf's way too high," he announced in this real military-like tone, sort of like he was the one who invented the whole wave set-up and the tides and all that crap. "It'll be this way 'til tomorrow noon or so."

Just then he saw some guys climbing out on this pile of rocks to the left. It don't know why the shit they dumped the rocks in there like that. It was sort of like a short pier made out of these huge boulder-like rocks, and you could walk out on the flattened tops of them. I think they call it a jetty. Yeah - I heard somebody call it a jetty once.

Anyway, these two clowns were taking a hike out onto the jetty and the crashing waves were sweeping really close to them.

This lifeguard stomped forward a little bit and yelled like hell for these two dopes to get the fuck off the rocks. He was pretty tough about it too. The two morons hesitated a minute, then slowly hiked back in.

"Some people," the lifeguard said to me with this sort of really tired, pissed-off shake of his head. "They don't have a brain in their heads. They'd kill themselves if it wasn't for us. Just two months ago a kid about your age was climbing out there at the end of the jetty and a wave much smaller than these came along and just swept him right out to sea. They never even found his body."

I stared toward the jetty and bit down on my lower lip. I'm not exactly sure why I did that. But I did.

"He drowned?", I quietly asked him.

"Sure - what else."

"Drown. Do many people - have many people drowned here?"

"I'd say probably three or four since I've been here," he very casually replied. "In the last eight years or so. That's not so bad, I guess."

"Must be pretty awful, I guess," I sort of was muttering to myself without even really thinking, "to drown - to sink down into the ocean like that and die like that - just breathing in all that water - awful."

"Ah," he kind of shrugged, "I don't think it would be so bad. If you've gotta go, it's probably one of the best ways. Yeah. Just suspended in the water like that - all peaceful and quiet and calm. It's probably not bad at all. Maybe it's even the best way to die - I think. You just go to sleep in the water. It must be a pretty comforting way to go out. They say it's very much like the way we're born. A lot like our birth. You know, being in the water inside our moms the way we are. So drowning must be like being born again - only it's the end - not the beginning. A calm, relaxed, quiet end. I guess maybe it's kind of a perfect coming around full circle and completing our life. Returning to where we came from."

"Maybe that's why so many people kill themselves that way," I said without even thinking.

"Maybe," he very casually agreed with me.

I stared at the wave that was crashing down into the shore and just kept looking at it and wondering.

The lifeguard turned around and glanced down at me with a friendly smile. He was sort of a medium guy. Medium age, medium height, medium weight, medium hair - a real medium looking guy. The kind of dudes you see everywhere.

But suddenly it struck me.

And then this freezing chill went down my spine.

He looked just like that guy last night. He looked almost exactly like that medium guy last night at the bar.

That guy I killed.

3:41 pm

After that lifeguard looked straight at me and suddenly reminded me so much of that guy I murdered last night, I just jumped up and got the fucking hell out of there - jogging across the sand back toward the path to my truck.

I flew into my truck and just tore off down Vista del Mar. I was driving really fast and kept staring out the right windshield at the huge waves breaking along the beach. And when I finally slowed down a little, I began thinking about what that creepy lifeguard guy had said - how drowning was the best way to die. How it was so calm and peaceful and comforting - just gently swirling in the water and sort of falling asleep.

I couldn't quite remember his exact words. But I did remember what he said about how it was like being born. How drowning was like being born again - only it would be the end instead of the beginning. The completion of life - the cycle of life.

Just the pleasant, peaceful end of the cycle. I kept thinking and thinking about that. About how maybe that was what was maybe meant to be - where everything had been leading.

I really thought about that.

And about that lifeguard, and how much he looked like that guy Steve last night. Steve. I never did find out his last name.

I wondered what Steve would have thought about drowning. What he would have said about it.

Or was that lifeguard really Steve?

Was that lifeguard real? Or was he Steve? Steve's spirit come back to tell me what to do?

I was beginning to think maybe I had imagined the whole thing. Had I been sleeping there on the beach and did I dream it?

Did it really happen?

Maybe it was kind of like last night. It seemed like a dream too. When I woke up this morning I was sure it was a dream. Until Jeff came in and made it real.

Goddamned, fucking Jeff!

I was almost tempted to turn around and go back to that spot on the beach and look for that lifeguard. I wanted to find him and make sure he was actually real, and not something from my brain.

But I didn't.

I just kept driving and looking at those giant, rolling waves - sweeping away, back and forth - just peacefully sweeping everything away really all nice and clean.

I started wondering what it would feel like to be just totally swept away under one of those beautiful curling waves. Just step right out into it and let it gently sweep you out and away into eternity.

That might not be such a bad thing at all.

Not a bad thing at all.

It wasn't until I swerved along the gentle curve of the highway and entered Manhattan Beach that I suddenly remembered the soccer game back at the university.

Shit! I looked at my watch. The game had begun ten minutes ago.

I jerked the wheel into a U-turn and really floored it back up Vista del Mar towards campus. Shit!

It took fifteen minutes to get back to the university, and by that time the first half of the game against UCLA was more than half over. Shit!

I was already trying to think up some good fucking excuses for being so late.

I tore into the parking lot next to the Lion Training Center and jumped out of my truck and just left the thing sitting there in the fucking middle of everything and ran like shit through the gate and onto the field.

So far, my mind hadn't jacked into gear with any good excuses. As I ran, I kept thinking what the hell I could possibly say to explain why I had totally blown off the beginning of the game. I was sort of tossing around that 'getting sick' gag that I'd used for yesterday, but it struck me it might seem a little stale by now and kind of hard to sell again to a hard-nosed, son-of-a-bitch like Coach Bonner.

Before I had a chance to come up with anything convincing, old Bonner stomped right over and practically smashed right into me.

We stood there nose to nose.

I waited for him to speak, but he didn't. His face was like a piece of hard, red cement.

He just stared at me with this completely empty expression. Then he glanced down at my left bicep.

"Where's your armband?", he asked me in this kind of weird, slightly shaky voice.

I took this really deep breath and clenched my whole fucking body, like somebody was about to hit me.

"I threw it away," I quietly answered him.

Bonner stared at me for a moment. It was exactly like the way my dad looked at me a long time ago when I burnt down the garage with his new Lexus inside it.

Then he slowly turned around. He turned his back on me. The fucking guy just stood there with his back to me. Shit!

"Go to the locker room," he mumbled. "Get off the field."

I couldn't believe it. I looked around and saw Marco and Josh and some of the other guys sitting nearby on the bench. They'd seen the whole thing, and they just sort of looked down at the ground or off toward the teams on the field.

What else could I do? I started slowly walking back toward the Training Center. As I moved, I could feel my legs trembling a little bit. I don't think I was scared or anything. I think I was just feeling a lot of emotions that I didn't realize I was feeling. It was more an emotion thing than a thought kind of thing.

But while I was walking away, there was one thought that came into my head. It was a really powerful, strong kind of thought. It was a thought about something that I was suddenly feeling. Something that I had never felt before.

I didn't care.

I just didn't fucking care anymore.

Not a bit!

Fuck the game! Fuck soccer!

I was just fucking tired of the whole shitty thing.

I wanted my life back.

And I wanted my name back!

I was done with that stupid 'Number Nine', 'Niner' shit. I was fucking done with it. That was all the hell I'd become anymore - to the whole fucking school! To everybody! Number Nine! Niner! Shit! What kind of an asshole answers to a number? Even a dog doesn't answer to a number. A goddamned dog has a name! And everybody calls him by his real name - not some half-shit number or something!

Suddenly I didn't give a fuck if we won or lost today.

I really didn't!

I didn't care.

It seemed like a pretty long walk to the locker room. When I got back to the gate, I glanced over at the scoreboard. UCLA was already ahead by two points. Shit! I was the best fucking player on the whole fucking team. They really needed me today. Fat-assed Bonner should have pulled out Jeff or Will or one of a half a dozen other guys and put me in. Fuck! We only win when I'm playing! Everybody knows that.

But I didn't give a shit. I just marched on into the locker room and sat down on the cold wooden bench. Let Bonner blow the whole fucking game, for all I cared. It was his funeral - not mine. Let the fat asshole lose the whole fucking League Championship. All just because of one fucking stupid little black armband! Fuck!

I'd have rather been back at the goddamned beach, anyway. Looking at the pale blue lockers in front of me, I started seeing those tall, sweeping waves again. Those beautiful, glowing waves.

As I sort of relaxed and closed my eyes a little, the blue glow of the lockers looked almost exactly like one of those huge waves - bending and rolling and reaching out to me and gently surrounding me and carrying me peacefully away to nowhere.

I sat there for a long time feeling a sort of odd, nice sensation of being softly swept away.

My mind had never felt so peaceful.

I forgot about everything.

Even time.

"What the fuck are you doing!", a voice loudly sounded from behind me in this really angry tone.

I opened my eyes and quickly spun around.

It was Will. He looked super pissed.

"What'a'ya mean?", I asked him, all innocent-like. "The coach sent me in here. I'm just doin' what he told me to do."

"You're just gonna lose the whole fucking game for us, you asshole! That's what you're doin'!"

I just shrugged and gave him a tight little smile that said 'go fuck yourself.'

"All because of that goddamned armband?", Will asked me in a slightly calmer voice. "I don't get it, Niner. I swear - I don't even begin to get it. It's an armband. It's just a fucking armband. It's only a symbol. It's what we all said we wanted to do."

"I never said . . . "

"Yeah, I know - you never said, you never agreed. Fine! You don't want to. I got it! But we're a team. We're a team, Niner. This isn't the kind of shit where we all do exactly anything we please. Where we just all go out and do anything we want. We're a team. We have to stick together and become one thing. We have to do things we don't want to. And this is one of them. You have to do it for the team."

"The team?", I asked, sort of confused by Will's logic.

"Yeah," he said in a strained voice, starting to lose his patience again. "We're a goddamned team. That's what this whole fucking thing is about. That's why we're playing the fucking game. We're a team. And we all have to stick together. I fouled out of the game, and I came in here to use the head. But I really came in here to talk to you. We're really slipping behind now. UCLA just made another fucking goal. We really need you. So - here - take my armband - and go out and let the coach see it."

Reaching up, Will slid off his black armband with the big 'KM' letters on it and held it out to me.

I stared at it and hesitated for a moment.

"No," I quietly said.

Will looked at me with this shit-faced amazement, and he seemed almost speechless.

"You gotta be kidding," he finally managed to sort of croak out. "You're telling all of us to go screw ourselves? You're throwing away the Championship? All because you have some fucking silly, half-assed reason for not wanting to wear this little piece of black cloth? Are you crazy, Niner? Are you clinically insane!"

"Maybe," I mumbled with a dry little laugh.

"Look - so we all made a mistake! So you weren't Kyle's best friend! OK! So you didn't even like Kyle! Fine! So I guess maybe you fucking hated the guy! Great! You've already showed all that by now. We can all see now that you didn't give a fuck about the guy. You were the only one of us who didn't even cry about it. In fact, you've almost been fucking laughing about it ever since it happen. I heard that shitty crack you made to Dave about Kyle's accident - on the fucking day they told us about it. That crappy joke about how it was probably the first time a Lion was ever turned into roadkill. Funny! Really funny! We get it. OK? You didn't like the guy. But you gotta do it now! You gotta wear it, Niner!"

He tossed it down on the bench and stormed out the door.

I glanced down at the twisted piece of black cloth lying there. It gave me this really horrible feeling.

I shut my eyes again.

About ten minutes later the whole fucking team came charging into the locker room like a herd of crazy horses.

When each one of them looked over at the lockers and saw me sitting there, they gave me this really crappy expression - like ya do when you accidentally step in a pile of dog shit. Fuck!

It was half-time, and Coach Bonner was slowly following behind them looking like he was wearing a jockstrap five sizes too small. A real pained look on his fat face.

I heard some of the guys saying to Will that the score of the game was - us - 1, UCLA - 3.

Shit!

All the guys on the team sort of clustered together on the other side of the locker room - about as fucking far away from me as it was possible to get. Nobody was even looking in my direction, except Marco, who kept taking this nervous little peek at me, and Josh, who gave me the eye once or twice and couldn't help flashing this tight, sort of disappointed grin.

Chad was the only one who deliberately detoured around my bench and walked right past me. He slowed to almost a stop as he went by and stared down at me with this really friendly look on his face.

"Fucking asshole!", he said to me in this hushed, really nasty tone.

"Fuck you!", I replied almost automatically without even thinking.

Coach Bonner began gathering everybody together over there in the corner and he stood at the front of them and started delivering the shittiest, most god-awful pep talk you've ever heard in your life. He never mentioned my name, but a couple of times I noticed that he made some lame, half-assed comment about how their ship had been 'deserted by the captain' and it was up to them alone now to either sink or swim.

146

Fuck!

This shit went on for about five minutes. I could hardly stand it. I thought the fat slob was gonna break down in tears near the end when he was really cranking up the rah-rah stuff and bowing his head as he mentioned the honor of the school and all that crap. Shit!

I guess I never really listened to one of these things from a distance before. You know - not being all mashed together with the other guys and sort of like being just one mindless body when we always listened to this emotional bullshit before. You just always believed it and you never stood back and thought about it. Not as just one person - one individual.

But now - for the first time - I did.

And it sure as hell did sound like a bunch of fucking bullshit. A bunch of meaningless, stupid bullshit.

The honor of the school. The glory of the team. The triumph of the spirit. The victory of mind over matter. Fuck me! Give me a break! What a load of shit!

Bonner ended his little brainwashing exercise with all these moronic whooping shouts as he wildly shook his fist in the air. All the guys instantly followed right after him and did the same mindless, bullshit thing. It all kind of reminded me of a scene from out of one of those old war movies they're always showing on TV real late at night.

"Let's go, men!", the coach finally yelled at the top of his voice, trying to be all fierce and warrior-like and everything - but coming off just really all pathetic-like - sort of like this hysterical little girl. Really lame.

The guys quickly began breaking out of the tight little group they had been in and moving toward the door to the field. When Reicher got up and turned, I could see Jeff for the first time sitting there behind him.

147

He was staring right at me.

Fucking asshole!

That same shitty stare - like he was trying to read my mind or something. Or like he was trying to set me on fire and destroy me exactly like those old Voodoo guys do down there in South America. It's really kind of scary, if you really think about it. It was almost like Jeff was evil. Yeah - evil. The more I thought about it - the more I was wondering if he was really evil.

And then something suddenly came into my head that really kind of confused and upset me. It was an idea. An idea that just bit into my brain like a fucking snake might have struck it. Just this simple idea - that it should have been Jeff that I killed last night, instead of that other guy - that guy I killed named Steve. That's what he told me his name was - Steve. Yeah - I should have murdered Jeff last night instead of Steve.

I pushed all that crap out of my head real fast. It was sort of even more scary than that Voodoo thing.

But all I really knew for fucking sure was that I hated him. I hated Jeff. I hated him more than I've ever hated anybody.

And the more he stared at me that way - the more I wished he was fucking dead. I really did.

He kind of hung around a little bit after the other guys began leaving the locker room. Then, really slow-like, he started walking over to where I was sitting on the bench.

I quickly stood up and turned my back to him. I didn't want to say a fucking goddamned word to him. Not one goddamned word!

Jeff came up right behind me, hesitated a moment, then softly spoke to me in this really rat-assed creepy voice:

"Midnight, Niner. Right after your great big happy birthday party. Meet me at midnight at the flagpole. We'll take my car. I think the police will be want to keep you there in jail - at least 'til your step-dad starts bribing people to get bail for you. Midnight! Got it? If you don't show up, I'll go down there alone, and then the police will have to come here and get you. And if they have to do that - then I think you can forget all about bail, and probably about the rest of your whole fucking life, for that matter."

Jeff said the total fucking thing without even taking a second breath. He just said it just like that. Like he was announcing the goddamned evening news or something. Then, he just walked away. Just like that. I guess he must of followed the other guys out the door. I didn't look. I didn't even turn my head and glance out of the corner of my eye. I didn't want to see him. I hated the sight of him.

I really wanted to kill him! To murder him!

It seemed like it was gonna be either him or me. That's what it was down to now. And it was all his fault. He broke his promise. He broke his sacred fucking promise he made to me last night. He swore he'd never tell anybody. He gave me his goddamned fucking word that he'd never tell another human being about what I did.

And now look at the fucking guy! He's breaking his sacred word and he's going off to rat on me to the police!

Holy fuck!

What a piece of worthless shit Jeff was! He's blackmailing me now! The crappy little punk is telling ME what to do! Threatening me now! Amazing!

Christ! It was really all Jeff's fault in the first place! He should have stuck with me last night. He shouldn't have gone off to the car like that. He never should have left me alone. It was really all Jeff's fault.

Fucking shithead!

It was all his fault! And now he's all determined and everything to destroy my life. What does he think the law is gonna do to me? Shake my hand and give me a cigar or something? Right! More like toss me in a cell and throw away the key!

And all because of Jeff!

It was just too bad that he couldn't break his fucking neck or something out there on the field right now in the second half of the game. That would really solve everything. It'd be perfect! If only he'd get hit really hard and die out there during the game. That would be the best god-damned thing that could happen for everybody. Except Jeff, I guess.

I was really thinking about how perfect that would make everything if he did die. If he was killed out there. If he was just suddenly gone.

That would have been perfect.

Like in movies and books where the rat-faced, coward asshole who betrays all his friends always gets the ax at the end of the story. Yeah. That's what always makes a happy ending. The bad guy gets slammed to shit at the end.

Yeah. I wanted a happy ending like that to my own story.

Standing there in front of the blue metal lockers, I slowly started thinking again about those huge, curling waves down there at the beach just sweeping everything away so peacefully. I felt all of my muscles just sort of tingle in this funny way and go all kind of slack-like.

All of a sudden I wasn't feeling so angry anymore. In fact, I wasn't feeling mad or angry at all. Just sort of all floating and drifting. You know - like I didn't care about anything anymore. Not even about Jeff. Not about his dying or getting killed or anything like that.

For some reason, my mind began thinking about this book I read a couple of months ago for my English class. Well - I mean, I read some of it. Sort of here and there. Lots of the pages. It was a pretty long book. Hell - it would have taken me five years if I had read the whole thing! But I hurt my shoulder in a soccer game, and I couldn't go to practice for a week, so I decided that while I was just sitting there in my room I might as well start reading the book that the other guys in class were supposed to be reading.

It was this big book by Ernest Hemingway. One of his most important books, and the teacher was making this big fucking deal about it all the time. You know - a real classic. But it really wasn't that bad. It was sort of OK, I guess. It had a bunch of action stuff that was always going on in the story, and I could understand most of the words Hemingway used. And it had pretty short sentences. So I really liked that.

I think the book was called 'The Ringing of the Bells', or something like that. Or, no - I think it had a question in its title. Yeah. It was called 'Who's Ringing those Bells?' Yeah. That was it.

Anyway, looking at the blue lockers and thinking of the giant waves at the beach made me think of the Hemingway book . It was kind of this corny story set way back in olden times - I think it was during World War II, and it was somewhere in Europe - in Italy, I think, and all these Italian people who lived up in the mountains were fighting against the Nazis who were coming over the mountains and trying to take over everything. And the main guy is this American Army guy who comes up to the mountains and tries to help all these Italian people fight back against the Nazis.

I remembered that the part that struck me the most about this weird book was how the American guy was willing to die instead of being caught by the Nazis. He didn't want to be captured and become a fucking prisoner, so he just let himself die, and he went down like a ship, so to speak. He sort of killed himself at the end all because he couldn't escape from the bad guys. I really remembered that. How the book was saying that maybe dying isn't so bad after all - at least, not if you don't have any other choice. It was saying that a guy is better off dead than caged up like some fucking animal in a goddamned zoo. That it's better even if you have to off yourself. Yeah. I was thinking maybe that made a lot of sense.

And this book, 'Who's Ringing those Bells?', also had this traitor guy in it just like Jeff who tried to ruin the hero. I forget what happened to him. I sort of think somebody blew him up. I hope so.

But then I started thinking that maybe that hero guy could have kept living at the end of the story - maybe he wouldn't have had to fucking kill himself after all, if only he had been able to kill that shithead traitor guy, that asshole Jeff, or whatever his name was. You know - push him over the side of a cliff or something and make it look like an accident.

I don't know. It all sort of kind of confused me.

I sort of really wanted to live. But not in some fucking cage.

And the blue metal lockers in front of me seemed to be actually moving now, and gently bending and swirling and looking exactly like one of those beautiful, peaceful waves at the beach. I shut my eyes really tight and I could see the shining water coming towards me.

And I could feel it. I could really feel it.

152

It was warm. Nice and warm. And it was kind of hugging me gently the way the water does when you're in a jacuzzi. And it made everything else just disappear from my head and just go really far away.

"Can't you fucking hear me!", a loud voice really startled me all of a sudden.

I spun around and there was fat-assed Coach Bonner standing there in the outside doorway. He looked like a really unhappy cat who couldn't find a good mouse to snack on.

"Huh?", I said, all surprised-like.

"I said to get out there on the field. You'll be starting the second half."

As he said that, he darted his little pig-like eyes up at the ceiling and didn't look at me. In fact, he didn't look at me after that for the whole fucking rest of the day.

For the whole fucking rest of my life, for that matter.

"I'm not wearing the armband," I said firmly in kind of this sort of dumb, shaky voice.

"Just get out there and join the game," he said really quiet-like, as if he was sort of sad about something.

I gave this sharp nod of my head and sprinted past him out the door.

At first, I sort of had this happy feeling - like I had won something or done something good. But then I had this hollow, empty thing totally fill me up, and it made something deep inside of me really ache and hurt. It was the funniest thing. I never cry. I've never cried in my life. But slowly this feeling was coming over me - and I thought maybe this is what it feels like just before people start crying. Maybe this is the thing that makes them want to cry.

The thought of it made me suddenly feel really angry and bitter. And the madder I got, the more that kind of funny, empty feeling went away. Pretty soon I couldn't feel it at all anymore. All I could feel was this really huge, burning anger inside of me. Like what they call 'rage' in all those dumb books we have to read in my stupid English class.

Yeah! I felt all this rage when these thoughts about everything keep flashing through my head - Kyle, and Jeff, and Coach Bonner, and that guy last night, Steve, and Beth, and Chelsea, and my dad, and my mom and my step-dad, and everybody! Fucking everybody I knew, or who'd I ever know!

It sounds crazy. But that's how I felt.

I hated everybody.

And I hated myself.

Jogging out onto the field, I ignored the other guys on the team and took my place in the center of the mid-field.

Jeff was in position just to the left of me. In Kyle's place - the position that Kyle always played. For three years. For three years he played there in mid-field right next to me. We were a team. A team within the team. Him and me - side by side in the mid-field. Totally in sync. Totally relying on each other. Doing stuff that none of the other guys could even dream about. It was amazing. We could almost read each other's minds. We knew exactly what to expect - how to move - where to go. It was so perfect. Kyle and me. So fucking perfect!

And now . . . .

I freaked me out to see Jeff standing there in Kyle's place. It was awful. It was fucking awful!

I tried not to think about it. But Kyle kept coming into my head. I could see his face. Nobody had a face like Kyle's. It was always so calm and so gentle - so fucking gentle, even when he was kicking the hell out of the ball and charging into the other team. Nothing seemed to ever upset or bother Kyle. He was just always so happy and sort of kind, if you know what I mean. I never once saw him lose his temper. Not once. He just seemed to love everything so much. He seemed to . . . .

I didn't wanna fucking hell think about the whole goddamned thing anymore! I remember that I bit down really hard on my lip, and I gave Jeff this really disgusted look. And as I stood there waiting for the half to begin, I stared up at the bright blue sky and felt the hot sun on my neck and began thinking I was at the beach again, and that Kyle and I were there on the sand at the shore waiting together for that huge wave to come crashing down on us and peacefully sweep us away - out to sea and way beyond - forever and ever.

And I started thinking about that guy in Hemingway's book. How he should have been fighting down by the beach instead of up in those mountains. Because if he'd been down there by the shore, he could have offed himself much easier. He could have just walked out into the waves and swam and swam until he was beyond everything and it was finally over. Like that lifeguard was telling me - that lifeguard that looked just like the guy I murdered last night - he said it's the best way to go. It's the nicest way to die. You just sort of go to sleep - all gentle and soft-like. Like drifting off into a beautiful dream.

I kept thinking about that.

155

4:41 pm

We'd been playing for less than a couple of minutes when I started losing it. I just didn't want to play soccer anymore.

I got the ball and was just beginning to kick and dribble it down the right side of the field, and I suddenly thought to myself - why am I doing this? This is so fucking stupid! What does it mean? What does it matter?

It just all seemed so fucking stupid all of a sudden.

And this was what Kyle and I had devoted almost our whole fucking lives to for the last three years! Kicking this fucking ball back and forth up and down the grass. What a waste of time! For what? To win? To win what? What did the fucking word 'winning' ever get ME? A lot of phony, fake smiles around campus? Was that why I had all these 'good friends'? Because I could move a stupid ball around better than a bunch of dumb assholes? Because I could help win a goddamned soccer game?

Was that all I was? Just some machine - some fucking machine?

Jesus Christ!

I could barely go on playing.

When this tall, red-haired UCLA forward came charging at me, I was able to pivot and slide right by him. But it was just out of dumb habit. I just did it automatically without thinking. Not because I wanted to. I didn't. If I had thought about it - if I'd had time to think, I would have just let the jerk have the ball. Who the fuck cared? I didn't.

I guess I couldn't help playing the best that I could - even if I didn't want to. I didn't want to be there. For some reason, I didn't want to be out on the fucking soccer field playing anymore. It wasn't fun anymore. In fact, it fucking felt fucking awful.

This was the first game on our home field that Kyle wasn't there. And it suddenly hit me that he'd never be there again. Only - he sort of was there. I can't really explain it. It was like I could feel him there - but I couldn't see him. It was kind of just like he was still there.

And feeling him there made me hate the game. It made me hate playing. Hate everything.

Jeff made it even fucking worse. Much worse.

He kept shadowing me all over the fucking field. I guess maybe he was just doing what he was supposed to - but he didn't have to keep staring at me that way and moving in so close to me every time I got the ball. He was really throwing me off. Kyle never did that. Kyle always knew exactly when I wanted help and when I needed an assist. He always gave me plenty of space - always let me do my thing.

But Jeff was acting like a total asshole. When we started racing down the field through an open space, he kept cutting too close to me, and he even tried to step into my kick and take the ball away from me.

Fuck! I felt like Jeff was playing against me - like he was a guy on the other team. Fuck! He kept doing that shitty thing where he'd fly up right behind me or in front of me and almost block my kicks - sort of trying to move in and take the ball away from me. I mean, Kyle and I used to always kind of do that to confuse the other team, but Jeff wasn't Kyle - and Jeff was doing it all shitty and angry-like, and he was only trying to ruin everything. He was only trying to make me look bad. To destroy me.

So the next time Jeff got the ball and charged off with it, I started doing it to him. Only I did it even closer and harder - just to show him how much I fucking hated what he'd been doing to me, and to teach him a fucking lesson.

But I guess maybe I kind of over-did it - because I actually kicked into the ball when he was kicking it, and my foot hammered really hard into his leg. Really hard. Hard enough to make him scream out in pain.

I really liked that. I really liked hearing him yell with pain, and I liked seeing his narrow, boney face suddenly scrunch up into this tight, red, twisted lump. I really liked that.

So I kicked his leg again - and again - even harder.

I didn't even fucking care about getting control of the ball anymore. In fact, the ball had disappeared. I think some UCLA guy must have slid in and stolen it. But I didn't even the hell fucking care about it at all. I was only interested in balancing back on my left foot and giving Jeff just one more full-ass blast in his shin bone that would break it in two and put him in the fucking hospital right now. And keep him in there forever.

But Jeff saw me wind my leg back - I guess I put a little too much spin on it, you know, all dramatic-like, as if I was getting ready to try to kick this amazing ten thousand yard field goal or something - and he flew up his fist and hit me in the jaw and knocked me over backwards.

Shit! What an asshole! He didn't have to do that - all just because I was gonna give him a little kick in the leg. Shit!

I got up from the ground and my chin kind of hurt, but it was OK - it hadn't been a full-on shot - just this half-assed hit off the left side of my front jaw. But I was really mad. Fucking mad! I heard this whistle blow and I remember seeing Chad and Reicher over across the way with these totally stunned expressions on their faces.

As soon as I was back up on my feet, I dived at fucking Jeff and tackled him. He's twenty pounds lighter than me, so it was easy. I tackled the asshole and held him down on the ground, and he started yelling this crazy stuff at me and trying to hit me in the face again.

I think Jeff was screaming something like, "Are ya gonna kill me, too? Are ya gonna kill me?" Something totally crazy like that. He was so excited and everything that he was nuts. He really was nuts. All I remember is that I kept hearing the words "kill" and 'killer" from him - all crazy-like in this hysterical scream.

So I just grabbed him by his throat and started choking him as hard as I could to get him to fucking stop - to make him shut the fuck up!

His scream kind of just collapsed into this really loud moan. He really couldn't make any words anymore - so I kept choking him really hard until I felt all these hands all over me from every direction pulling me and yanking me, and before I knew it, I had been tossed over all rough-like on my back and Reicher and Chad were holding me down so I couldn't move, and these two referees were kneeling next to Jeff.

As I was lying there on the hot grass and trying to catch my breath, I could hear Jeff making these soft choking noises. I turned my head to the side and I noticed that Jeff was stretched out on his back too. But he was totally still. He wasn't moving a muscle. Just totally all still-like.

At that moment, my heart kind of froze. Just like it did last night when I saw that guy Steve lying there on the sidewalk.

I really wasn't feeling scared. It was something much more than that. It was like I'd lost something. Like I wasn't a human being anymore.

Like I couldn't feel anything inside of me anymore.

Like it was just all hollow and empty.

I guess several minutes passed, and nobody really said anything out loud. All the guys on our team and UCLA's team were sort of all crowded around and looked like they were trying to figure out what the hell had happened. They were all glancing over at me like I was some kind of weird creature in the zoo or something.

Coach Bonner was excitedly talking to all the referees and following them nervously back and forth across the center of the field. The other coaches were also talking to them and each other. It looked like a hell of a mess.

Chad and Reicher finally asked me if I wanted to sit up, and they kind of awkwardly told me to just stay there. I sort of numbly mumbled that I would, and they backed off and I sat up and gazed over at Jeff.

He was still lying there on his back about ten feet away from me, but I noticed that his legs were moving now - just sort of flexing a little bit, and his right foot sort of lifted up a bit and twitched back and forth.

I felt this huge breath of cold air burst out of me when I saw him move. And suddenly I didn't feel that numb anymore.

Then this medical ETM guy who had been kneeling next to Jeff leaned back and pulled Jeff up to a sitting position.

Jeff looked really pale and white, and he was stretching his neck and rubbing it with his hands, and he was taking long, deep breaths of air and coughing.

Bonner came hurrying over to them and looked anxiously at the medical guy.

"Is he gonna be OK?", the coach asked him really all excited and nervous-like.

"He'll be fine," the medical guy said with a smile. "He's OK now."

The coach nodded, then looked over toward me with a blank expression and then slowly came over to me. He stopped when he got a few feet away and stood there staring down at the ground next to me and sadly shaking his head. He never even looked me in the face. He just kept staring at the dirt area right next to me.

He didn't say anything for about a minute. And that was one long fucking minute, let me tell ya!

"You're through," he kind of spit the words down at me in this sort of disgusted, whispering voice. "Get out! You're out of the game. You're off the team. I don't ever want to see your ugly face around here again. You got that? You're done - for good!"

He turned and walked away, moving over to where most of the guys on the team were all clustered together at the far side of the field.

Jeff was up on his feet now and the medical guy and the assistant coach, Todd Andrews, were helping him slowly walk over to the bench. Jeff glanced back at me. He had this weird expression on his face. I don't know how to describe it. But it made me feel really bad. It gave me this ache deep in my chest. It was this really sad kind of thing.

I walked over to the side of the field and started heading for the gate. Then I stopped for a second and glanced up at the bleacher stands to my left. They were packed with a couple of hundred people. Mostly kids and parents. I knew most of the faces of the kids and some of the parents.

My eyes just sort of drifted back and forth across all of these fans. My fans. They were the ones who always cheered for me. They were a big part of why I had always been out there on the field playing this stupid game.

I stood there wondering what would happen now. This was the last time I would ever be in front of them. They wouldn't be my fans anymore. I wondered if they'd even still like me after today. Maybe they wouldn't. Maybe they wouldn't even want to talk to me again after today.

As I started to turn toward the gate, I suddenly noticed Kyle's parents. They were sitting right in the center of the bleachers. And they were looking right at me. They weren't smiling at all. I guess I'd have to say that they kind of looked like they were in another world. Like they were in some sort of distant place. The President of the university was sitting right next to them and a couple of other guys from the athletic staff that I recognized were sitting in front of the Martinsens.

I suddenly remembered that some big fucking honor ceremony had been planned for after the game. They were going to remember Kyle with some big fucking award or something. They told us we were gonna line up and the President and all the other big phonies at the university were gonna march out on the field and present Kyle's parents with some sort of fake plaque or trophy or something. And then we were all supposed to form a circle around them and sing the school song and all that crap.

Jesus! I remember when the coach told us about it two days ago. It made me want to barf. It really did. The guy is getting this fucking special award for being run over by a truck? Being run over by a fucking truck! And they give him a stupid wooden plaque or some dumb trophy!

Fuck!

I was glad I'd been kicked out of the game. All of a sudden I was glad. And I was glad I was getting out of there.

Kyle's folks were beginning to look at me all kind of curious and con-cerned-like. Mr. Marlinsen even started standing up and trying to move toward the aisle.

So I got the hell out of there.

I jogged over to where I'd left my truck.

Shit!

There was a parking ticket on the windshield.

I left it there and jumped in my truck and really floored it and went soaring off out of the parking lot and back toward my apartment on the other side of campus.

5:09 pm

Driving back to the campus apartments, I felt totally empty inside of me. The only thing I was feeling at all was this incredible burning anger. It seemed to be everywhere in my body, and almost made me feel like I had a fever or something. Like I was sick with something. You know - like when you have the flu or something and this fever burns right through you and makes you feel like you're on fire and you just keep getting hotter and hotter until you feel like you're gonna be totally eaten up by it and die.

It made me think about those waves at the beach. That really would be the best way to die. To be gently carried away in that soft, cool, beautiful water, instead of being burned alive by a fever.

My parking space was gone. Naturally! Some asshole in a blue Toyota Camry had parked there. So I circled around the lot a couple of times, but it was no use. Parking at this place totally sucks! There's parking lots all over the place, but there's never an empty slot. I swear there has to be ten times as many cars on this campus as there are students. Fuck! You pay for a parking permit and you can never find a fucking parking space! And when you finally do find one, you never want to leave it, 'cause when you do, you'll never get your place back again.   N e v-
er!

Fuck!

I finally pulled around to the faculty lot by the chapel. There were plenty of empty spaces there. There always is. Anything for the faculty. They fucking count! I knew I was gonna get a fucking ticket for parking there, but I didn't give a shit. Not today. So I pulled in one of the slots.

The chimes, or the recording of the chimes, were ringing the quarter hour when I climbed out of my truck. I stood there looking up at the tower and listening to them.

I sort of stepped over onto the grass and went into the shade of these huge, leafy trees. It felt so nice and cool. The sun was just dipping down behind the red tile roof of Sacred Heart Chapel and everything looked all kind of glowing and peaceful. I could hear the shouts of a bunch of guys playing frisbee football across the way in the Sunken Garden. They were really yelling at each other and making a lot of noise. It was all friendly-like and everything, but I didn't want to hear guys having fun playing a game right now.

I really didn't want to hear it or even think about it.

So I quickly walked over to the side stairs by the bell tower and climbed up to the east door of the chapel. It was wide open, so I kind of wandered in.

I haven't been in churches very much. I got dragged by my mom to a couple when I was a little kid. But I always sort of hated them. They kind of really scared me when I was really little, and, then, when I got bigger they just seemed really stupid and boring. And phony. Really phony!

It was really dark inside. None of the lights were on yet. But the sun from the west was shining through all the narrow stained glass windows lined in a row on the upper wall right across from me. These windows had little pieces of different colored glass - every color you could think of. You couldn't believe how beautiful they were with the light of the sun behind them. It was one of the most beautiful things I'd ever seen in my life.

I sat down in one of the chairs on the side of the altar and just stared up at the windows for several minutes. It made me feel good.

166

Pretty soon these two elderly women came walking down the center aisle and sat down in one of the front pews. They looked over at me kind of nervous-like, then smiled shyly and closed their eyes and bowed their heads and started praying, I guess.

It made me feel kind of weird. I didn't know how to pray. I can't remember the last time I prayed. I must have been about six or seven. It always seemed like such a bullshit thing to do.

Sitting there, I kept looking at the windows and wondering why I'd never noticed them before - the three or four times I'd been there in the chapel for school stuff - you know, lectures and award ceremonies and all that shit. And, of course, the memorial service for Kyle yesterday. But yesterday I was looking down at the floor all the time. I never looked up yesterday.

After another couple of minutes passed, the door behind the left side of the altar opened, and a guy I recognized as Fr. Evans came out and began fussing with a bunch of crap on this huge table in the center of the altar. Fr. Evans was the jerk who ran the whole show in the chapel. I forget exactly what they call it - but he's the big cheese in charge of everything. He was the guy who got up and spoke and did all the official stuff yesterday at Kyle's service.

Fuck! What a phony this guy was. Fr. Evans - what a total fake. A real Olympic champion phony. The way that guy stood up there and carried on like some actor or something.

Fr. Evans was a good looking guy - kind of all perfect and neat and clean all the time. Like a GQ model or something. His hair was always perfectly styled and in place and his cloths were perfect. He always looked like one of those dummies in a store window - the kind they have in the men's stores. It was like he wasn't real. Everything about the guy was just so precise and controlled and sort of like a machine. Even his smile. That tiny smile of his. Always the same.

Phony.

He was looking at me out of the corner of his eye from across the way while he straightened all the junk on the table. He knew who I was. I mean, everybody on campus does. I never talked to Fr. Evans before, but once or twice when I was walking around and came face to face with him, he gave me his tight-assed smile and nodded his head and said my name. So I knew that he knew who I was.

But I don't think he liked me very much. I don't think he liked anybody very much. He was just one of those guys who want to be up in front of an audience and all admired and everything all the time. But that's as far as it goes. They don't like to get too close to people when they're off their fucking stage. They only want to impress people. Real assholes!

A lot of the girls call Evans 'Fr. What-a-Waste'. Girls can't imagine why a young guy that good looking would want to be a priest when he could be out screwing all the girls he wanted. I guess it pisses them off that Evans doesn't give a fuck about women - I mean, sexually. Most of the guys on campus think he's gay, but I don't think he is. He never seems to go after any of the guys. He just likes to stand up there in the light and hold his head up high and show everybody his profile and his flashy teeth and his phony smile. But it doesn't mean anything. He's really just this actor guy, and this is his theater. It's a pretty good gig, I guess.

When Fr. Evans, or rather Fr. What-a-Waste finished fussing over the table, he knelt before the cross and turned and looked right past me, totally ignoring me. I was glad he did. Whenever he does force himself to look at anybody, he always has this really piss-ass superior expression on his face like he's looking at somebody who just shined his shoes and didn't do a very good job on them. He's the kind of guy who would have made a great head waiter at the Ritz Carlton.

I really felt like talking to somebody who could help me. I really wanted that right now. But there was no way I could ever talk to this priest. What the fuck could he know about somebody like me? And I didn't want to hear all that religious crap again like in Campus Ministry.

So when Fr. What-a-Waste came rigidly walking past me like a soldier on parade, I looked down. He slightly hesitated, then quickly went on. I glanced up from the floor and noticed that the two old women were gone too. They probably left while I was staring up at those beautiful stained glass windows.

I was alone now.

Leaning back in the chair, I tried to relax. But I couldn't. I was too upset. It was even hard to think. I kind of didn't know what I was doing there - why I had come inside there and sat down. Then I remembered it was to get away from the sound of those guys playing frisbee nearby. All that laughter and yelling. Yeah. And then that made me think of Kyle, and the memorial service yesterday.

Fuck! Was it really yesterday? It seemed like it was such a long time ago. Years ago.

But it was only yesterday. And I was sitting just back there in the pews on the left side. I looked across the way and saw the empty space where I had been sitting yesterday. All the guys on the soccer team had sat together up front. They planned it ahead of time, and they had two pews all marked off for us up front. So fucking stupid!

169

But I came late and kind of quietly snuck in the back and sat down there by the open window. I came late on purpose. I almost didn't come at all. But when I finally decided to, I wanted to be all by myself.

I remembered how some of the guys kept turning around during the service and glancing around for me. I was the captain of the team, so I sure the hell was expected to be there with them. Marco finally saw me kind of hiding back there and he kept waving his hand at me to come and join them, but I looked away and pretended I didn't see him.

Mostly I just stared out the open window next to me during the whole service. The warm wind had begun blowing yesterday afternoon and it was already hot and dry. I just looked out the window at the ocean and the Marina in the distance and really tried not to listen to what everybody was saying about Kyle. But a few times I couldn't help hearing some of the stupid crap they were dishing out.

Especially when Fr. What-a-Waste got up there and started cranking it up all heavy-like. Christ! What a ham! It was like he was in some fucking debating contest or a shitty politician running for office or something. Just on and on and on with all this god-awful sentimental shit and sticky spiritual stuff - his voice going all up and down really dramatic-like. It was fucking terrible! I tried my best not to listen, but how do you keep all that loud shit out of your mind unless you're wearing earplugs - which would have been a pretty good idea, had I thought of it ahead of time.

Kyle and Fr. What-a-Waste had been friends. Not good friends. Just friends. Kyle was friends with everybody. He liked everybody and I never talked to anybody that didn't like him. He was just always happy and interested in everything and everybody, and nothing ever made him upset.

170

I honestly don't think there was anything mean or bad inside of Kyle. Like the saying goes - he didn't have a mean bone in his whole body, and . . . .

Goddamned fuck! I didn't want to think about Kyle! Why was I thinking about Kyle? It was this damn place! I jumped up from the chair and headed out the door and started thinking about something else.

Jeff. I started thinking about Jeff. How every time I'd pass by the front of the chapel here on Sunday nights, I'd see old holier-than-thou Jeff standing out in front on the steps ushering all the students in for eight o'clock mass. Standing there with his phony smile and wearing his stupid maroon Crimson Circle sweater and passing out programs and shaking everybody's hand like he owned the place. Like he was god or something.

That really made me angry again. I hadn't thought anymore about what I'd done out on the field. I didn't want to.

I just quickly went down the stairs next to the tower and headed across the lawn. The chimes were ringing a quarter to six, and I couldn't hear those guys in the Sunken Garden playing their game of frisbee anymore.

The sun was still setting and giving the sky a deep golden burn, and I slowly started walking back to my room over in the apartments.

5:50 pm

171

Josh and Will and Marco and Reicher and Dave Rogers and Chad were all gathered inside the room when I came in. Everybody sort of stared at me all awkward-like and waited for the other guy to say something.

I really didn't look directly at anybody. I just went over to my bed and started taking my soccer uniform off. Instead of folding my shirt and my shorts all neatly like I always do and putting them on my dresser, I just took them and threw them down on the floor by the window.

The guys all silently watched me do it. Nobody said a word.

I was standing there in just my jockstrap. Then I took that off too and tossed it down on the floor next to the other things, and I headed quickly over to the bathroom door.

"Are ya takin' a shower?", Josh asked me with this concerned look on his face. "I was just gettin' ready to take one."

"Of course," I snickered. "You've only had ten of your usual twenty showers. And it already must be more than five minutes since you took your last one. You're really overdue. But you'll have to wait. I'll just be a couple minutes."

"Don't you want to know how the game came out?", Chad asked me in a kind of angry tone.

"No," I calmly replied with this really cool, casual shrug.

"We lost," Will said very bitterly.

"Wonderful," I snickered with a big smile.

"Thanks to you," Reicher snarled at me like some pissed-off dog. "All thanks to you - you fucking crazy asshole!"

"Why did you do it, Niner?", Marco gently asked me like a little disappointed kid would have. "Why did you go after Jeff like that?"

I shrugged.

"You almost killed the guy," Dave said in a kind of concerned voice. "I know you got into that stupid kicking thing with him - trying to get the ball away from him. I know you two got into that slugging thing with each other. I was watching you from the goal line. But why did you start choking him like that? Why'd ya do it?"

"You almost killed him," Will added with a kind of weird look on his face.

"Yeah," Marco emotionally agreed.

I turned and went into the bathroom and started shutting the door, then turned back and kind of blankly gazed over the top of everybody's head.

"Is . . . Jeff OK?", I asked very quietly.

"He's OK," Chad cooly answered me. "He had to sit out the rest of the game. He got his voice back and everything, but his leg was pretty bruised and swollen where ya kicked him. They had to ice it for a while and put bandages on it. He's walkin' with sort of a limp right now. But he seems to be OK."

"Why'd ya do it, Niner?", Marco asked me again in this really pathetic voice. "Why'd you ruin everything for us?"

I just shut the bathroom door and took my shower.

About seven minutes later when I came back into the room, everybody was still there all slouching around like they had been when I'd left them.

I was hoping they'd all be gone. Shit!

I just wanted to get away from all this crap. I was done with soccer and the team and all that shit. I just wanted to be left alone.

I dried the rest of my back with the towel and put on a pair of jockey shorts, then got the grey cotton pants my mom got me out of the closet and my favorite turquoise blue knit shirt, and I quickly put them on.

Moving around Reicher and Marco like I didn't even care if they were there or not, I stepped over to the mirror above my dresser and adjusted the collar of my shirt. I loved this turquoise shirt. It was really a size too small - but it fit me like a glove - a tight glove. And it made my pecs really stand out and look all sexy and everything, and the sleeves cut in perfectly just at the top of my arms, so that my biceps bulged out just at the right angle and looked huge. I really loved that shirt.

After I put on my black leather shoes, I heard this really faint knock on the door. Dave was the only guy who wasn't texting or talking on his cell phone, so he sort of darted over and swung open the door.

Freddy - I mean Fred was standing there in the hallway. I was really surprised when I glanced up and saw him. And he was sure as shit surprised to see all these morons piled into my room. Poor old Fred was so shocked, in fact, that he looked like he was going to shit in his pants. Shocked and sort of terrified.

He tried to say something, but couldn't. He was looking anxiously around the room at all the faces and it wasn't 'til he jerked his head to the right that he saw me sitting on my bed kind of hidden behind the hulking frame of Reicher.

"Yeah?", Dave asked really impatient-like.

"Uh . . I . . . isn't . . uh . . ?", Fred stuttered.

"Whataya want?"

"I . . uh . . wanted . . . uh . . ", he sort of really all shy and embarrassed tried to continue.

"Hey, Fred," I called out to him with a slightly uneasy smile as I finished tying the strings of my left shoe. "What's up?"

"Uh . . hi, Niner. I just . . I just wanted to talk to you for a minute. Just for a minute. But I can come back later. OK?"

"No - that's OK," I said, hurrying toward the door, trying to think fast. "I got a minute or two. We can talk out in the hall."

I pushed past Dave and went out the door and firmly shut it behind me. Fred and I were standing there right next to each other in the hallway and I could hear all this loud laughter and cat calls and bullshit whistling coming from inside the room. What a bunch of assholes those guys were.

"What's that?", Fred asked me with a kind of scared and hurt look on his face, gesturing toward all the noise coming from the other side of the door.

"Uh - that's just the guys. They're reliving something really funny that happened at the game. You know how they are. Real morons. Let's go down the hall."

I led the way and moved quickly down the dark hall with Fred on my heels. As we moved, I could distinctly hear a couple of the guys inside loudly laughing the name "Freddy the Faggot." I sure hoped that Fred hadn't heard that. I really hoped he hadn't. But I wasn't sure.

We slowly walked down about four or five rooms and sort of just stopped there. I looked at Fred and gave him a "what's up?" smile. The guys back in my room were getting so loud that you could hear a shout or a laughing yell every now and then. Assholes!

Fred was kind of shaking a little, and he took this big, nervous breath and started excitedly stuttering:

"Niner - I . . I . . just wanted to . . to . . to give you . . to give you a birthday present - before the party - before the party tonight. I just wanted to give it to you - you know - in private - without anybody else around."

Christ! What the fuck was this! My mind kind of raced and I didn't have the god damnedest idea what the fuck this weird little kid was gonna give me. Shit! I didn't even know him! I never even met him or even talked to the fucking guy before a few hours ago! And now he's giving me a present?

Fuck!

Fred gave this really pathetic little smile - all sensitive-like - sort of as if he might break down and cry any minute. He kind of awkwardly reached into his shirt pocket and pulled out this small, white piece of twisted paper and timidly handed it to me. I held it up and took a close look at it.

There was nothing written on it, thank god! I was afraid it was gonna be some kind of love note or something. But it was just this totally blank piece of twisted paper. I leaned closer and really gave it a good eye-balling.   It was nothing. Absolutely nothing. Just a scrap of paper.

What the hell! This gay guy is giving me a paper scrap from the trash for my birthday? Is he kidding? Fuck! What's the story?

I didn't know what to say. So I didn't say anything. I just sort of stood there looking at him like he was this kind of strange bug on a window or something. And he was looking back at me like I was god.

"I made it in my art class this afternoon," Fred finally said in this real-ly girly, excited voice.

"Yeah?"

"Yeah. Do you know what it is?"

I examined it again. I thought it might be a trick question.

"Uh - a piece of paper?"

"Yeah - but not just any piece of paper," he said kind of proudly.

"No?"

"It's a Mobius Strip," he said with this huge smile. "I made it."

I looked at it again.

"A . . what?", I asked him.

"A Mobius Strip."

"Oh. Yeah."

I wondered to myself what the hell a Mobius Strip was. I just sort of held it there in my hand all careful-like and kept gazing at the thing - a tiny scrap of twisted paper, as far as I could see.

"Have you ever had one before?", Fred shyly asked me with this weird kind of tender smile that made me feel really uncomfortable.

"Naw, I don't think so. Nope. First one. Thanks. Thanks a lot, Fred."

"Maybe it'll bring you good luck," he said all hopeful-like. "You know what it's the symbol of, don't you?"

I kind of widened my eyes and shrugged confidently, but I didn't have a clue. I'd never even heard of the goddamned thing before.

"Uh . . . sure," I mumbled with a smile.

"Yeah. Infinity. The infinite. The endless and timeless essence of existence. It's the symbol of that and the eternal - the eternal beginning."

"Cool."

"And it can be the symbol of a friendship - a friendship like ours," he started getting all excited in this really silly and embarrassing way - kind of like the way a little girl does when she gets a new doll.

"I guess," I casually agreed in this really deep, macho voice.

"A friendship that's just beginning like ours, and will keep beginning every day and lasting forever and forever - for all eternity."

Holy fuck! Did this idiot get his hands on some of Cutter's weed? What was the story? I couldn't believe what I was hearing. I actually took two steps backwards to get a little more distance between me and this nut case.

Fuck!

"Well," I said with this bright, phony smile, "I gotta go now. I gotta talk to the guys. Thanks again, Fred. That was really thoughtful of you to give me this . . uh . . to give me this. Thanks. I appreciate it."

I held it up in the air and shook it a little, like it was a prize I had just won or something. Then I turned and stuffed it quickly into the right pocket of my pants.

"Sure, Niner," Fred excitedly gushed, smiling at me kind of dreamily with his eyes glowing all adoring-like, sort of like the way a girl looks at you right after you've finished fucking her.

"Later," I mumbled and started quickly walking back to my room.

"At the party?", he asked all anxious-like. "It's still OK for me to come to your party tonight?"

Shit! That's right! I invited him to my birthday party at the Bird Nest tonight. That damn Einstein! Why did I listen to that maniac! Oh, well - I thought maybe it wouldn't be so bad after all. There was gonna be about a hundred people there, so what was the harm of one little fruitcake?

"More than OK," I yelled back with this cocky grin. "It won't be a great party without you. See ya there, buddy!"

"Thanks, Niner. Thanks. I'll be there, Niner. Thanks. Thanks."

178

I could hear his 'thanks' all the way down to the door of my room as I walked along the hall. It kind of made me feel funny. Sort of almost sad and lonely. I don't know why. It was like my mind wanted to think about all this other stuff that I never let it think about. Kind of like that. And it sort of made me feel something that hurt really deep down inside me.

But it flashed away as quickly as it came as soon as I opened the door of the room and went inside and slammed it behind me.

"What did the Mrs. want?", Josh sarcastically laughed with a grin.

"Yeah - what's up with Mrs. Niner?", Reicher asked with this really fucked sneer. "Since when has your wife been giving you room service?"

"He just wanted to give me something for my birthday," I casually explained, hoping to change the subject.

"So what did he give ya - a blow-job?", Chad asked me, almost falling down from laughing so hard.

"That was a pretty fast blow-job," Marco managed to gasp through his stupid laughter. "Probably needs more practice."

"Niner will help him with that," Will snickered. "His cock's had a lot of practice. He's like Domino's - he delivers."

"Nice set-up," Reicher laughed. "Old Number Nine probably has Freddy the Faggot on call 24/7."

"His name's Fred, you fucking asshole!", I yelled in this really angry tone, pushing past Dave and putting my face right up to Reicher's. "Don't call him that shitty nickname anymore. Just call him Fred. That's his name. And while you're at it, quit calling me Number Nine and Niner!"

Reicher stared at me like I was crazy. He seemed really pissed off at the way I was talking to him.

"What's wrong with you, anyway?", he kind of snarled at me.

179

"What's wrong with you?", I really angrily shot back.

"Nothing! And if I want to call him Freddy the Faggot, then I'll call him Freddy the Faggot like everybody else does."

"No you won't. Not in front of me."

"Why not?"

"Because . . . . he's my friend. Fred's my friend."

"Your friend!", Josh said with amazement. "Since when?"

"Since today. And I don't want to hear anybody calling him that fucking nickname anymore. Got it."

"I'll call that little faggot anything I want," Reicher slowly announced in this really threatening way, like he was a gangster or something.

"No you won't," I said in this kind of quiet, firm voice.

"Who's gonna stop me?"

"Me."

"You?", Reicher gave this huge, mocking laugh.

"Yeah. Me."

"And how ya gonna do that?", he asked even more threateningly, leaning right into my face. "How are ya gonna do that, Pretty Boy? I'm not as fucking easy to choke as Jeff is. He's a little guy. I'm NOT."

"If I hear you call him Freddy the Faggot one more time, I'm gonna punch you right in the center of your ugly face and break your fucking nose. I'm gonna hit your nose so hard that they'll have to dig it out of the back of your head."

I was nose to nose with Reicher and glaring right into his eyes.

"Yeah?', he said kind of real uneasy-like as some of the other guys sort of nervously laughed a little.

But the room really went quiet all of a sudden after that. Nobody said a word for a while until I spoke.

"Yeah."

Reicher took a deep sigh and moved back from me - then scratched his head and sighed again.

"Big deal," he kind of muttered.

Chad and Dave and Will were talking on their cell phones now and kind of escaping the tension in the room. Josh had gone over and started fooling around on his computer, and Marco was fidgeting with his iPod.

I went over to the window and looked out at the trees for a moment or two, then turned back and faced everybody.

"Fred's gonna be at my party tonight," I casually told them. "I want all of you to act OK around him. He doesn't have to be your friend or any-thing, but I want you to treat him OK. I want you to act like he belongs. He's my friend - and if I belong, he belongs too. Got it?"

They all stared at me like I was nuts. I was really getting fucking pissed off with being given that shitty look all the time.

"That little queer is going to your party?", Josh asked me with his eyes bulging out in amazement. "You actually INVITED him? You've been dodging him like the fucking plague the whole semester. Why the fuck did you invite him?"

"I think old Niner is finally coming out of the closet," Reicher said with a real wise-guy smile.

I clenched my fist and pumped it real solid-like into my other hand, then took two steps toward Reicher as I gave him this really mean glare.

"Just kidding," he said kind of nervously. "Fuck - you can't even take a joke anymore? Shit!"

181

"And I don't want to hear anybody calling him 'queer' either," I angrily told everyone. "Or any other asshole name like that. His name's Fred."

"OK, Niner," Chad said with a kind of arrogant yawn as he continued texting on his phone, "you're the boss. Or, at least you think you are."

"Yeah - who made you the boss of us all of a sudden?", Marco asked in this childish tone. "Just 'cause you're captain of the team."

"WAS," Dave corrected him.

Josh's cell phone rang loudly just then. He'd been talking on it off and on ever since I entered the room. It had this really stupid ring tone - you know, that cavalry charge bugle thing. And it sounded just like a bugle too. Really half-assed, if you know what I mean. Irritating as hell.

"It's Beth," he said as he held out the phone to me. "This is like the tenth time she's called in the last hour. Why the hell don't you turn on your fucking phone? You must have a million messages on it by now. Christ!"

"Tell her I'll call her later," I said uneasily.

"Tell her yourself," he sort of hissed, holding the phone closer to me.

"I'll talk to her later," I said firmly, trying to steady my nervous voice.

Josh gave me this really dramatic, suffering expression, and then talked to Beth again and relayed my message to her. From what he was saying, it didn't sound like it went over very well.

He hung up and flashed me this way-sympathetic phony look.

"She wants to meet you in the library at eight. She'll be upstairs by the fireplace. Fuck, man! Not answering your phone like that - you've really pissed her off. She thinks you're deliberately trying to avoid her. I sure wouldn't want to be in YOUR shoes right now."

"Thanks," I mumbled, feeling really uneasy and uptight and everything. "Neither would I."

"And don't forget to turn your phone on. I'm fucking sick and tired of taking all these fucking messages. Turn it on right now and take it with you when you leave."

I slowly went over and looked at my phone sitting there on the shelf above my bed. I just kept looking at it. I didn't want to pick it up. I didn't even want to touch it.

All the other guys were busy talking and texting on their phones. Even Josh had quickly called somebody up in the last few seconds.

You know how it is. You can't waste a single moment - not a fucking single moment. You have to stay connected to everything. You have to stay connected all the time. All the fucking time. If you disconnect for just a second - just an instant - it's like your heart stops beating. And you die.

That's what everybody believes - without even thinking about it. But they believe it. Most on them may not believe in God - but they do believe in staying connected. They'd rather die than be not connected every fucking moment of every fucking day and night. And that's exactly how I always felt - without ever even thinking about it.

But I was thinking about it right now. Watching Dave and Reicher and Will and Marco and Chad and Josh all jabbering away into their tiny fucking phones and sending messages - I felt like my head was gonna explode. It kind of just suddenly overwhelmed me, like that huge crashing wave at the beach this afternoon. Only it wasn't a peaceful, beautiful sweeping thing like the wave - something that I wanted to warmly embrace me. It was just the opposite. It felt like it was suddenly smothering and crushing me - all this mindless noise. All this meaningless chatter.

I kept staring all numb-like at my cell phone sitting there on the shelf. Finally, I gently reached over and forced myself to pick it up. Out of habit, my thumb pressed against the 'on' button at the top of the phone. Almost the instant it connected and went on, the ring tone started loudly wailing away.

I looked at the number on the screen. It was Beth.

I just stood there with it in my hand and didn't answer. I just let it ring and ring and ring.

Scrolling down the menu, I saw that there were now 87 messages waiting for me. 87 fucking messages!

My cell phone continued to ring, but I completely ignored it.

"Fuck - answer it already!", everybody started yelling at me, only not using the same exact words.

I ignored them, and that made them yell even louder - especially Reicher and Chad.

"If you don't fucking answer it," Josh shouted at me, "then I'm gonna! Give it to me!"

He kind of angry-like reached out his hand.

Right at that instant, it felt like something snapped inside me. Like something really deep inside of me was sort of suddenly released with this huge violent burst.

Without even thinking, I moved over to my desk and set my ringing phone gently down on the shiny wood surface.

Then I reached over and picked up this really heavy ceramic statue of Mickey Mouse that Beth bought me at Disneyland.

I took Mickey and smashed him down right on top of my cell phone there on the desk. Really hard. And I smashed down on it again and again and again and again and again and again and again.

I must have smashed the fucking thing at least a dozen times. And as hard as I could.

You should have seen the cell phone - or what was left of it. You couldn't recognize what it had been. It was as flat as a dollar bill. And the Mickey Mouse statue wasn't so hot either. His big yellow shoes were broken completely in half, and one of his ears had totally come loose.

When I was finally done smashing, I just stood there staring down at the crushed mess that used to be my cell phone.

It wasn't ringing anymore.

All of the guys had stopped what they were doing and they were silently staring at me with these huge, shocked expressions.

Before anybody could say a word, I quickly reached into my desk drawer and snatched out my brand new iPod. I tossed it down next to the wreckage of my cell phone, and I picked up Mickey Mouse again and began smashing away on top of my iPod.

Smash, smash, smash, smash, smash, smash, smash, smash, smash, smash.

All the guys didn't look shocked anymore.

They looked totally frightened.

And none of them said a word. They just all started moving slowly toward the hall door.

Dave was the first, and he gently opened the door, and the others were all right behind him. All except Josh, who kind of backed up into the bathroom, looking like he was being stalked by a lion.

Marco, giving this timid little scared laugh, was the first one through the door and out of the room. He was followed by Will, and then Dave, and Chad, and then finally Reicher, who turned and faced me as he left.

"You really fucking need help," he said all resentful-like. "You really need to talk to somebody. Get some help, dude. You're really fucked up."

He shut the door very quietly as he left.

I looked over at Josh. He gave me this incredibly tense grin that didn't resemble a smile even in the slightest.

"Well - I think I'll take a shower," he said kind of nervously as he closed the bathroom door and locked it.

6:19 pm

What Reicher had said to me made me think of what Dr. Shepherd had said to me on Regents Terrace when I'd been on my way to my Philosophy class that afternoon. He said I could come by his office tonight between 6 and 7 if I needed to talk to him.

I looked over at the clock on Josh's desk and saw that I could just make it if I drove over there to his office in U-Hall in my truck.

So I took off out the door and down the hallway and the stairs and across the quad to the faculty parking lot next to the chapel where I had illegally parked.

Shit! Another fucking parking ticket was on my windshield!

I dove in my truck and hauled ass over to U-Hall, nearly running over somebody again in the crosswalk by the library.

Lucky for me, the basement garage of U-Hall had a whole shitload of empty spaces at that time of evening, so I didn't have to park illegally. In fact, I got a space right next to the elevator lobby.

I dashed over and caught the departing elevator up to the ground floor of U-Hall. Shepherd's office was on the fourth floor, but the elevator from the student parking garage only goes up to the ground floor. Don't ask me why. The elevator from the faculty garage goes all the way up.

That seems to be the story of the whole fucking university. The faculty gets everything, and the students are always second rate - they get shit. Especially when it comes to the fucking parking situation.

I hurried out of the ground floor elevator lobby and entered the huge atrium of U-Hall.

I really don't know how to describe this place. U-Hall, or rather University Hall as it's technically called, is like this gigantic enclosed area that looks like one of those Hyatt hotels they have all around the country. Especially the one in Honolulu that I saw two summers ago when I went with the soccer team to Hawaii.

It's about a mile long and a thousand feet high. Well, at least four stories tall. The whole ceiling is glass, and a forest of trees grow in a long row right down the center of the bottom floor. And there's all these trees growing all over the place on the sides, and crap growing along the balconies of every floor. It's pretty incredible, when you come to think of it. You don't know if you're fucking inside or outside. It really gives you sort of a funny feeling - like you're in outer space. I guess kind of beautiful and spectacular, but really kind of fucking weird.

It was pretty quiet. Not too many people were there yet. There were about a hundred classrooms on the upper three floors, and they were either already in session or weren't gonna begin for another forty minutes or so. You could only hear the low grinding hum of all the stupid lazy-ass escalators going up and down.

I was in a hurry to catch Dr. Shepherd, so I quickly walked through the wide atrium and passed underneath all those tall, leafy trees to the main elevator down aways and took it up to the fourth floor.

At the top, when the elevator doors opened, I rushed out and suddenly came face-to-face with the Vice President of the University. I forget his name. I hardly knew him. I'd only talked to him once - it was last spring when he presided at a meeting with my parents when they were trying to kick my ass out of the university for smoking pot and flunking three classes.

"You're quite early," he smiled, looking at me in a superior way through these really thick glasses that magnified his eyes so much that they made them look like these huge chocolate cupcakes.

"Early?", I asked with surprise.

"Our meeting isn't until tomorrow at two o'clock. I take it you're not on your way to the Presidential Conference Room?"

"Uh - no," I said - really all kind of confused. "I'm going some place else. I'm meeting with the Dean tomorrow. I didn't know you were gonna to be there. You're gonna be there?"

"Of course. Wasn't I last year? This has become an annual event. I wouldn't miss it. Your step-father's been very busy."

"Busy?", I asked, even more confused.

"He's a busy man," he said in this really stiff, piss-assed voice. "An important man. Evidently one of his law partners is the legal council for two of the regents of the university. And another of his partners is a very good friend of the Chancellor of the university."

"Oh, yeah?"

"Yeah," he said in this real condescending, almost angry tone. "The Dean of your college seems to think that he's being out-gunned. He wants you expelled. He doesn't think you deserve another chance. Not after last year. But your step-father's already pulling strings to keep that from happening. You know how it works. It's all who you know."

I didn't know what to say.

"Yeah?"

"Yeah," he was getting more pissed. "Once again it looks like you're not going to get what you deserve. But we'll see. We'll see. The Dean is committed to taking this one to the carpet. Maybe it won't be all fixed for you this time. Maybe you'll finally have to take your medicine. What do you think about that."

"Uh . . I don't know."

"Do you even care?"

"Uh . . . sure."

"You know, you could do the right thing yourself, young man. You could resign tomorrow. You can resign and make it easier for everyone. Yourself included. Just resign. How far do you think you're going to go in life with your family saving you every time you get in trouble. Never having to take responsibility for what you've done. You're a man now. Why don't you act like a man and step up and do the right thing."

"Uh . . . "

"You must be almost twenty-one, aren't you?"

"I'll be twenty-one tomorrow," I mumbled uneasily.

He just stared at me with this really fucking cold, disappointed expression.

"Happy Birthday," he said kind of softly in this really bitter, phony voice.

"I gotta go - good night," I mumbled with a nervous smile, moving off down the hallway to my right toward the Psychology Department.

"Think about what I said," he firmly called out to me as I left.

I continued hurrying on my way without looking back.

When I got to the Psychology Department, I went through the wide open doorway and followed a short maze of hallways to the large central lounge. I'd only been to Dr. Shepherd's office twice before when I had him for a class a year ago, so I really wasn't quite certain where it exactly was. It seemed like it was one of the doors along the far wall. I remembered that it had this great view of the city and the ocean, so that meant it had to be one of those doors.

I started walking fast from one office door to another looking quickly at the names. I couldn't find it, and I was getting worried, because it was getting late and I really wanted to talk to him. I really needed to talk to him.

To anybody. I was beginning to feel like I couldn't go on. I needed some-one to help me - to tell me what to do about everything.

Finally I found his name at the very end of the row of doors. I knocked really loudly. He called out 'come in'. And I did.

His office was like a fucking movie set. Everything perfect. Every-thing neat and tidy - not a single piece of paper out of place. The desk was clean and empty, and all of the books were carefully arranged on the shelves almost as if they had never even been touched or read.

When I opened the door and stepped in, I gave one of my best smiles and tried to go into my super-cool act.

"Ah, the Handsome Scholar," Shepherd warmly returned my smile, looking really happy to see me. "I'm glad you came. I honestly didn't think you would. Welcome, sir. Please sit down."

I sat down.

"Uh . . . ", I began, not quite sure what to say.

"Problems. Right?"

"Yeah," I mumbled, sort of hopelessly hanging my head.

"Shoot," Shepherd said with a very sensitive smile.

"Uh . . . it's hard to know where to begin . . . "

"Begin anywhere. The beginning, the middle, or the end. Wherever you'd like. Just start talking. What's happening?"

"Well - right now - they're trying to kick me out of school. Tomorrow my folks are coming to meet with me and the Dean and some other big shots. I don't know. I guess maybe my step-dad might be able to help me. He seems to have a lot of pull with the high up guys."

"He's coming with your mom tomorrow?", he asked with interest.

"Yeah."

"What about your real dad?"

"No."

"Why not?"

"Oh . . . I don't know," I said all uncomfortable-like, sort of twisting in my chair. "He called last week and left a message, but . . uh . . . I sort of never called him back. I didn't want him to come."

"Why not?"

"Oh - he's never anything but a bunch of trouble and crap."

"Why's that?"

"I don't know."

"Sure you do," he gently smiled, "or you wouldn't have said it. Why is he so much trouble and crap?"

"He's always been trouble," I said sort of all irritated-like. "Ever since I was a baby. Christ! He divorced my mom when I was only two. Ever since then he's done nothing but try to make me unhappy."

"Really? How has he done that?"

"I don't know. He left me and my mom all alone, and then he'd force me to go and visit him and he'd be all mean to me."

"How was he mean to you?"

"He'd try to force me to do what he wanted me to do. He'd make me study when I didn't want to, and he'd make me do all these crappy jobs around the house. I mean - fuck! Uh - excuse me! I mean - he was rich and had a maid and everything, but he'd make me do all these jobs around his house - like making my bed and picking all my stuff up and cleaning my bathroom and helping do stuff in the kitchen. He didn't care how I felt. It was only what he wanted. And I couldn't stay up late. He made me go to bed early and get up early, and take walks with him. He's this really brutal, selfish guy, and I always hated him. I always hated him. I hate him!"

"What does he do for a living?

"He's a doctor. You know - for kids - whatever they call it."

"Pediatrician," Shepherd very quietly said.

"Yeah, That's is. I think he chose it because he really likes hurting little kids."

"Why do you say that?"

"Because he always hurt me."

"How?"

"He used to punish me when I refused to do all this stuff he wanted."

"How did he punish you?"

"Oh . . you know - he'd make me stay in my room and keep me from watching TV or playing video games. He even took away my CD player once and never gave it back to me. He really hated me."

"But he never hit you?"

"Uh . . no - not exactly. He shook me once - once when I broke the windows on the neighbors car across the street. I told him it was an accident. I was throwing these rocks. But he didn't believe me."

"How often do you see him?"

"I haven't seen him since I was eighteen.   Three years, I guess. That's when the court couldn't make me see him anymore - you know, that visitation thing."

"Do you talk to him on the phone?"

"No. He calls me all the time, but I don't answer and I ignore his messages. He's got this really whinny pathetic voice. I can't stand it. It's a joke with all my friends. Every time he makes one of his phony phone calls. They all call him 'Bob the Bastard'. That's what we call him. Yeah. I call him 'Bob the Bastard.' And that's what he is."

Dr. Shepherd kind of knitted his fingers all together and frowned a little and looked like he was really thinking hard about something.

"Do you . . know why your parents divorced?", he asked me sort of careful-like.

"Not really. But it was his fault. I can tell ya that. He's the one that caused it."

"Is that what your mother told you?"

"Uh . . . yeah - but not exactly. She never said exactly what he did. But he divorced her."

"To marry someone else?"

"No. He never remarried."

"Interesting. And when did your mother remarry?"

"When I was thirteen."

"Do you like your step-father?"

"Yeah - he's OK. He leaves me alone - doesn't make me do stuff."

"And did your mother make you do stuff when you were growing up? Did she make you do things that you didn't want to do?"

"No. Never. She always did stuff for me. She loves me."

Shepherd gave this little laugh that kind of disturbed me. Then he just gave me this really steady gaze for almost a minute.

"I see," he finally said softly. "I see."

"Yeah - but that's not why I'm really here. It's gonna be unpleasant tomorrow with the Dean and everything, but I think my step-dad can straightened everything out. I'm not that worried about it. But I am really worried about something else."

"Yes, I know," he said very quietly, with this really sympathetic look on his face. "Of course I heard all about it."

That really shocked me. I felt hot all of a sudden and I'm sure my face must have really turned red because I could feel sweat on my forehead. I sort of panicked. My mind was scrambling all around trying to think of how he could have known already about what I did last night. Fuck! My heart started racing and I could feel my mouth go dry. Fuck me! How could he know? How could he have heard about it? Did the police find out about it? Did that fucking Jeff already go to the police? Was Jeff so pissed off at what I'd done to him out on the field this afternoon that he just went and told the police, and then the police called the school and they told everybody on the faculty and they were all waiting for me to show up. And now Shepherd was gonna reach for the phone and call security or call the police and tell them that I was there and . . and . . .

"What's the matter?", Shepherd asked me with a look of real concern. "Are you OK? You look like you're getting ill. What is it?"

"I'm OK," I was barely able to mutter. "I just didn't know . . . that you knew about it . . . about what happened."

"Everybody does," he said all matter-of-fact-like. "And I would have gone to the memorial service yesterday, but I had an important class."

"Memorial service?", I asked, totally confused.

"Yes. Kyle Martinsen's memorial service in the chapel. We are talking about Kyle, aren't we?"

"Yeah - sure," I nervously sort of mumbled.

"He was a wonderful young man. I know how close you two were and it must be a terrible thing for you."

"Yeah," I said really abrupt-like.

"You know, I had Kyle for two classes and we became good friends. We used to talk quite a bit. I know what you meant to him, and I . . . "

"Yeah - yeah," I said kind of harshly. "But that's not my problem. He's gone, and that's it. Nobody can do anything about it now, so there's no use talking about it. He's gone and it's done. My problem isn't about Kyle - it's about . . . it's about . . . my girlfriend, Beth."

"Oh?", Shepherd said with a sort of flash of surprise. "Your girl-friend?"

"Yeah. She's pregnant. Three months. She wants us to get married this Christmas - during the break."

"And . . what do you want?", he slowly asked me.

I shook my head and put my hands up to my face for a moment.

"I don't the hell know. I just don't know."

He got up from his chair and stepped over and sat down on the edge of the front of his desk, and then he put his hand all gentle-like on my shoulder and gave it a couple of pats and just left it there.

At first, it felt really good. But when he left his hand there on my left shoulder, it felt kind of funny. Kind of strange. It made me feel a little un-comfortable. I don't know why. But I remember wishing that he'd just take it away and go back and sit down behind his desk again.

"You youngsters have it so hard today," he began saying, as if he were in front of his classroom. "Almost everyone's against you."

"Yeah?", I asked, really liking the sound of what he was saying.

"Yes. It's true. First, most of you are raised by parents who put all their time and energy into both their jobs, and then they think that they can make up for not being there for you by giving you a big chunk of all that money they've made. And what do young people do with this money? Is it a good idea for youngsters with no experience in life - with no wisdom or knowledge of what has value and what doesn't have value - is it a good idea to just give them all this money? To let them become the biggest consumers in our society - for them to have this power to create popular taste by their compulsively mindless purchases? To give them the ability to buy drugs and have sex and act like adults before they've even had the chance to begin discovering who they are - what they are? I think it's cruel. I think it's despicable to force them into adulthood by giving them money, and force them to make commitments and life-changing decisions when they are mentally and emotionally still children who don't have an ounce of self-knowledge and don't really have the slightest clue who they really are and what they really want."

Shit! What a lecture! I was following him at the beginning, but fuck! By the end, I didn't know what the hell this guy was talking about. It was almost like I was back there in Campus Ministry. I sort of wanted to leave.

"Well, it's a problem I'll just have to work out myself," I said with a confident shrug, kind of gently moving my shoulder away from his hand.

But his hand swayed and stayed there as I moved.

"Bottom line is - do you love her?", he asked me very firmly.

"Uh - yeah - I guess I do. Yeah, I guess I do - a little."

"As much as you loved Kyle?", he said in almost a whisper.

"What!"

Fucking shit! Was this guy crazy! What the hell! What fucking horse shit was this! I couldn't believe I heard what he said!

"As much as you loved - ?"

"Yeah - I know what you fucking said," I answered really angrily. "But are you crazy! What the fuck are you talking about!"

"You know what I'm talking about," Shepherd said very calmly. "It's like what I was saying about self-knowledge, and how you youngsters don't acquire any until way after you've become adults."

He began very softly and sort of all tender-like rubbing his hand on my shoulder.

Fuck me! I wanted out of there right now!

I jumped up from the chair and backed away from him a little.

"I gotta go meet Beth now," I nervously announced.

He stood up and slowly moved towards me with a kind of smile I'd never seen him give before. I think maybe it was more the kind of look he had in his eyes.

"Look - pretty boys like you and Kyle - I mean, boys like you who are practically works of art you're so perfectly beautiful - you're always made to be loved by your own sex. It's a law of nature. Biologically, we're all bi-sexual - part man and part woman - that's what we came from - part from our mothers and part from our fathers. And when a man is as beautiful and made so finely as you are - well, he wants to be made love to by another man. Another man is the only one who can truly appreciate him and satisfy him. It's not a question of what you want. It's that you were created to be made love to - for other men to love. It's as simple as that."

I was staring at him like he had a gun in his hand and was pointing it at me and about to fire it. My heart was in my mouth.

"You're nuts!", I screamed. "You're fucking out of your fucking mind! You crazy asshole faggot!"

I just turned and quickly went over to the door and began to open it.

But before I could, his strong, large hand came around the side of my head and slammed the door shut.

"First time is always the hardest," he whispered excitedly to me, taking his hand and yanking me around so that I was standing and looking him directly in the face. "You know that's who you are. You know that's what you've been wanting. You've been trying to seduce me ever since you were in my class. The smile. The flexing of your chest every time you talk to me. That melting look you always give me. You've wanted this for a long time. Get onto yourself. You can't deny it anymore."

I went to speak, but I didn't have time.

In an instant, Dr. Shepherd put both of his hands behind my head and sort of held me in a headlock like a professional wrestlers or something. His eyes looked like they had some kind of weird fire in them - like he really was crazy.

Then, all of a sudden, he leaned forward and roughly pressed my head forward, and he kissed me on my mouth. He pressed his lips against mine and kissed me really passionately. He kissed me so passionately and for so long that I thought for sure that my lips would start bleeding.

I tried with all my strength to push him away. I desperately tried to get away from him, but I couldn't. He was pressing his body so tightly against me that I could barely move my arms. And he was a big guy. He must of worked out, because he was really strong and a little taller than me, and he had me pinned there against the door for what seemed like an hour, but I think it was really only fifteen seconds or so. I don't know. It all happened so fast. And I think I was in shock. I'm sure of it. Because I started going nuts. I totally lost it.

At last, I twisted my head really violently and broke that disgusting, slobbering kiss he was giving me.

199

He seemed startled for a moment, but quickly went to kiss me again, sort of making this repulsive, passionate little moan.

But I jerked back my head and freed my left arm and shoved him back. Then I started screaming like a maniac, pushing and pushing and hitting and hitting and pounding madly against him to get him away from me.

"NO! NO! GET AWAY FROM ME! GET AWAY! STOP IT! NO! STOP IT! STOP IT OR I'LL KILL YOU! NO! NO! STOP IT! STOP IT! STOP IT! STOP IT!"

I really totally lost it. It was like I was somebody else. I just went completely nuts.

I really frightened myself. And I really frightened Dr. Shepherd. He seemed really scared of me - by what I was saying and especially how I was acting. He didn't know what to do, and being so afraid, he really backed away from me as I kept screaming and insanely yelling at him.

"It's OK - calm down - calm down," he kept telling me in a frightened, shaky voice. "OK - OK - calm down. I'm sorry. I'm sorry. It's OK. Stop acting so crazy. Calm down and be quiet."

I lunged forward at him and cocked back my right fist and was all ready to really punch him hard right in the center of his face.

There was this complete look of horror in his eyes. It made me freeze. It made me freeze dead. I stood there hatefully looking at him, then I lowered my hand and I turned and ran out the office door.

It was like I was in a daze as I kind of staggered and ran through the maze of hallways and took one wrong turn after another until I was back out into the huge atrium of the building.

I kept running, across the bridge to the balcony on other side, then down to the opposite end of the fucking gigantic place. With all the trees everywhere and soft, dim lighting, I had the feeling I was in another world. A nightmare world. Nothing seemed real. And my mind wouldn't focus on anything. It wouldn't work. It just totally shut the fuck down.

When I came to the pile of escalators at the other end of the building, I caught my breath, then racing down the 'up' one to the third floor and then started running around the gallery balcony back to another bridge and crossed it and started running back again.

I didn't know where the fuck I was going, or where I wanted to go. I just wanted to run, and I didn't want to stop. I was afraid to stop.

If I stopped, I'd have to start thinking.

And I was afraid to think. I didn't want to remember what happened in Shepherd's office. I didn't want to remember anything that asshole faggot had said, and especially what he had done to me.

But I finally slowed and lost some speed when I went down the stairs to the second floor, and I started thinking. I started thinking of that guy last night. That guy Steve that Jeff and I met at the Warehouse bar in the Marina. I started thinking about him.

And I started thinking about why I had killed him.

7:05 pm

Going down the stairs to the ground floor of U-Hall, I was doing everything I could to get all that crap out of my brain.   All the shit about Dr. Shepherd and everything.

The atrium was crowded with kids on their way to class. I started walking down the center under the trees, but I kept seeing people that I knew. I had this kind of weird smile on my face. It was like I was thinking

202

that everybody I saw coming towards me knew what had happened upstairs in Shepherd's office. Like they were looking at me kind of funny because they knew what Shepherd had said to me - what he had done.

As I slowly walked, I didn't want to look anybody in the eye. I didn't want to talk to anybody. So I kind of wandered over to the side and started moving along the windows of the offices. I just kept staring at the windows and ignoring everybody. Whenever I saw anybody I knew out of the corner of my eye, I stopped and turned and faced the windows and sort of tried to hide. Several guys said 'hi' to me, but I just sort of gave them a quick thumbs up sign and then turned away and kept moving on.

My mind was just all totally blank. When I suddenly saw this narrow passageway to my right, I began walking down it until I came to an alcove that was a doorway to the cafeteria. The cafeteria was closed and the door was locked and nobody at all was around, so I just sort of stood there a minute, then squatted down and sat on the floor with my knees up against my chest.

That made me feel a little better. Kind of warm and protected. I didn't feel anymore like my insides were gonna fucking fall out all over the place. I sort of felt safe now. At least a little safe, I guess. I took several really deep drags of air into my lungs. I was kind of breathless from all that running and stuff. Then I wrapped my arms around my knees and kind of rocked back and forth a little bit as I sat there on the floor.

Thoughts started coming into my head again about what happened last night down at the Marina, so I quickly bit down hard on my lower lip and I started humming one of my favorite songs to myself to make the awful memory go away.

After a few minutes, I started feeling a whole fucking lot better. I started feeling like I wanted to beat the crap out of the next guy that looked at me or smiled at me. My juices were just exploding. I was angrier that I could ever remember being. Angry as hell. And I even thought for a few minutes about going back upstairs and beating the shit out of Dr. Shepherd. Not killing him or really putting him in the hospital or anything, but just getting a few really good shots at that fucking lying face of his. Just maybe two or three punches in the mouth, and a couple of good ones to his stomach.

I swear to god I was all set to jump up and go back upstairs and do that. Just pulverize that handsome, faggy actor face of his, but then I kind of remembered that he had said he had a seven o'clock class tonight and that was why I'd rushed up to his office like I did. So what was the use? He wouldn't be in his office anymore. He'd be in his fucking classroom, probably lining up the best looking guy in the class for a blow-job or some other faggy thing later on. Yeah - I could just see him now playing up to one of his handsome students exactly like he had played up to me last year. Fuck!

I thought for a minute that maybe I could go up there and expose Shepherd for the molesting jerk that he was and really let him have it with my fists right then and there. But then I thought that I just couldn't come storming into his classroom and pound him out in front of everybody.

That wouldn't have been cool. And I was the one that would probably get in trouble. The cowardly fag would definitely call campus security and it would be my ass that would get fried by the whole fucking thing. Shit! A guy can't even pound out a creepy jerk of a professor who attacks him. Fuck! Life is just so unfair.

Plus, I sort of also remembered that he was a pretty big guy. Bigger than me by probably more than thirty pounds. And he wasn't fat or anything like the coaches were. He worked out a lot. Probably at one of those fag factory gyms up in West Hollywood. I was thinking I was lucky to get away from him. He was holding me so tightly against the door that it was a fucking wonder I managed to push him away and hold him off with those kind of sissy punches I was making against his chest.

So - everything considered - I decided that going up there and trying to whip his ass in front of his psychology class wasn't a very good idea. There was no way I could have come out of it well. So I just decided I'd come back another day and beat the fucking faggy shit out of him. And make him take back all that crazy shit he said about me and everything. Yeah. I liked that idea a lot. It really made me feel better thinking about how I'd do it. How I'd get him to beg and plead and all that shit. And maybe even make him cry. That would be great! To see a grown man like him cry.

I've never cried in my life. No matter how bad I ever got hurt. Nothing can make me cry. But to see Dr. Shepherd get clobbered really good and break down and cry and cry. That would really be sweet.

That would be fucking great!

I was really feeling better now. Almost all better.

I stood up and straightened my shirt and tucked it in, then walked all confident-like back up the narrow hallway and came out into the atrium ready to conquer the world.

A girl with long brunette hair was walking toward me and I shot her one of my killer smiles. She smiled back. I could tell she instantly wanted me, so I moved in front of her and sort of blocked her path, flexing my chest and tilting my head back a little so my eyes would shine in the light.

"Hey beautiful," I sort of half-sung in this really sexy, throaty voice. "Why haven't we met before?   I'm sure I'd remember someone like you."

Actually - she was really plain and not the least bit good looking, if you know what I mean. But I wasn't in a critical mood right now. I just felt like I really wanted to make some girl want me. To want me to make love to her.

"Sure you would," she laughed. "I'm in your philosophy class, stupid. I sit right across the row from you. You've seen me all semester."

Shit! Yeah - now I sort of recognized her a little.

"Yeah - sure," I said all kind of awkward-like. "I was just kidding. It was a joke. Sure I remember you."

She rolled her eyes and gave me this really tired, impatient look. She wasn't buying any of it. I tried my million dollar smile again, but she wasn't buying that either. Tossing her head, she continued walking on her way at a slightly faster pace.

"That was some performance in class today," she called back to me in this really snotty, sarcastic tone. "Just leaving right in the middle like that without even saying a word. Delaney was pretty pissed. I think he's gonna give you an 'F'. Congratulations."

Just my luck I chose that bitch to talk to. That's what you get when you try to be nice to ugly girls. They always fucking hate you because they know deep down that they don't really deserve you. You can't win.

I started walking back toward the elevator, kind of taking my time and sort of strutting under the trees right down the center of the atrium. One girl after another returned my smile, but they all seemed to be in a hurry, and even when I said 'hi' to them, they just brightly said 'hi' back, but quickly continued on their way to where they were going.

This really gorgeous girl was going up the escalator to my right, so I hurried over and got on and hiked up the steps until I was right behind her.

"Hi", I said to her, all kind of cocky-like. "What's up?"

She completely ignored me. Didn't even turn around.

"Hi," I repeated - a little louder. "Where ya goin'?"

She still didn't respond.

We were getting to the top and she sort of stepped off the escalator in this really fart-assed way - like she was the queen of something. I swung around and got in front of her and flashed her my sexiest smile - you know, putting a lot of teeth into it and sort of holding my lips just right.

"Excuse me," she said in this stupid, bored voice. "I'm late for my class. Have a good evening."

And she just turned away and went waltzing off.

Shit! I swear! You can't win! These girls all have so much fucking attitude. The ugly ones don't like you because you're more beautiful than they are, and the gorgeous ones don't like you because you're as beautiful as they are and they don't like the competition. They want some ugly guy who'll crawl around after them and be their slave and all that fucking crap. Fuck that! I never met a gorgeous girl who wasn't like that. I hate gorgeous girls. They're nothing but trouble.

I was feeling really pissed now. Walking over to the down escalator, I sort of cut in front of three guys who were about to step onto it. They were these three nerdy guys, so they really didn't give a shit. Riding down, I noticed this pretty girl near the bottom who was watching me. She sort of started moving over to where I was going to be exiting.

207

"Hey," she said as I was getting off at the bottom, coming right up to me with this really warm smile. "How's it going?"

"It's going great," I said really cocky and confident-like. "How's it going for you, pretty lady?"

"It's going great too," she said with this nice little flirty laugh. "But I think it's gonna be going a lot greater. Are you ready for a big night?"

Jesus Christ! Eureka! Talk about having a good thing land right in your lap. I didn't even have to do anything. It just walked right up to me.

"I sure am, pretty lady," I sort of moaned in this incredibly sexy voice. "Where should we have our 'big night'? Your place or mine?"

"Well - how about the Bird Nest?", she giggled.

"Huh?", I was suddenly confused.

"The Bird Nest. That's where you're having your birthday party, isn't it? That's what Beth said."

"Beth?", I nervously gulped.

"Yeah," she said, kind of looking at me funny, then breaking up into laughter. "Don't you remember me? At the concert last month? I'm Liz Martinez - one of Beth's sorority sisters."

"Oh, yeah - sure," I kind of choked. "Hey, Liz."

"I just wanted to wish you an early Happy Birthday and tell you I'll see you later at the party. Happy Birthday, Number Nine."

"Thanks," I said in kind of a weak voice, trying to smile. "It's actually tomorrow - but thanks."

"See ya later," she said brightly, rushing off beneath the trees.

Fuck! What the hell! This was getting fucking pathetic! I usually had to scrape girls off me everywhere I went. Now, tonight - I couldn't even find ONE. Not one fucking girl to kind of wash away that shit that happened upstairs. I really wanted to find a girl that would go off with me and help wash all that crazy, fucking shit away. To show what a fucking crazy liar that Shepherd faggot was. I really needed that.

I began walking toward the elevator again. I knew I was gonna see Beth a little later. But I also knew that wasn't gonna do it for me. She had to love me now. With the kid on the way - she had to love me. She didn't have any choice. But I needed another girl to want me. Someone new that just wanted me for the stud that I was. Someone who just wanted me to fuck her because I was such an incredible man. A totally masculine, manly man who could fuck her better than any other guy on the planet. I needed some new girl to tell me that right now. Just to tell me what I've always known. I wanted to hear it again.

Sort of dodging around this really thick, leafy tree to my left, I noticed a girl sitting at one of those little patio tables. She was really nice looking - kind of pretty and soft and not too much make-up. The kind I usually liked best. And she was alone. And she looked up from her book and smiled at me.

Having been shot down three times in a row, I was kind of losing my steam. I mean - fuck! I couldn't even remember the last time I was even shot down once. Not fucking once! I think maybe back in the 11th grade when I asked some super-rich snotty bitch to a school Christmas dance. That was the only time I could remember. And, now - tonight - I felt like some fucking target in a goddamned shooting gallery. Fuck!

But this friendly, pretty girl looked really safe. So I slowed down a little and edged over a bit to her table and gave her a smile. Not a huge, sexy smile. Just a normal happy smile - the kind you give the clerk at the market or somebody you pass on the street.

"Hi," she said.

"Hi," I replied.

"You're on the water polo team, aren't you?", she asked softly.

"Soccer. I'm on the soccer team."

At least - I was until this afternoon. But I didn't go into that.

"I knew it was something," she said with this really warm, gentle little laugh. "You have such a beautiful body."

Now that sort of really took me for a fucking loop. I mean - they always get around to telling me that crap - especially when we're in bed together. But right out of the gate like this? Almost the first words out of the mouth of this chick that I don't even know? Shit! It really took me for a fucking loop! But in a good way. A great way. I really liked it. It made me feel great. It was exactly what I needed right then.

"Thank you," is the only thing I could think of saying back to her.

I wanted to return the compliment, but she was wearing this sort of baggy sweater and she was sitting down, so I really could tell what kind of body she had. But I was hoping it was pretty good. I had a feeling it probably was. Yeah. For her type - it seemed like it must be pretty OK.

"Going to class?", she gently asked me.

"No," I replied with a shrug and kind of a shy smile.

"Coming from class?", she smiled back.

"No."

"Then what are doing here in U-Hall?", she asked with this really flirty, playful expression.

There was no way I was even gonna fucking go into any of that. I didn't even the fuck want to fucking think about it again. Shit!

"Meeting you," I sort of cockily answered. "Isn't that a good reason for being here?"

"The best," she said in a really low voice, smiling and leaning back in her chair and combing her fingers through her long hair. "You're psychic?"

"Huh?"

"You can see into the future and know what's going to happen?", she asked with this soft laugh that really turned me on.

"I wish," I laughed a little. "Sure save a lot of problems, I guess."

"I guess."

"What about you? Is the book for your class? Are you going to a class pretty soon?"

"No - I just got out of my anthropology class. I was just waiting for my friend Nina to finish her yoga class and give me a ride back to my dorm."

"Which dorm are you in?"

"McKay"

"Well, I got my truck downstairs and I'm goin' back that way. Why don't you let me take ya?"

Usually girls go through this whole fucking half-assed routine when you make your first move on them. You know - the old 'couldn't possibly care less' shit. You can tell if a girl wants you to fuck her about two seconds after you first look her in the eye. But they always have to play this fucking colossal pretend game of not really being that interested and kind of just going along with you because you're all forcing them to. You know - the old 'hard to get' act. But it's really not so much that. They can usually be got pretty easily. It's just that they have to pretend that they're not dying to be fucked by you. I guess it's an ego thing or something. But this chick wasn't like that at all.

"That'd be great," she kind of instantly accepted. "I'd like that. Let me make a quick call to Nina and leave a message for her."

She pulled a green cellphone out of her purse and made a very quick call and left a brief message. Very nice and all that.

I really liked this chick.

She got up and gathered all her junk and stood there smiling at me with this very direct, really friendly and warm, open look.

I really liked her.

And she had a pretty good body too. I was right. I could see her tits when she bent over to get her book, and they were really nice. All firm and tanned and curving just where they should. And really big! You know. Kind of like grapefruits.

I just reached over and took her backpack from her and carried it in my left hand. It was kind of heavy. Probably had her laptop inside of it.

When I did that, she looked up at me with a slight smile and gave me this really warm, inviting gaze. Right deep into my eyes. I recognized it immediately. I'd seen it before hundreds of times in other girls. It was 'the look'. And it always meant the same thing. That sex was less than an hour away. I definitely was gonna get laid. It was a sure thing now.

Feeling that made everything instantly better.

I forgot about all that other shit.

The moment was all that counted now. And living in this fucking moment and making the best of it was going make everything great, and it was going to make all the other shit go away for now. Totally just dissolve out of my brain.

We walked over to the elevator, and then took it down to the first level of the parking garage. Sort of strolling over to my truck, I put my left arm gently around her shoulder as we walked. She didn't put up a fuss. In fact, she really seemed to like it. She gave me that look again.

We got in my truck and I hesitated when I put the key in the ignition. I turned and looked at her and she was sort of all melting-like and leaning a little towards me. So I leaned towards her, and without either of us saying a fucking word, we just sort of both kissed each other on the lips at the same time. It was a really passionate kiss, too. I didn't even have to grab her head or anything. She was all there.

It felt so great. And I really made it a wet kiss - just all wet and deep and everything, mainly because I wanted to get rid of the feel of that awful shit-ass kiss that Shepherd had given me. I'd kept wiping my mouth for the past half-hour trying to get his slime off my lips, but I still felt it no matter how hard I rubbed. I was going to go the bathroom and wash out my mouth with water and use a lot of soap and stuff, but that was just before I met this girl. Now - kissing her - everything was OK.

And I knew it would really be OK right after I fucked her.

7:44 pm

After making out a little in the front seat of my truck, I drove this hot girl back to her room in McKay Hall. I almost hit one of the campus security patrol cars when I was taring out of the parking structure. My cock was getting harder every minute, and I wanted to blast off as soon as possible.

I parked in the faculty lot behind McKay, and the girl and I quickly climbed out and just kind of stood there looking at the dorm building for a few awkward seconds. Then we glanced at each other with these really hot looks and started walking toward the entrance. She took my hand as we walked. And neither one of us said a word. Not one fucking word! I couldn't believe it. It was like one of those dopey scene from one of those stupid romantic chick flicks. Incredible! Fucking incredible!

When we got to her room on the second floor, she just went in and held the door open wide and waited for me to follow her in. Fuck! I couldn't believe it. No games. No phony feminine shit. She just turned and shut the door behind me, and we started making out again and taking off our clothes at the same time. We each took off our own crap. It was a lot easier that way. I think it took us less than ten seconds. It was so great!

Naturally, her roommate wasn't there. I don't know where she had gone, and I didn't ask. I didn't the fuck care. Shit - if she came back in the middle of the whole fucking thing, she could just buy a ticket and watch, for all I cared. Maybe she could take notes and learn something. I've been told a million times that I do it better than anybody. I have no way of knowing if that's true of not, but I always suspected it might be. I really know how to please a girl, and I have my own special technique that always drives them wild. I guess maybe it's what they call a natural talent or something. Whatever it is - I've sure got it. I always have.

So there we were, all totally naked and everything, standing there and kissing like crazy and putting our hands all over the place all excited-like. And I was totally hard now and ready for action, so I sort of lifted her up a little and positioned her down on the nearest bed.

She was on her back, so I knelt over her and pulled up her legs and took my cock and smoothly guided it with my hand right into her. Nice.

She'd been all ready for it, so it was really fucking awesome. I reached down and started squeezing her gorgeous tits as I began gently rocking away on her. I was so turned on that I was really kind of surprised and upset by what happened in less than half a minute.

What happened was that my cock just all of a sudden went soft. In less than a fucking minute! There I was totally out of gas, if you know what I mean. Banging away on this chick like a total stud for twenty seconds or so, and then my goddamned cock just started going totally soft. And the softer it got, the more I tried to stoke myself up, licking her tits and putting my hands under her butt. I was doing everything I could think of, but nothing was working. Not a fucking thing.

Finally my cock just fell right out of her and sort of hung there like a deflated balloon. It was really embarrassing. I didn't know what was happening. It started making me really pissed-off. Shit!

I whacked off a little and tried to get my hard-on back, but that almost made it worse. My cock just sort of seemed to shrink a little into my crotch, like it was trying to protect itself from something. Fuck! Then she started giving me this really rough hand job, yanking on it pretty hard and squeezing it until it hurt. Fuck!

I finally pushed her hand away and told her to stop it.

"What's the matter?", she softly asked me.

"Nothing."

"Is there anything special you want me to do?", she asked very gently, rising up on her elbows and giving me a really nice little smile.

"No," I said kind of all angry-like.

I was sitting on the side of the bed and she slowly twisted herself up and sat beside me. Neither of us said anything for almost two minutes.

We just sat there and didn't touch each other either. I was just looking the fuck down at the goddamned floor. Her dorm room had the same shitty grey carpet that my apartment had. I was thinking that the university must have hired the same cheesy company to do the carpeting for the whole fucking campus. And they were really cheesy carpets too. Shit!

"You know," she finally said in almost this tender whisper, "we don't really have to do that. It's no big deal. We can just lay down here and hold each other and kiss. Just whatever you feel like. And maybe - after a little while - you know - maybe you'll feel like you can . . . . "

Fuck me! Shit! What a fucking goddamned thing to say to me! Yeah, right! Maybe I can get it up a little later? Maybe I can become a man again! Fuck! I was really pissed! Who did this bitch think she was! Talking down to me like that - like a was this fucking pathetic loser or something! Being all nice and everything. And pretending she wasn't the fucking slut whore that she was. I mean, fuck! What kind of girl would just jump into bed and fuck a guy she's never seen before in her life? A guy that just came walking by. I mean, fuck! What a whore! No wonder I couldn't get it up. I didn't want to fuck a skanky slut like that. No wonder I couldn't keep my hard-on with her. It was her fault. It was all her fault!

I stood up and quickly started putting my clothes back on.

"I gotta go," I coldly announced.

She looked kind of stunned by that.

"You have to go?", she asked with surprise.

"Yeah - I do."

"Can't you stay a little longer? Weren't you planning on . . ?"

"I have plans to meet my girlfriend," I said in this really arrogant, bad-ass tone, raising my voice a little and putting a lot of emphasis on the word 'girlfriend' when I said it. "I'm already late. I don't know why I came up here in the fucking first place."

She looked really hurt by that. In fact, she even hung her head a little and sort of softly moaned this really bogus, fake disappointed little 'oh.' That's all she said. Just 'oh' - really soft and all crushed-like. It seemed so real that I almost believed it. But I didn't.

It took me only a minute or so to dress, and after I tied my shoes and stood up again, I didn't even look back at her as I headed over to the door and opened it.

"It was nice meeting you," she said in this ridiculous, hurt little voice.

"Right," I sort of spit it out at her without even turning around.

I went sort of storming out the door, and when I turned around to slam it shut, I suddenly thought of something to say.

"Ya know - I had a fucking soccer game today! I played all fucking afternoon and on top of that I've had the shittiest day on the planet! So, like I'm fucking exhausted - OK? I'm fucking exhausted, and I shouldn't even be fucking trying to do anything right now anyway, because I'm fucking goddamned exhausted and can hardly even walk! Got it? Shit!"

I slammed the door really hard because I was so royally pissed at this whole fucking thing! I really was!

And I never wanted to see her again. What a whore!

I rushed out of McKay Hall and went back to my truck. There was another fucking parking ticket on my windshield. But I didn't care anymore by then. From now on I was gonna park any fucking place that I wanted to, and if campus security didn't like it, they could shove it up their ass.

The library was just across the way, so I thought since I really couldn't park any closer to it, I might as well leave my truck where it was and walk over.

Walking along the narrow faculty parking lot, I cut through the Peace Garden as a shortcut. I knew it was late and I wasn't wearing my watch, so I wanted to see what time it was on the bell tower clock. You had this really neat view of the distant bell tower from there, sort of all framed by these tall pine trees. Kyle used to always say that they were called Italian Stone Pines. He'd been to Italy twice with his folks and he really knew all kinds of crap like that. It was funny.

To be able to see the tower clock, I stepped off the sidewalk and onto the little grassy lawn that was pretty much the entire Peace Garden. It was a pretty strange place. Somebody said that one of the professor guys had a son or something who was killed by terrorist somewhere or other, and he gave a bunch of money so that this weird little garden here could be created and dedicated to peace.

I never really got it. How can you dedicate something to peace? Especially a plot of grass and some trees and a bunch of stone slabs. That's mainly what it was. These huge chunks of stone just laying around there like it was a cemetery or something. And on each stone they carved the words of some really phony, fake sentence. You know - the supposedly wise words of these famous phony guys who lived a thousand years ago like Gandhi and Churchill and all these other big thinking brainiacs. Just so dumb and fake.

I never paid any attention at all to these weird stone things in the Peace Garden, but Kyle always liked to carefully look at them, and we used to come up here a lot last year to study under those tall pine trees.

That's what I remember most. Those beautiful huge pine trees.
Kyle and I used to sit on the grass with our books and kind of talk over our assignments as we looked up at the trees and the clouds in the sky and the bell tower in the distance.

I totally ignored all those stones with those half-assed inscriptions on them, but Kyle seemed to really like them. While we'd be there, he'd go around reading them. Every fucking time we were there. I thought for sure he would have memorized all of them, but he'd still get up and walk over and slowly read all of them - sometimes out loud in that really gentle, deep voice of his.

His favorite stone was the one with the quote from the Dalai Lama. It said something like - "My religion is simple - it's to always be kind," or some horse shit like that. I don't remember exactly. But some crazy idea like that. As if you can always be kind. Fuck! Good luck to any jackass that believes crap like that and tries to do it. Imagine what your fucking life would be like if you tried being kind all the time to everybody. You'd last about three minutes before you'd totally get creamed.

But Kyle was kind of dumb that way. I think he really believed it and he really tried to do it, from all I could see. People were always taking advantage of him, but he really never seemed to mind, I guess. He just . . . he just sort of . . .

Holy fuck! Christ! I'd come to look at the fucking clock on the tower to see what time it was. Why was I thinking about that loser Kyle and all his dopey ideas. Fuck! I didn't wanna think about any of that crap. I just wanted the time. Beth was waiting for me in the library by the fireplace. I should've been there at eight.

I stepped over beneath a pine branch and got a good view of the clock. It was almost 8:20.

Shit! Beth was gonna be so pissed at me. I was already twenty minutes late.

Racing off down the three flights of stairs at the side of the garden, I crossed the street and ran up the sidewalk of the gently sloping hill and looked toward the brightly lit library right in front of me. It was pretty new and all super modern and everything. It was built kind of in the shape of this huge spaceship - at least it looked like a spaceship to me. It was totally round - just like a frisbee - and three stories tall and with walls of windows all over the fucking place. Nothing but windows. It was kind of a really weird-looking place.   Like a spaceship or something.

I really pressed it into gear and flew in the exit door as these two guys were coming out, and I leapt up the stairs three at a time to the second floor lounge where Beth was waiting for me by the fireplace.

8:24 pm

Beth was sitting in a chair next to the fireplace where these huge flames were sort of raging away. As soon as I walked up to her, I could instantly feel that it was hot as hell there in that lounge area, thanks to her and the fire. She was really pissed, and even though she was kind of trying to hide it, I knew right away when I saw her tight face how angry she was.

221

"Howdy," I sort of shyly said.

She didn't say anything for a long time. In fact, she didn't even look up at me. She just sat there with her chemistry book in her lap and almost pretended like I wasn't even there.

"You're almost a half-hour late," she finally said in this flat, cool voice. "I didn't think you were gonna come by."

"Sorry - I got caught up with stuff," I softly apologized, all kind of whipped-like.

She glance up at me at last and had this really intense look in her eyes that kind of intimidated me. It wasn't so much that she was pissed. It was more like this kind of desperate thing. Like she was really determined to do something or to get something.

I sat down in the chair next to her and looked at the blazing fire for a few moments, then glanced back at her and gave a big, awkward smile.

"My favorite shirt," I said with this kind of playful fake pride, reaching up and slightly tugging on the collar.

She ignored it and didn't smile.

"We have to talk," Beth said in this really dramatic, serious-as-hell tone. "You said we'd decide what we were gonna do. I can't wait any longer. Everybody's gonna know. I'm starting to . . . "

She glanced over at this tall, blond girl with these bright pink tennis shoes sitting in a chair across from us. The girl was intently working on her laptop and she didn't seem to be paying any attention to us, but she was close enough that she could fucking hear everything we were saying.

"Do you wanna go someplace else?", I whispered to Beth.

She shook her head 'no', beginning to get a little emotional. Her eyes started glistening and I could tell that tears weren't fucking far away.

Shit! That was all I needed tonight. Some over-emotional, crying basket-case on my hands. How the fuck was I supposed to deal with this! I mean - she was forcing me to make this fucking important decision that was gonna change my whole fucking life forever, and she sat there starting to cry and make me feel all fucking guilty and everything. Fuck!

I sat back in my chair and looked at the fireplace.

The girl across the way set her laptop down on the low marble table that all the five chairs were gathered around, and she smilingly looked over at me and Beth.

"If you're going to be here awhile, would you mind watching my laptop for a few minutes?", she asked us really all nice-like.

"No problemo," I smiled back at her.

She got up and walk off and went down the stairs.

"You promised it'd be OK," Beth said real emotional-like. "You said we'd figure this thing out. I'm not getting an abortion. I may not be a very good Catholic, but no way am I gonna get a damned abortion."

"Yeah - yeah - I know," I said kind of all uneasy-like. "I never told you to get an abortion. I never said that. I just said that we should think about putting it up for adoption. You know - right after you have it - we can hand it over to one of those baby agencies. Kids are really scarce around here. They sell right away. We might even get some money for it."

"Stop saying 'it'!", she sort of yelled at me - loud enough that two guys sitting at a table pretty far away looked over at us.

"OK - him or her," I lowered my voice. "That's what we should do."

"No!", Beth said loudly. "Nothing doing. I'm keeping the baby. I won't give my baby away."

I took a deep breath and stared up at the high ceiling and the girls who were walking along the balcony right above us.

"What do you want me to do?", I finally asked her in this really intense whisper. "What am I supposed to fucking do?"

"Marry me. During Christmas break. Like we talked about last week. Like you said you wanted to. Like you promised me."

"I said we'd think about it," I sort of stammered anxiously. "I said we'd think about it. It's a huge fucking step."

"You promised," she moaned with this god-awful desperate look on her face. "You said you loved me. You told me you loved me. Don't you love me anymore? Is that it? Don't you love me?"

"Yeah," I sighed, "of course I love you. I kind of love you."

"Kind of?", she asked all-upset and pissed looking. "What do you mean 'kind of'? You either love me, or you don't."

"I do . . . . . but . . . "

"But what? What the fuck are you trying to say?"

I put my hands up to the sides of my head and painfully winced.

"I don't know," I mumbled. "I'm all fucking confused. I don't know about anything anymore. I'm not fucking sure if I even know what love is. You know I've always had problems with that. I told you right off the bat last summer - when we hooked up and became a couple - I told you what that counselor I used to talk to said to me - that I had trouble loving people. That I had this major fucking problem with love - feeling it for other people. I told you all about that - and I sort of warned you about it - and you kept telling me that I'd learn - that you'd teach me and show me how to love. Remember? Remember how we talked all about that last summer?"

Beth's eyes went really narrow-like and she gave me this kind of really fierce stare, leaning back in her chair and crossing her arms.

"And haven't I?", she almost whispered. "Haven't I taught you? Haven't I loved you so much and showed you what it was like - and how to do it? I thought I had."

"I do love you, Beth," I sort of half-heartedly argued. "I love you. Sort of."

"Sort of!"

"I mean - I think I do. I'm not sure. I'm still not sure exactly what love is. What it fucking is. I'm still just a kid, really. I'm only twenty. I really don't know the fuck about anything. I'm only twenty."

"Twenty-one - in less than four hours," she sort of corrected me real harsh-like. "A full-grown adult. A man. At midnight tonight. And you're gonna have to start acting like a man tonight. Taking responsibility for your life - and our baby's life."

"I know - I know," I painfully whispered.

"I've gotta go back to my room and get ready for the party," she suddenly announced, abruptly standing up and picking up all her stuff.

"OK," I mumbled, solidly staying put in my chair.

"Aren't ya coming with me? So I can show you a couple of the things I was thinking about wearing."

"That's OK," I gently smiled at her. "I think I'll stay here and relax a little. It's been a bitch of a day. The game and everything."

"Yeah - I heard all about the game," she said with this kind of superior, shitty, scolding look. "Everybody says you went fucking nuts out there. We can talk all about that later. And about getting married."

"OK," I sighed.

She turned and walked around the low marble table, then stopped and looked back at me with this really sharp look that I instantly hated.

"You're gonna have to decide tonight, Niner," she almost hissed, or maybe it was my imagination. "After the party. You're gonna have to decide. I mean it."

She walked off toward the elevator and I watched her as she went until she disappeared behind the doors. I was thinking to myself that I really liked her. She was fun. She was really considerate all the time, and always doing special shit for me. Just like my mom. We always had great times together. She was fun. She was a good person. And I started trying to think of her as the one that I'd be spending the rest of my life with. Like she'd be the only one from now on - from now on until the end when I checked out. It made my stomach knot all up, and I felt all hot and funny.

You know - when I saw that elevator door closing shut in front of her face, Beth just didn't seem as pretty as she was last summer. I mean, she's a really nice-looking girl and all that - but she just didn't sort of knock me out and everything the way she did when I first met her last summer.

That first month we were together, it was so great. I didn't want to be away from her for a second. I would have been in that elevator with her. I would have gone back to her room with her. She couldn't have kept me away. But, now, I sort of didn't feel that way anymore.

I sat back real hard in my chair by the fireplace and sort of started wondering what that meant - why I felt differently now.

But I really didn't want to think about it, so I sort of leaned forward again and stretched and flexed my arms and saw these three girls from my English class passing by and I flashed them this super-sexy smile and they giggled and made these cute little hand waves back at me.

There were a lot of kids moving back and forth through the library lounge and I knew almost every other one of them. Funny. I really didn't know any of them - not really well. It was just that they knew me. They knew me and were sort of like 'fans'. Fans of mine for one reason or another. The guys, because of the sports thing. They admired me and wanted to be me. The girls, because of the sex thing. They wanted me. Plain and simple. All these girls wanted me to fuck them. So - I guess they were all sort of really like fans. Not really friends. Just fans.

After a few minutes, I noticed all these young guys in really jacked GQ-type suits all coming up the stairs and gathering kind of all nervously together over by the check-out counter.

A fraternity.

I hate fraternities!

It was pledge week - and that meant that the world's greatest collection of fucking moronic assholes would be all over the place strutting around like the super-dorks they really were. What fucking idiots! All these stupid losers who were afraid of their own shadows.

All the frats had always been after me to join their phony shit houses. But I always refused. I just cut 'em dead. I wouldn't join a frat if you paid me a million dollars. Fake and phony. Just a bunch of losers all huddling together like sheep. You see 'em every place ya go - they travel in packs like wild animals. They're too chicken shit to face life on their own, so they all cluster together like a flock of baby chicks.

Besides - all of us guys on the sports teams all stick together. We don't join these fake, phony frats. We have each other, and we're all tight and loyal to each other and the team. We live together and we eat together and we party together and we hang out together and we study together.

So we don't need to join any stupid fraternity club and hang out with a bunch of cringing cowards who can't go it alone and be fucking free and independent like us guys on the soccer team are.

Shit! Frats! What morons!

These pledges in their lame little suits eventually all waddled off in a herd, and I sat back and tried to relax a little.

Sitting there by the fire, I noticed everyone going up and down the stairs and walking this way and that. It kind of made me dizzy. Everybody seemed to be in such a fucking hurry. Like a bunch of galley slaves in one of those old Roman movies. Fuck! What a life! These pathetic suckers really took this education crap totally serious. Day and night. That's all they did was fucking study and punch away on their goddamned computers writing shit that they'd forget before they even fucking turned it in to their professors. What a goddamned waste of fucking time!

I was watching this really gorgeous dark-haired girl in this incredibly short skirt going up the stairs when the elevator door opened across the way and I noticed someone stepping out. My heart suddenly exploded.

It was Jeff.

He was talking to another guy, and they hung a sharp left and went off toward the book shelves. I didn't think he saw me. He wasn't looking my way, and I was sitting down and not really out there in open sight. But I wasn't positive. And I started thinking he'd probably see me when he came walking back from the shelves because then I'd be straight ahead of him. Yeah - I knew he'd see me when he came back.

And I noticed he was limping. He really seemed to be having a hard time walking. Thanks to me. But at least I didn't break his leg out there on the field. And I should have. The phony bastard!

I wasn't afraid of him, but I didn't want to face him again, and I didn't want to hear his threats and his ultimatum about going to the police later on tonight after the party. I just didn't want to hear any more of that fucking shit. So I thought I'd better get out of there quick.

I kind of jumped up from my chair and slowly backed around the nearest corner and hurried off down a dark, long hallway that led to this huge floor to ceiling glass window.

Coming to the end of the hallway, I leaned against a recess in the wall. I was pretty well hidden, and I was right next to the glowing, tall, dark window. I turned my face toward it so that nobody passing by would recognize me.

I just stared sort of peacefully at the window. Beyond, right outside, there were these three big pine trees that caught my attention. They were kind of hard to see because it was so dark outside, but you could see them there if you really looked carefully.

My eyes started acting a little funny, though. One minute they seemed to be sort of all focused on the pine trees - then they weren't. They would sort of suddenly relax and be a little out of focus, and then they would be looking at just the glowing glass of the window. There were two light posts outside that were shining towards the glass and making that weird glowing thing - kind of a dark blue - a soft, dark blue glow. Just like the waves at the beach this afternoon.

And as I stood there looking up at the glass window, it was just like being there on the sand at the edge of the beach today and watching those giant, gentle waves breaking one after another right in front of me. Those sort of friendly waves - warm and peaceful and wanting to surround you and carrying you softly away.

I couldn't get those fucking beautiful waves out of my brain. They had kept coming back to me and coming back - just like waves always do. And these waves seemed to be talking to me and telling me to come back to them, to return to them. It was like they really wanted me. They wanted me to come back. Like it was what was meant to be.

Looking up at the glowing window, I felt like it was this huge, towering wave that was curling up and getting ready to come crashing down on top of me. It gave me this fucking thrilling sensation. And kind of an overwhelming feeling. I wanted it to happen. I really wanted it to happen like that. To escape like that.

Then, I suddenly got a little dizzy and I shut my eyes and leaned my head back against the wall, and my mind sort of jumped around and started thinking of all this other shit. Just flashing back and forth all over the map of my life.

All of a sudden I started thinking back to that time when I was a little kid of seven, and my dad came by my mom's house to pick me up for his holiday time with me - to take me back to his house way on the other side of the city to spend two weeks with him.

I was remembering how much I hated to go with him, and how I'd gotten sick right before he came by, and how I told him how sick I was when he showed up, but the bastard ignored me and insisted I go along with him anyway, and how I told him I couldn't, but how he kept fucking insisting that I had to go, and then how he yanked me up and took ahold of me really rough-like, and how he put me under his arm like a fucking piece of luggage or something, and how he carried me out to the car, and how I was crying and screaming, and my mom started crying, and my dad kept raising his voice and telling me to keep quiet and to stop screaming and

230

crying, and how that made me cry even more, and how he then jammed me into his little car and really hurt my leg, and how he almost made me throw up when he tightened my seat belt so tight that it almost killed me, and how . . . .

I don't know what made me think about all of that crap. I hardly ever thought about about my dad at all. I can't remember when the last fucking time was that I thought about my bastard father. Bob the Bastard. My fucking cruel father. I didn't even like saying his name. It was kind of weird why I was thinking about him now, with the glass window curling over me like an ocean wave and those stupid tall pine trees outside.

Bob the Bastard. I almost smiled. I remembered how sick I felt when we finally got to his god-awful place, and how he put me right to bed.

And how the bastard made me stay in bed the whole rest of the fucking day and night - the stupid jackass. And I remember how I wanted a hamburger and french fries and ice cream and cake that night, but he wouldn't let me have anything that I really wanted. He never did. Bastard! Instead, he just forced me to eat all this garbage he brought up to my room on this tray - you know - crap - like clear soup and a baked potato and all this green shit and enough vegetable to choke a horse. It was like the pathetic fucker was trying to kill me.

And, then - instead of letting me watch all my favorite TV shows, he unplugged the television and he went and got this really shitty ancient book about some really dumb animals - something about willows in the wind, or something like that. And I remember how much I hated it. But the more I suffered, the more he liked it. I remember how he laughed and smiled as he read that dumb, stupid book. Just to make me feel worse.

And I remember how he sat by bed afterward and sort of gave me this creepy stare when I was trying to go to sleep. He just sat there and stared hatefully at me, and he had this really evil smile on his face. He thought he was fooling me, but he wasn't. I was afraid to shut my eyes and go to sleep because I knew he wanted to hurt me.

Thank god he finally got up and left. But it's really kind of funny. Right before he did, he leaned over me and came down real close to my face. His smile was all gone and he really looked all serious and everything. I remember that he took his hand and really gently stroked my hair and my face for a while. I remember how I thought he'd never stop. How he just kept doing it. I was so scared. I thought he was going to really let me have it and really hurt me. I remember being all tense and afraid.

And then he did the most fucked thing. The bastard really tried to get me off my guard. My asshole father really faked me out. He gently kissed me this really long kiss on my forehead, and he pulled back his face a little and looked down at me with this really weird expression and he said in this really creepy tender voice, "I love you, son."

What an asshole that guy was! It was all just part of his fucking psychological torture routine - just like all that other crap that he always did to me - like all the chores and all the games he used to force me to play and the boring places he forced me to go with him - those goddamned boring museums and book stores and all that stupid shit.

Jesus! Bob the Bastard! What a complete asshole! Boy - did he hate me! He really hated me! And he still does. I know he does.

I leaned back really hard against the wall and kind of felt this sharp pain in my chest. It was really weird. I never felt that before. It was like this knife or something - especially when I took a breath - maybe it must have been something in my lungs. And it sort of choked me a little when I looked over at those big pine trees outside and they seemed to suddenly be part of that huge, curling ocean wave that the glowing blue window had become. And I was thinking about my dad again.

I could feel that kiss on my forehead. And I could hear him saying those words. It was just like he was here right next to me and he was fucking saying it to me again in that really fake tender voice of his.

I shut my eyes and I could actually hear him saying it. Just like he was here and had just kissed me on my forehead. I could really hear him saying those fucking phony words to me.

"I love you, son."

I sat down on the floor and sort of crunched up into this little ball, tightly hugging my legs and leaning my head down and pressing it against my knees.

I stayed that way for two or three minutes, then suddenly jumped up to my feet and slowly walked back up the long hallway.

When I came into the lounge I carefully looked all around.

Jeff wasn't there.

He wasn't by the shelves anymore, and he wasn't in sight anywhere else. The only person around was the girl in the pink tennis shoes who was back sitting in her chair by the fireplace. She looked up from her laptop and saw me and gave me this really dirty look. I had forgotten all about the promise I made to her to stay there and watch out for her computer. But obviously no one had swiped the fucking thing because she still had it, so I don't know what she had to be so pissed off about. Shit!

I carefully looked around again for any sign of Jeff, then I hurried off down the stairs and beat it pretty fast out of the library.

233

9:07 pm

It was still warm outside. But it wasn't as dry as it'd been all day. I could begin feeling a little moisture in the air. I could begin feeling a nice, soft warm breeze from the ocean.

I walked through the the quad area and cut through the Hilton Building and started going along the sidewalk around the Sunken Garden. But I saw this priest in the distance coming my way and I suddenly recognized him. I forget his name, but I'd talked to him a dozen times before. He was this really weird, ancient guy, and he still wore that creepy black priest costume. I didn't like him. He always stared me right in the eye like he was trying to read my fucking mind or something, and he always put his hand on my shoulder and left it there.

Shit! That's all I needed now - another fucking goddamned queer to put his paws all over me and do their faggy thing.

So I sort of just shot out into the street and barreled down into the Sunken Garden. It worked pretty good. The queer old priest didn't even see me. At least, I don't think he saw me. He seemed pretty whacked anyway, so I probably could have waltzed up and stood on his shoes, and he wouldn't have known what was happening. He was pretty out of it. They only hire the best at this school. I don't think they retire the professors until they turn a hundred and ten. That'd be my guess.

Since I was already there, I decided to take a short cut across the huge lawn, and I started walking slowly toward the chapel.

I kind of stopped after only a few steps, and I looked out across the grass. It was bigger than a football field. That's really all the Sunken Garden really was. Just this flat, giant grass lawn. With pine trees around the edges. But no flowers. Not a fucking flower in sight. So I always wondered why they called it a goddamned garden. It wasn't any garden. How can something without flowers be a garden? It was just a lawn. Just a plain fucking lawn.

But I really loved it there ever since I was a freshman. I really did. It was mainly used as an athletic field for kids to just fool around on. None of the teams ever used it. Just kids who hooked up with each other and played fun games on it. All day long. There was usually somebody playing something on it all day long. And sometimes even in the evening. Though there wasn't anybody there now. Except me.

I stood there just kind of glancing all over the grass field, kind of re-membering all of the games of frisbee football I had played there during the past three years. I bet I played more than a thousand fucking games there on that grass. I bet I did. The thought of it made me feel sort of hap-py-like, but then suddenly I felt really kind of sad, for some reason.

Turning my head, I started checking everything out around me.   I looked up at a tall pine tree just behind me. They were the same fucking ones that were in that Peace Garden up on the hill - the place that Kyle and I used to study. I think they were. They looked exactly the same. The ones that were Kyle's favorite tree. The Stone Pines. What did Kyle used to call them? Italian Stone Pines. Yeah - that was it. Italian Stone Pines.

Fuck! Did Kyle love those trees! He used to talk about them all the time - about this great place in Italy that he really liked that had a whole shitload of these kind of trees.   It always kind of made me wonder how somebody could like a tree so much.   I mean - fuck!   What so special about a tree? Trees are all pretty much alike. I mean - you got the trunk and the branches and all that leafy shit on the branches, and well - they're just trees.   Some are kind of crappy, and some look kind of nice.   But they're just trees, for Christ sake!   What's the big fucking deal?

But Kyle always seemed to notice stuff that nobody else did. He al-ways liked the stuff that nobody else even noticed or even knew was there. He'd just look at those pine trees and look and look, and, I mean - fuck! It was like he was watching a fucking movie or something.   It sort of made me laugh sometimes - the way he seemed to love those pine trees.

I looked up at the crooked pine on my left and saw how the thick trunk kind of splintered off half way up and formed this really cool twisting little flat area.   It looked like this giant wooden hand with the palm facing up. Sort of like a platform. It instantly made me want to climb up it, and the thought sort of slowly spun in my head, and it made me start remembering stuff that I hadn't thought about in years.

When I was about nine, my dad built this treehouse for me in this big giant pine tree in his backyard. This tree was the biggest tree in the world. And he spent all spring building this really neat treehouse so that it would be there for me when I came there for my forced visitation during my summer vacation. Fuck - did I have fun in that treehouse. I spent almost every minute of the day up there. I even slept there sometimes at night. I loved that treehouse so fucking much. And the best part was that my dad wasn't allowed up there. He never came up there one fucking time. I wouldn't let him. Not that he ever even asked. I don't think he ever asked me one fucking time if he could come up. I guess he didn't care. But if he had asked, there was no way in hell I would have let him come up there. That was the greatest thing about my treehouse - that I could completely get away from that miserable bastard father of mine.

Thinking some more about that, I remembered how I used to think that my dad built that neat treehouse just so I'd go climbing high up there and maybe fall off - that he was really hoping that I'd fall and really hurt myself - or even kill myself. Kill myself.

I started walking across the grass again and looking up at the chapel and the bell tower. There wouldn't be any more chimes tonight. They stopped at 8:30 every night. The fucking neighbors in the houses near campus complained about the noise, so the university stopped the bells from ringing early in the evening just so these crazy jackasses wouldn't get all bent out of shape about a few chimes tinkling away in the distance. What morons! Those fucking neighbors complain about everything.

I began thinking that I'd probably never be hearing those bells again. They were gone for me. All done. I was certain that I'd never hear them again. It was just like it was in "Who's Ringing Those Bells?" - that Hemingway book we read in English class two months ago - that one about the American soldier who ends up killing himself rather than being captured by those evil Nazis.

Standing there looking at the bell tower, I knew for certain that I'd never hear the ringing chimes ever again. And I thought - maybe they might be real. Maybe they really might be real bells or chimes or whatever. Maybe it wasn't a CD recording after all. Maybe it wasn't just some recording that they played all day. Maybe the bells were real.

When I was a freshman - my whole freshman year - I always believed they were real. I wanted to believe it. Then one day at the beginning of my sophomore year my friend Terry O'Connor who lived down the hall in Rosecrans told me he'd been up there at the top of the bell tower with one of the workers to replace a wire on the loudspeakers, and he told me that it was totally empty up there. That there weren't any bells or chimes. There was nothing. Just a bunch of fucking loudspeakers. I didn't believe him, but some of the other guys had been up there too and they all said the same thing. They wanted to take me up and show me, but I wouldn't go. I wanted to believe the bells were real.

I loved those bells so much, I wanted to believe they were real.

But after I became a junior, I kind of wised up a lot and I finally knew that there weren't any bells up there in the tower. And as much as I enjoyed hearing the ringing sound, it never was the same again after that.

And, now - right now when I was looking up at the top of the tower, I would have given anything if I could have just heard those bells ring one more time.   I would have given fucking anything.   Because I knew deep down inside me that I'd never be hearing them again in my life.

It was over for me.

They'd be ringing for somebody else from now on.

 For somebody else.

 Not for me.

9:23 pm

My birthday party in the Bird Nest was gonna be starting pretty soon now, so I started walking again - up to the chapel steps, then down across the lawn in front of the bell tower and over to the faculty parking lot where I cut through the corner and walked along the curving road past this really goofy looking monument that somebody threw together about a hundred years ago. I hardly ever walked this way, and I'd only seen this weird thing a handful of times, so I sort of slowed down and gave it a careful look as I passed by.

I kind of felt like I was seeing everything on campus for the first time that night.   And I'd never really paid any attention to this weird looking monument before. Whenever I'd asked anybody about it, they'd told me that it was a memorial to what sounded to me like "Fat Ma".

Shit! This school has more fucking memorials scattered all over the place than any other goddamned place on the planet.

I never did understand what or who "Fat Ma" was. There were three white statues - all life-size and everything. One was a lady, and the other two were small kids - a boy and a girl - kneeling down in front of her. Somebody told me once that there used to be another little kid statue, but some idiot snuck up one night and whacked its head off and stole it. So they had to haul away the headless kid and bury it someplace or something. I wondered who'd want to whack a little kid statue like that. Takes all kinds, I guess. But fuck! It was just this innocent little kid. What kind of a goofy sick fuck would do something like that?

And I was also wondering if the lady was these kids' mother? And if she was - why build a statue to her? And was she the "Fat Ma" they'd told me about? I kind of looked at her real carefully.   She looked like this really nice lady - and she was really skinny. I mean - really thin. She sure wasn't fat. I guess I'd never know now why they called her the "Fat Ma."

Stepping up on the curb, I started slowly walking across the small lawn that was right in front of the Bird Nest. I sort of hesitated and felt my stomach tighten as I stared at all the lights shining from the weird looking little building. It really did look just like a broken umbrella.

I didn't want a party anymore. It was the last thing I wanted. I just didn't feel like being with anybody - especially at some fucking phony party where I'd have to be all fake and full of bullshit for a couple of hours. And I didn't want anybody celebrating my goddamned birthday. What was the use! It didn't mean anything anymore! Not a fucking thing.

But I had to go. I had to. I didn't have any choice. I'd just have to be a man and go through with it. How bad could it be? And it wouldn't be for that long. It'd be over in just a couple of hours.

Everything would be over in just a couple of hours.

So I kind of made myself move forward and head toward the wide open doors.

As I approached, I glanced over toward the edge of the bluff a dozen yards away and I notice Einstein sitting alone on one of the low benches and gazing out at all the lights of the city.

I slowly went over and sat down beside him.

"Hey," he said with a surprised smile.

"Hey, dude," I sort of mumbled, trying to return his smile.

"Ready for the big party?"

"Yeah - sure."

He glanced over at me and sort of gave this sensitive look.

"Still down?"

I took a really long, deep breath.

"I guess."

"Anything you want to talk about?", he asked me like he really cared. "Might make you feel better."

I just gave this pathetic little laugh.

"I wish."

"Can't be that bad", he said kind of gently. "Is it Kyle?"

"Why do you keep fucking asking me if it's about Kyle?", I raised my voice all angry-like, pounding my fist on the bench. "It's not about Kyle! It's about something totally fucking different than Kyle! Kyle's gone! He doesn't matter anymore! Got it? The world didn't fucking stop revolving because one guy checks out! OK?"

"OK," Einstein said very quietly, turning and looking at me like I was some sort of fucking baby in a goddamned crib or something.

"It's something that can't be fixed," I mumbled. "There's no way out of it. Nobody can help me. Nobody. It's hopeless."

"It's a pretty night," he said in a tone so soft that it was almost a whisper. "Stars are out. You can see all the way to downtown. There's the Getty Museum over there. See that cluster of little lights on the top of those hills across the way. Have you ever been there? It's great. And look over there - those lights there. That's the Hollywood sign. They really light it all up at night, don't they. We can see the whole city. It looks like the whole world, doesn't it."

I didn't answer him. I'd suddenly become aware of this really loud noise way down below in the forest of tree and bushes along the creek at the base of the steep bluff. It was this incredible fucking racket - sort of like a high-pitched electrical kind of buzzing noise. It was amazing. Really loud. And coming from all the bushes and green stuff about a hundred feet right below us.

"Why are those crickets so fucking loud tonight?", I asked him in this really kind of pissed off, irritated voice.

"They're not crickets," he answered with a smile.

"Grasshoppers then."

"No. They're frogs."

"Frogs?", I said with this big look of surprise.

"Yeah. Frogs."

"Frogs don't fucking make a goddamned racket like that," I sort of argued, all incredulous-like.

I thought he was kidding me, so I let it drop and just yawned like I didn't care. I was pretty sure me was just making a dumb joke about it.

"Sure they do," he patiently started to explain. "They're in the water and the swampy area down there. That's where they live. And they come out at night and look up here at the top of the bluff, and when they see any of us looking down at them, they start talking to us in their own language, hoping that we can understand their wisdom.

OK. Now I knew he was punking me. Fuck! What kind of moron did he think I was! I was feeling so shitty that I decided to play along with him, so I acted like I was all interested in all the fake crap he was dishing out.

"Wisdom?", I asked, pretending to be really all kind of curious and everything. "What kind of wisdom could a frog have?"

"You'd be surprised," Einstein said all super serious-like.

"Try me."

"Frogs have been around a lot longer than we have."

"Yeah, well sure," I agreed. "They've probably been down there a long time in that creek. Maybe ten years or so. We've only been here on campus for a few years."

"No. I mean that the frog has been living here on earth much longer than we humans have been in existence. They were here way ahead of us. Millions of years before we humans came stumbling along."

"Shit. Really?"

"For certain, Niner. And they've had all that time to get to know what life is really all about. To learn the secret of living. And that makes them the wisest of all the creatures on the planet. Those frogs know what it's all about. The Wisdom of the Frogs. It's a pretty powerful thing."

I was probably looking at Einstein like he was nuts, because he gave me this really bright smile and blinked his eyes a couple of times.

"So - good for the frogs," I sort of sarcastically laughed. "But if they're so much smarter than we are, why are they still sliming around down there in a swamp? How come these genius frogs aren't running Microsoft or Exxon or living in the White House? Huh? Answer me that."

"Because they're still frogs - and frogs is what they were created to be. They can't make use of their own wisdom and knowledge. They were just made to find all this stuff out about life and pass it along to us humans. That's the plan. That's how it works, Niner."

He was so all calm and serious and everything that I almost thought he was for real. I mean - well, I guess I really didn't know. Einstein's like the fucking smartest guy this goddamned school has probably ever fucking seen, so even if it sounded like horse shit to me, who the fuck knows if it could be true or not. With Einstein, you never knew.

"Pass it along?", I asked him, sort of putting this huge chunk of doubt in my voice. "How do these fucking frogs pass all their wisdom along to us. Tell me, Einstein - just how the fuck does that work, anyway? I don't know too many guys who have frogs as Facebook friends, or that get text messages or phone calls from any fucking frog."

He just smiled really calm and confident-like at me.

"They don't come to us," he said very simply. "We have to go to them. That's how it works."

"We have to go to them? You mean we have to climb down the bluff and go into that thicket down there and go splashing out into the creek and catch a goddamned frog and set him down for a nice, good talk?"

That idea really made me laugh.

"No - of course not. That never works at all. In fact, they'd shut up completely if any of us came marching into their home and got too close to them. You can never do that. They don't like it.   That always ruins it."

"You're losing me, Einstein," I snickered with a smile.   "This crap doesn't make any sense at all. I think your joke's running out of gas. Better call it off."

"It's no joke," he said really serious-like. "The Wisdom of the Frogs is no joke. They pass on their knowledge to us by simply talking to us. What you're hearing right now - down there."

"It's a fuck-awful noise - that's all. It sounds like a hundred high voltage electrical wires fell down there. I hate all that buzzing noise. I really hate it. That's why I never come here at night and sit by the side of the bluff. All that goddamned racket - it's really fucked. I hate it."

"I know you do," Einstein told me in this tone that almost sounded a little sad. "I know you do. You didn't know. You didn't understand. You thought they were just crickets or grasshoppers.   You didn't know they were frogs. You didn't know they were trying to talk to you."

"Einstein - you're so totally full of shit!"

"Maybe," he smiled, "but the frogs aren't.   They know what they know, and they're talking to us and trying to get us to listen."

"Sorry - I don't speak 'frog'," I said with a sneer.

"It's not a language. It's beyond language. They don't speak in the words of any language. They don't speak in words."

"Well, yeah," I sneered again, really getting tired of this stupid horse shit. "So how the hell are we supposed to fucking understand them. Hey - I know. Maybe they want us to read their minds. Is that it, Einstein? Did you take some fucking class or read some goddamned book that told you how to read a frog's mind?"

He just patiently smiled at me, like he was talking to some fucking idiot child. That kind of pissed me off a little, and I decided I was sick and tired of his moronic bullshit joke. So I turned away from him and just gazed out at the miles and miles of lights in the distance.

"No. No mind reading. Just listening. Just careful listening. Listen to the sounds they're making. They're making those sounds for us. That's how they talk to us. That's how they communicate with us. That's the voice they have. Their own special voice. Their own unique voice. And we have to listen to it and learn. They're talking to us."

"And how the fuck do they know were up here? Huh, Einstein? How the hell do they know I'm sitting right here by the edge of the bluff and can hear all the croaking, buzzing shit they're making right now? Huh?"

"They can't see you," he said very quietly. "They sense you. The frogs have all these senses that humans don't. They can sense when you're here at the bluff. And they know who you are and what exact wisdom you need. They know what your problems are, and they're talking to you and trying to tell you what you need to do - to solve your problems and be happy. They're talking to you right now, Niner. Listen to them. Listen to the Wisdom of the Frogs. Let it go deep inside of you, and think about what they're telling you to do."

"Right," I snickered. "All I hear is a bunch of fucking god-awful noise. You're so full of shit, Einstein."

"You have to let it come deep inside you. And then you can hear their voices. When their voices start coming through to you - you hear them from inside of yourself. You'll know when you can finally hear it, Niner. It takes some people a lot longer than others to be able to do it. It's sort of a a time thing. When the time is right - you'll be able to hear it. You'll be able to discover the Wisdom of the Frogs. It'll come - just try to be patient. They'll tell you what you need to know."

"What the fuck do I need to know?", I asked kind of angry-like.

"That's what they'll tell you, Niner. That's the Wisdom of the Frogs."

"Stop repeating all that crap!", I raised my voice and stood up.

Einstein didn't say anything. He just looked at me all calm and satis-fied-like. And that pissed me off even more.

I clenched my fists and stared kind of numbly at the huge view of the city and the hills and the mountains. It was super clear and still warm, and the breeze was blowing really soft and gentle. I looked toward the west and I could actually see the horizon line of where the dark sky met the ocean. The moon was almost full, and it was shining on the water.

"You can see the ocean," I sort of mumbled out loud.

Einstein stood up and stepped over by me and squinted his eyes.

"Yeah. How 'bout that. You usually can't see it from here at night. We're not high enough up. But there it is."

"It's beautiful," I said in this really quiet whisper to myself. "So peaceful. It's so peaceful."

"Yeah," Einstein agreed, sort of surprising me that me could actually hear what I had said.

I kept staring at the distant moonlit water and felt my whole body just sort of going all soft and relaxed and calm-like.

"Einstein - did you ever think about . . ?   Did you ever think about just . . ?

"Hey birthday boy!", Beth shouted from behind me. "The party's officially begun! Come on! You don't wanna be late for your own party!"

I turned around and saw her standing smiling in the open doorway of the Bird Nest and waving at me. I slowly started walking towards her, and Einstein followed behind me.

"Did I ever think about what?", he asked me with this sort of really concerned and curious voice.

"Never mind," I numbly answered. "It doesn't matter. It's not important."

7:39 pm

When I walked through the door of the Bird Nest, there was this giant sign on the opposite wall with bright blue hand-printed letters that said - NUMBER NINE IS TWENTY ONE, and a smaller sign across the way that said - HAPPY BIRTHDAY NINER.

Fuck! They couldn't even write my real name for my own birthday. It was still all that stupid nickname shit.   And I wasn't even Number Nine anymore. I wasn't even on the soccer team anymore. So the joke was on these idiots. And on me, I guess.

Beth was standing nearby next to a small table with a large sheet cake on it. I moved over for a closer look. The cake was this real assembly-line looking thing all done up in this thick light yellow frosting. On the top, in big letters, it said -   HAPPY 21st   BIRTHDAY TO GOOD OLD NUMBER NINE.

Shit! 'Good Old Number Nine!' Fuck! They couldn't even put my goddamned real name on my own fucking birthday cake! Shit!

Beth asked me how I liked it, and I just gave a little smile and lied and said 'great!'

But it wasn't.

Staring at the cake, I bobbed my head up and down like a moron, and I tried to amp up my phony smile.

Beth put her hands all tender-like on my arm and sort of nuzzled into me like she always does, pressing her head against the side of my shoulder and moving one of her hands softly over across my chest.

That usually always gets me. Really stokes up the old ramrod, if you know what I mean. But it didn't do anything to me right then. It didn't do a thing. I just sort of felt all numb through my whole body. Just all numb. And kind of angry. I don't know why. But just really angry with everything and everybody.

I just didn't want to be there.

There was another little table with food and junk behind me, so I kind of gently peeled Beth off me and slid over and started woofing down whatever I could get my hands on. I was really starved. I hadn't had anything to eat today after pigging out at the Team Breakfast this morning.

All these sorority sisters of Beth's were there sort of swarming around, and most of them kept coming up and talking to me and wishing me a happy birthday and all that kind of crap in their excited, babbling, high-pitched voices.

I just didn't want to be there.

A few minutes later that other sorority sister of Beth's - that girl I tried to pick up in U-Hall a couple of hours ago - came all waltzing in the door, and she saw me and came flying over and gave me this huge, fake hug and slobbered all the usual phony crap about my "special day."

There were probably about twenty-five people there - mostly Beth's sorority friends and a few other guys from the apartments and from some of my classes. But all my friends hadn't arrived yet. All my bros from the soccer team. They usually came a little late to dumb stuff like this, so I wasn't surprised at all that they weren't there yet.

Josh was really the only soccer guy that was there already. That's because he was my roommate and my buddy and our apartment was just across the way and all. He sort of had to come early.

I looked over and saw him standing on the far side of the big room. He was talking to these three girls and they seemed all fascinated by what he was saying. When he finally glanced my way, he sort of nodded his head a little and kind of looked like he was sort of nervous about something. He tried to grin, but it didn't come off at all. He only managed to make this kind of sick-looking, wincing expression.

Josh without a grin. That was kind of a first. And it made me feel really weird. Sort of like if one morning the sun never came up. Just strange.

I walked over toward him and he stopped talking as I approached. The girls seemed a little nervous too, and they kind of gave me this fishy look. I wondered what the hell was going on.

"Hey, bro," I said all cocky-like to Josh.

"Hey, Niner," he sort of awkwardly replied, staring down at the floor. "Happy Birthday. Nice party. What's up?"

"Just the party," I smiled. "What's up with you?"

"Nothing. Uh - I think I'll go get a Pepsi. They got Pepsi, don't they? Yeah - I'm sure I saw a pack over there. Later."

Josh nodded at the girls and gave that really strained look again, his mouth kind of twisting into this sort of tense, upside down grin. Then he took off all quick-like and walked to the other side of the room.

I watched him. He didn't go over and pick up any Pepsi. He just stayed by the window and looked out at the lights of the city.

One of the girls that had been chatting up Josh kind of shyly looked at me and nervously cleared her throat.

"Did you really smash your cell phone and your iPod on purpose?", she asked me all kind of timid and uneasy-like.

"Huh?", I was really surprised by her question.

"Everybody's saying you deliberately smashed them to bits this afternoon. Is that true? Did you really do it?"

I didn't know what to fucking say.

One of the other girls standing there - I think her name was Doreen - moved over a little closer and looked at me like I was in some goddamned cage in some sort of fucking zoo.

"Why did you do it?", she asked me in this kind of demanding tone. "What made you so mad? My boyfriend went to the game this afternoon. He said you almost tried to kill one of the other guys on your own team. Is that why you did it? Did it have something to do with that? Is that why?"

I kind of sighed and bit down on the inside of my cheek. Fuck!

"No," I said in this really pissed voice. "I smashed them because I was fucking tired of having stupid, idiot girls calling me all the time asking me stupid, idiot questions."

The three of them looked at me all kind of shocked for a few seconds, then one of them gave this awkward little laugh. All of them seemed really pissed by what I had said, and they just sort of turned and floated away toward the fireplace without saying anything else to me.

I went back to the food table and scarfed down some more tiny sandwich-type things. Standing there, I noticed that those three girls were really all excitedly talking to their other sorority sisters. A few minutes later most of the sorority bitches started going over to Beth and looking all apologetic and stuff, and then they started quickly leaving out the side door.

Fuck! Talk about not being able to take a joke or something.

Pretty soon only about a dozen people where left there at the party.

Beth kind of anchored herself to me after that and stuck to me like glue. I sort of felt like a prized trophy or something, the way she proudly steered me around the room from one person to another, introducing herself and telling everybody that she was my girlfriend.

Josh and Einstein were sitting down in the seats around the fireplace. It was sort of this cozy little pit in the center of the room where you could step down and sit close to the fire. They seemed to be talking pretty-serious like and I really wondered what they were saying. So when a friend of Beth's from the dorm came up and started gabbing away, I made a quick exit and went down into the pit and sat next to the fireplace.

They instantly stopped talking and seemed all kind of uptight. Einstein managed to give me this nice, relaxed smile, but Josh didn't even look at me. He just glanced sort of nervously around the room and looked at his watch.

"Thanks a lot for spreading the word," I said really sarcastically to Josh, feeling pretty bitter about the whole shitty thing.

"Huh?", he replied with a surprised expression, giving me this sort of sideways little look.

"Huh?",   I mocked him with this really exaggerated fake-innocent, wide-eyed look.

"What'a'ya mean?"

"I mean telling everybody about how I creamed my cell phone and my iPod," I said really pissed. "That's what I mean."

"I didn't tell everybody," Josh weakly replied with a hard swallow. "They already knew. Everybody already knows. They just come up and ask me about it 'cause they know I'm your roommate and I was there."

"Thanks a lot," I sort of bitterly sneered.

"Well, what'a'ya want me to say?", Josh protested all kind of lame and defensive-like. "I gotta tell them what happened. I gotta tell the truth."

"Sure - of course you do," I shined him on again. "The truth. Always."

Josh sort of hung his head down like he was a little embarrassed or something and didn't say anything for several moments.

"You know - there were a lot of other guys there," he kind of mumbled. "The guys on the team. Marco, Chad, Dave and Reicher and all those guys. They saw it too. They've been . . . well, they saw it too."

"Nice," I gave a pained little laugh. "My good buddies."

"So don't blame me. I didn't say nothing about it to anybody who didn't already hear about it and asked me."

253

"Where are those guys, anyway?", I asked him. "Some of 'em should have been here by now. I thought a couple of groups of 'em would have been here a long time ago. What time is it, anyway?"

Josh nervously looked at his watch.

"It's about 10:20," he said in this really uneasy voice that made me feel kind of weird and confused.

"Some of them should at least be here by now," I repeated.

"Look," Josh said, anxiously getting up and walking a few steps away from me. "I gotta go. I got things to do. Happy birthday again."

"What'a'ya mean ya gotta go? The fucking thing isn't even in gear yet. Fuck! At least wait 'til some of the guys get here."

"Naw - I can't. Uh - Niner. Uh - I don't know how to tell you this."

"What?", I asked him as this sudden knot painfully strangled something deep down in my lower stomach.

"Uh - I'm . . . I'm moving out of the room tomorrow."

"Huh?"

"I'm moving out," he repeated really all calm-like as he stared over at the brightly burning fire. "To an apartment on the second floor. I'm not gonna to be your roommate anymore."

I was kind of really all stunned and everything by what he just said. I guess actually kind of shocked. I mean - what the fuck! What was happening with this guy? We were perfect roommates. We got along great. There'd never been any problem at all between us. I mean, the shower thing was sort of really annoying and inconvenient once in awhile, but it was just sort of a joke - Josh the Fish, and all that crap - it never really bothered me that much. Josh and I got along fine. What the hell was up with this shit all of a sudden?

"Why?", I asked him in this confused tone.   "We're buddies."

"It's just," he began explaining like it was really hard for him, "it's just that . . . . after today - after what happened today . . . I . . . we - all of us are really kind of upset with you. Disappointed. Kind of scared, I guess. You're doing all this shit - and we don't know why - and it seems really crazy and . . . and I don't know what. But I just don't want to be your roommate anymore. You were a really OK roommate up until today, but the way you've been acting . . . "

"So I got really pissed off and broke a couple of crappy things," I quickly replied all defensive-like. "They were mine. I can break 'em if I want to. Big fucking deal. That's no reason that you have to . . . "

"It's not just that. It's everything. The crazy way you acted at the game. First you refuse to wear the damned armband, then you don't even show up for the start of the game, and then you play like a maniac and attack Jeff and try to kill him right out there on the field."

"I can explain all that . . . "

"Can you? Can you explain why you were trying to choke him to death? Why you made us lose the fucking game? If you would have played just a fair game today we could have beat those UCLA guys. But you deliberately ruined the game. And even the coach doesn't want anything to do with you anymore. Everybody thinks you're crazy. Everybody thinks all you want to do is ruin stuff for everybody."

"But . . . "

"I'm sorry. I just don't wanna be your roommate anymore. I'm moving out tomorrow morning. I'll . . . "

"Don't bother," I said with this real cocky sneer. "I'm the one moving out. Don't worry. I won't be there after tomorrow. In fact, I won't even be back tonight. So just go back to your precious room and you can have it all to your fucking self from now on."

"Huh?", he seemed kind of stunned.

I didn't say anything.

Einstein was gazing up at me with this kind of really worried look on his face. He was sort of staring all intense at me like he was trying to read my mind or something.

"What'a'ya mean?", Josh kind of timidly asked me.

"Just what I fucking said. The room's yours. Enjoy."

"Where are you going?", Einstein gently asked.

I sort of just stared numbly ahead into space and gave a really tight little smile.

"To where I belong," I whispered.

"Where's that?", Einstein anxiously wanted to know.

"Yeah - where are ya going?", Josh instantly echoed him.

I didn't even look at them. I just kept staring blankly ahead at the window and the city lights beyond. And the dark sweeping sky.

"You'll know soon enough," I sort of numbly answered.

Josh nervously looked at his watch again, then gave this really un-comfortable little shrug and quickly stepped up out of the pit area. He turned back towards me as he started to leave.

"Sorry," he said in this really weak and strained voice. "Good luck, Niner."

I didn't say anything.

He hurried out the open doors of the Bird Nest and left.

Resting uneasily back in my seat by the fire, I watched a handful of kids entering the room. I couldn't remember ever seeing them before. I guess it was the free food and sodas. They scarfed a ton of stuff and took their plates up the stairs to the loft and sort of hid away out of sight.

A couple of minutes later this huge crowd began filing in through the doors and stood all clumped together right in front of the entrance. There were probably two dozen guys.

I stood up and stepped over for a closer view.

It was all the guys on the soccer team. All my teammates.

10:30 pm

I felt this thrill sort of run through me like a bolt of electricity. It was so incredible. Every guy on the team was there. All standing there in this tight bunch right in front of me. All my buddies. All my best friends.

The first thing I thought of was that they were going to sing me 'Happy Birthday'. That it had been all carefully planned. I could see that. They'd planned it this way. All meeting together someplace else and coming over here as a group. And they were all wearing their soccer jerseys. How cool was that! It was just so incredible.

I think right then I was really happy for the very first time that day. I was so fucking happy. Fuck! I was over the moon.

257

Stepping up closer to them, I couldn't help giving this beaming, kid-like smile. Sort of like when you open your presents on Christmas. In fact, I was sort of looking around at them wondering if they really had gotten me some really neat present. You know - because I'd been their captain this year, and all that sentimental crap. I was sort of thinking that it was probably a pretty good present they got me. Maybe something for my truck, or a trip some place, or something like that. I didn't see any fancy wrapped boxes or anything, so I assumed it must be tickets to something that one of them probably had in his pocket.

I stood there facing them smiling from ear to ear, waiting for all of them to suddenly break into song and loudly sing me 'Happy Birthday.'

I kept waiting.

But they didn't sing.

In fact - I noticed that they weren't even smiling.

My own smile kind of dissolved as I started carefully looking at their faces. They were not only not smiling, but they were staring at me like I was some awful thing they had just run over on the road.

"Hey, guys," I called out to them all kind of uneasy-like. "Thanks for coming. Help yourself. Free food and cake. You're just in time for the big cake cutting ceremony. Come on in."

I moved forward and went to give a friendly slap on the shoulder to Chad. He pulled back. So I reached out to Dave, and he also sort of dodged away from my hand. Reicher and Marco were over to the left, so I held out my hand to them for a shake, but they didn't move or even acknowledge I was there. They and all the other guys just totally looked right through me.

258

I was getting ready to try to say something funny. Something that would break the ice a little. But I couldn't think of anything. And then it happened.

Suddenly, they all abrupt turned around at the same time, like they had carefully rehearsed it, and they stood there with their backs to me.

I so was shocked, I couldn't speak.

They stood there like that for a good minute or so.

Then - without ever saying a word or making a sound - they silently walked out the doorway together like a squad of fucking marching soldiers and suddenly disappeared into the darkness of the night.

I was so stunned that I honestly felt sick. I felt like I was gonna throw up. Like I was gonna barf right there on the floor.

I remember the weird feeling I had in the back of my throat. Like when you stick your finger down it. The way the muscles back there start flexing all over the place. Shit! It was so awful.

I just stood there and watched them all go off without ever having said one word. Not one smile. Nothing. Fuck! It was so horrible.

After several moments, I just went over and stood by my cake, and everybody else sort of quietly went off into corners and seemed really all embarrassed and everything.

My best buddies in the world. My teammates for life. The friends I always knew I could count on. The great and glorious soccer team.

As I stood looking down at my crummy birthday cake with the fucking nickname Number Nine on it, and the only thing I was thinking about was what a fucking idiot I had been.

Soccer had been my whole fucking life ever since I was ten years old. My whole fucking life. One junior league after another. One school team after another. High school. And now university. My whole life. And the guys I played with were my bros. The only ones I could ever count on. They were my family. I never had any brothers or sisters. Just the guys on the team. They were my family. And now - after everything we'd been through the last three years - now they were fucking me over like this.

Three years! And this is what these fucking assholes do to me!

I wanted to smash that birthday cake into the table until it was just a fucking yellow stain.

Fuck soccer! Fuck these assholes! Just one day - messing up a little just one day - and the motherfuckers treat me like I don't even exist. Like I'm just a worthless piece of shit. Fuck them!

I was done with the whole fucking thing. Forever! I never wanted to see or hear anything about soccer again.

And I was really glad that I was the kind of guy that never cried - that didn't even know how to cry.

Because if I had been a crier, I'm sure I would have broken down like some girly asshole and really cried right then and there.

Jesus! Thank god I never learned how to cry. I would have looked like a pathetic moron standing there and sobbing.

But, this way - I just kept getting angrier and angrier about the whole fucking thing. And I hated them. And myself a little.

Beth came over and put her arms around me. It felt kind of good. But not as good as it used to. I still felt totally alone in that big fucking room.

I went to say something to Beth, but what could I fucking say? There was just nothing really to say. I just wanted to forget it ever happened. Pretend that all those bastards never even came by.

"They're just all pissed right now at everything," Einstein said as he came up to me on my other side. "They all had their hearts in that game. It meant everything to them. They didn't mean it, Niner, They don't really hate you. They're just kids. That's how kids act."

"Who gives a shit," I sort of angrily snapped. "Big fucking deal. A bunch of morons don't like me. Who cares?"

I glanced over toward the door and I saw Fred - the little gay guy from the apartments - hanging around just outside, really all timid-like and everything.

"Shit!", I muttered kind of angrily. "It's Freddy the Faggot. I forgot all about inviting him. Fuck - I never thought he'd show up. And there he is just cruising around out there getting all ready to come in and glob onto me. Fuck. Thanks a lot, Einstein. This was all your idea."

"Stop it, Niner," he told me like he was scolding some idiot kid.

"I don't want him here now," I said kind of bitterly. "If Freddy the Faggot is your good buddy - YOU talk to him. Go on, I don't want to."

Beth sort of gave me this disappointed look, but she didn't say anything. She just sort of climbed off me and started talking to a guy we both knew from the Rec Center.

Einstein stepped up right in front of my face and gave me this awesome look - sort of like a general sending a private off into battle.

"Don't call him that," he slowly and really intensely told me. "Don't ever call him that again. This morning you really got it. You got it for the first time. What's happened to you, Niner? Why do you hate him all of a sudden? You really helped this guy this morning. He's been a different kid all day because of what you did. Because you made him your friend. What's wrong with you now?"

"I just don't feel like doing it anymore. It's too fucking much. After everything that's happened - I don't want to do it anymore. I don't want to. I can't."

"Well, here he comes, and you're going to have to - like it or not. I just don't get you at all sometimes, Niner. What's wrong with you?"

A second later, Fred was right on top of us, sort of nervously flapping his arms and goggling his eyes. He was so excited he could barely talk.

"Hey, Niner - hey, Niner - Happy Birthday - Happy Birthday," he gushed in this real sickening high pitched voice. "I came like you asked me to. I told ya I'd come. How's the party? Hi, Einstein. Is it a really cool party? Have many guys been here already? Where is everybody? Is it just us? Are more people coming? That's OK. This is cool. I was afraid all these people would be here that I didn't know. This is nice. Just a few. I like that. Happy Birthday, Niner. Great cake."

Fuck! I just wanted to get away from this little queer as fast as I could.

"Yeah," I numbly mumbled. "Thanks for coming, Fred. You talk to Einstein for a bit. I gotta go see to some stuff."

"Sure, Niner. Whatever you say. Thanks. Talk to you later. Thanks. Happy Birthday, Niner."

I left him sort of glued to Einstein and I made a fast retreat to the other side of the room and started talking to this guy named Elliott that I knew from the swimming pool. He was a lifeguard there for a while, and we used to work out together and play pickup games of basketball. Elliott was a nice enough guy, but he really didn't have much to say. Kind of boring and dull. We just sort of shot the shit about the latest water polo game against Pepperdine, and when he started asking me about the soccer game this afternoon and wanting to know what happened - why I got in the fight with Jeff - I got really antsy and started preparing to bail out.

Looking over at the doorway, I saw Megan kind of shyly coming into the room. I was pretty surprised. After I talked her into helping me cheat on my history test this morning and getting caught and flunking and everything, I didn't think she'd show up here tonight in a million years. It was really kind of amazing. I guess I really poured it on a lot thicker than I thought. And when she glanced over and saw me and smiled, I knew she was pretty hooked. I mean - I liked her a lot, and I really was sorry I messed her up with the prof and made her fail the class, but I really didn't want her to go all ape-shit about me. Not now.

10:42 pm

Megan slowly walked over toward me, and I slapped Elliott on the shoulder and shoved off towards her. It was then that I noticed she was carrying this fancy-ass gift in her hands - a small, brightly wrapped package with a shiny big blue bow on it.

Fuck! She brought me a gift! What was the story here!

When Megan kind of shyly came face to face with me, she smiled almost the way that Fred does, then quickly leaned forward and planted this incredibly soft, nice kiss on my cheek.   She sort of lingered a little when her lips were on my skin, and I really liked it.   It felt like she really had these feelings for me.   You know - not sex, or asking to get fucked or anything - just all the tender and gentle affectionate stuff that some girls once in awhile feel.

For some reason, I've never met too many of those types.   The girls I've always been with have their hands on my cock before we've even said 'hello'.   The sex is just right there as soon as we see each other.   Even with Beth.   It was wild fucking from the very start.   In fact, I couldn't really re-member Beth ever touching me as tenderly as Megan just did.

Megan sort of held out her present like she was kind of embar-rassed, and she very shyly wished me a 'Happy Birthday', and I thanked her and told her she shouldn't have gotten me anything because we had told everybody not to bring any gifts.   Guys hate giving gifts.

"I just wanted to," she said really softly.   "You were so nice to me this morning - after what happened in class.   I really enjoyed getting to know you.   I've seen you for so long - so to finally meet you and become friends was very special for me, and . . . "

Fuck! You ask some random girl to help you cheat on your history exam and she thinks she owns you! Shit!

Just then, Beth kind of dived in between Megan and me, and she put both her hands around my right arm and started massaging my muscles in this incredibly sensuous, sexy way.   Anybody would have thought that in a another couple of seconds she was gonna travel on down and start suck-ing my cock.   I mean - Beth was really in heat and playing it out for all it was worth. Fuck!   I could even feel my dick starting to get hard.

Megan seemed really all surprised and confused, and she suddenly looked sort of awkward and uncomfortable.

"Hi - I forget your name," Beth said to her in this real superior, kind of hot voice. "We had a couple of classes together last spring. You're that really smart girl. The human brain."

"Uh - I'm Megan McCarthy," she said really uneasily.

"I'm Beth - Niner's fiancee."

I was kind of stunned.

Fuck! Why did she go and say a fucking thing like that! We hadn't decided anything like that yet. Why was she announcing it to strangers all of a sudden like that? Fuck!

Megan's face really didn't do very much. It just sort of hung there all quiet and still-like. Kind of like she was trying to wake up from a nice dream. You know how it's always kind of hard to wake up when you're having a great dream? You always want to hang on in there and keep dreaming and believe that it's real.

That's how Megan looked.

Then, she peaked up at me with this really hurt little smile, and her eyes got really huge and moist. I was afraid she was gonna make some kind of scene or something. You know - start yelling at me for having lied to her, telling her that Beth and I were only just friends and everything. Or maybe punching Beth in the mouth or maybe pulling her hair or something. That might have been kind of cool. Them fighting over me. And if it did happen, suddenly I was thinking that I kind of wanted Megan to win.

But, no. Megan didn't say anything or do anything. She just really all sad-like dropped her head and stared at the floor, then slowly pressed the fancy little package with the blue bow into my hands and sort of almost tiptoed out of the room and off into the darkness outside.

Beth gave this really crappy little smug smile and leaned into me even firmer than before.

"What's that?", she sort of mockingly asked, nodding toward the gift in my hands. "What did Miss Brainiac give you?"

"How the hell should I know," I said really angry-like.

I went over and tossed it down on a nearby chair.

Two guys who lived down the hall in the apartments came wandering in and slapped me on the back and gave me the usual birthday shit. Their names were Roy and Tom - but I really wasn't sure which was which. Every time I'd always seen them, they were together - kind of like a traveling Siamese Twin act or something - so I just always said both their names when I talked to them.

One of them glanced over toward Fred who was still talking to Einstein across the way by the food table.

"Shit - what's Freddy the Faggot doing here?", he sort of sneered.

"Fuck - did you really invite that little freak to your party?", the other one - either Tom or Roy - asked me with this really disgusted look.

"Relax," I said all defensive-like. "Einstein brought him. He's Einstein's friend. You don't have to talk to him. Just ignore him."

They both stared at Fred and made these really shitty exaggerated expressions that totally showed how big a freak they thought he was. Then they both laughed this really mean laugh.

Fred glanced over toward us and he noticed what they were doing, and he got really nervous and kind of turned red. Einstein noticed the whole thing and quickly put his hand on Fred's small shoulder and sort of spun him around a little so he wouldn't be facing us.

But before he did that, I had laughed too. Not a big laugh. But I just laughed when Roy and Tom did because I was feeling so totally shitty and like I didn't care about anything anymore. And I just felt like I wanted to laugh with somebody about the whole stupid fucked-up world and all its goddamned half-assed people. I guess maybe I was laughing more at Tom and Roy than with them. But to anybody else, I'm sure it looked like I was laughing with them. Sort of sharing their joke about Fred.

And I'm sure Fred saw me laughing. I'm positive he did, because I saw this really intense and confused and sort of hurt look on his face just before Einstein turned him away from us.

It kind of made me feel funny.

I was so pissed about everything that had been happening to me that it was sort of like I really didn't have any feelings left inside of me. It was like I couldn't feel happy or sad or good or bad anymore. You know what I mean? I was just getting more and more numb, and more and more angry. I guess - kind of more and more dead inside.

More and more dead inside of me. Just - nothing.

Like I was beginning to get ready.

Beth was sort of hovering over the cake, and it looked like they were getting ready to put the candles on and all that crap.

I sort of staggered over to her and stood by her side. I really didn't give a fuck about all this stuff. It had all been her idea to begin with. Beth had planned the whole thing. I decided I was just gonna suffer through it until it was over. Until everything was over.

Twenty one white candles were placed across the center of the cake and Beth took this really deep breath of excitement and started looking all around the table.

"Oh, I forgot the matches," she said all helpless-like. "I need some matches to light the candles. Does anyone have some matches? Niner? You always carry matches in your pocket, don't you?"

She was right. I always had matches in my pocket. It was for the pot I got from Cutter. I never really knew when I'd have a good chance to smoke it. So I always carried around a small book of matches.

"Yeah, I think I do," I told her, sort of feeling down into my right pant's pocket.

I yanked out everything in there - my keys, a few coins, and that stupid twisted piece of paper that Fred gave me this morning as a birthday present. I forget what the hell he called it. Some queer name. And I forgot I even fucking still had the moronic thing. It really made me mad when I saw it. For some reason - it really pissed me off.

I held my hand out to Beth and showed her all the crap I had. She sort of rummaged through with her fingers and real curious-like picked up Fred's faggy twisted paper thing.

"No matches," she said with a disappointed but really confused look, "but what's this? What's this thing?"

"It's just some cheap piece of idiot paper that's supposed to be a big important fucking birthday present," I angrily said with this really mean snicker. "That stupid little faggot gave it to me. It's just a piece of trash."

I roughly ripped it out of her hand and threw it down on the floor. As I threw it, I suddenly noticed Fred and Einstein standing right next to me.

Something inside of me just sort of froze.

Fred was standing there and just staring at me like I was pointing a gun at him or something. Then he started shaking. I mean - his whole entire body just started shaking like he was having some kind of convulsions or something. He tried to talk, but he couldn't. He just made this kind of choking noise that made me sick to my stomach. I honestly thought he was gonna drop dead right there.

And then, all of a sudden, his face just totally caved in and he started crying - crying so hard that I couldn't believe it.

As Fred wept, he kind of made these strange noises and struggled to catch his breath. It really sort of frightened me.

Einstein put his arm around Fred's shoulder and tried to comfort him, I guess. But it didn't help. Fred kept sobbing and backing further and further away from me until he finally caught his breath.

"It was just a joke," he sort of tearfully moaned like he was really in some kind of intense physical pain. "I was just a joke to you. A joke. And I believed you. I believed you. But you're just like all the rest of them. You hate me. You only wanted to make fun of me. I wish I was dead."

He turned and started almost running out the door.

I wanted to call after him - to say something to him - to apologize. But I couldn't. I was so numb, I couldn't speak. I just stood there.

Einstein looked at me with this completely disgusted expression. It was the first time I ever saw him really angry and almost about it lose it.

"I'm taking Fred back to his room," he sort of gasped like he was holding his breath. "I think I've been totally wrong about you, Niner. I think I was wrong about you. You're really some piece of work."

His voice was trembling near the end, and he shook his head and charged off after Fred. I could see him catch up with him at the far side of the lawn. Fred was still sobbing and Einstein put his arm around him again, and they started slowly walking away together.

There were about a dozen people left inside the Bird Nest and most of them had been watching what had happened. Most of them were laughing, but a few of the girls looked pretty upset by it.

Beth kind of disappeared as soon as Fred started crying. I think she went to look for some matches in the cupboards behind the bar on the other side of the room. When she happily came back she proudly held up a couple of long wooden matches and struck one and started lighting the candles on the cake.

As soon as she had lit them all, she excitedly backed away from the cake and motioned everybody to come over and crowd around. Then she pushed me forward a bit so that I was alone right in front of my birthday cake. She took her cell phone camera out and began taking a million pictures of me, and some of the other people there started taking pictures of me too. There were these flashes everywhere I looked - just like a battlefield or something. I could barely see anything. Just a bright glow with all these sparkling colors around it. It kind of reminded me of that beautiful blue ocean wave that I kept seeing everywhere.

"OK everybody - on the count of three," Beth happily shouted.

She slowly counted to three, then started loudly singing Happy Birthday. Everybody else instantly joined in.

I stood there staring at my cake as they sang. The bright glare was evaporating from my eyes and I started feeling something really weird. I didn't know what it was at first, but then I suddenly remembered it was exactly the same way I felt when I was about ten and something happened in the street in front of my mom's house. It was a cat that got run over by a car. The cat had been coming by our house almost every day for a year. My mom didn't like animals and I never had a pet, so this cat kind of was like my own pet. I never fed it and it didn't sleep at our place, but it always came by and sat down next to me and wanted to be held and petted.

I really loved that cat. It was kind of the only pet I really ever had. And I'd hold it and rub its neck and sometimes kiss it on the nose. I never knew what it's name was. For sure it must have belonged to somebody else. I mean - it must have. So I never really ever named it. I never called it by a name, and that always made me feel like it would be OK if one day it stopped coming by and never came back again. I felt like it wouldn't hurt if I never saw it again. But a part of me really wanted to name it and make it my own cat - to belong to me and be mine.

It was a really small cat - sort of the size of a kitten. My mom said it was full grown and all, but something must have happened to keep it from ever growing up. It was just really small and kind of frail and helpless. And I really loved that cat. I really did.

Then one day when it didn't come by, later on I found it on the side of the street in a pool of blood just totally crushed flat. I remember how at first I couldn't stand to look at it, and, then, when I finally forced myself to, so that I know for sure that it was my cat, I kept looking and looking at it.

I guess that was the closest I ever came to crying in my life.

I mean - I sure as hell didn't cry. I'm one of those guys who just can't cry. I'm not made that way. But that's probably the closest I ever came, because I got that really strange feeling that I was having now. Like everything inside of you is about to cave in and collapse. Like your guts are soaring up toward the back of your throat.

Fuck! It felt so weird to be feeling that way again after all that time. I mean - in an hour or so I was gonna be twenty one. I was gonna be a man. A full-grown man. But I was feeling all this kid-like shit right now.

And especially when everybody was singing and they came to the part at the end where they sang either "to Number Nine" or "to Niner", it really made me think of that poor little nameless cat of mine that was killed by that car. And I could see it there in the street again. And that's exactly how I was feeling again. And when the singing stopped and lots of the people were whooping and clapping their hands, I heard this guy howler "And many more", and that made me feel like it all didn't mean anything. Like I finally knew for sure that there wasn't gonna be "more."

I sort of realized it was all over.

It was finally all over for me.

11:03 pm

Beth picked up a sharp knife and quickly carved up the cake. She lifted up a large corner slice and playfully tried to jam it into my mouth. It was really the last fucking thing that I wanted, but I ate part of it anyway, and tossed the rest of it onto a paper plate.

Then I looked down at the floor and I saw the crumpled, torn piece of paper that Fred had given me. It was near the railing opposite the fireplace, and two guys had just stepped on it without realizing it as they were talking and laughing and carrying their plates of cake over to the seats next to the fire.

I slowly moved over and bent down and carefully picked up the piece of paper from the floor. Holding it between my fingers, I noticed how its figure-eight shape had been ripped in the center and how it had now just become this ordinary scrap of paper.

I held it gently and stared at it.

Suddenly I remember what Fred and Einstein had told me about it. What is was called. They said it was a Mobius Strip. Funny name. But now I remembered it. It came back to me. How it was the symbol for infinity. Eternity. Something that went on forever. Like a friendship. Like the friendship Fred wanted to have with me. Forever. Like they tell you in church how your spirit's supposed to be.

Life. Infinity. Never ending.

Just like those huge waves in the ocean that never end - that just keep on coming and coming and breaking so beautiful and peaceful on the shore and keep wanting to sweep you away.

I looked at the Mobius Strip in my hand and almost smiled.

I don't know how I could smile right then, but I did a little. I guess there's all different kinds of smile. For all I know, maybe you even smile right before you check out and die. Maybe. Then maybe the end wouldn't be so bad after all. Maybe you sort of find that out just before you shut your eyes for the last time and kick off. Maybe you somehow know right at that last moment that your life really is like the Mobius Strip - infinity - something that's going to go on forever.

Maybe that's how it really is.

Maybe.

I squeezed my fingers tightly around the broken paper strip, then kind of gently stuffed it back inside the right pocket of my pants.

Glancing over toward the small group clustered around the cake table, I suddenly was looking Jeff directly in the eye.

Jeff was standing calmly against one of the thick wood columns, all alone and really relaxed looking. And just sort of peacefully looking at me.

It was funny. When I saw Jeff there, I didn't react the same way I had been doing all day. I wasn't scared anymore. I wasn't afraid. Or mad or angry or anything. I mean - I didn't react at all. It was like I was all totally numb and I didn't care at all anymore.

I just looked back at him for a little while. He had this really confident, pleasant expression on his face, and it didn't ever change. Once or twice someone would come up and talk to him, and he'd respond to them - but he kept looking at me as he talked with them.

Roy and Tom were standing by the far windows, so I casually hiked over to them and started shooting the shit again.

Every time I glanced back towards Jeff, he was still staring at me with that fucking calm, pleasant expression.

I finally couldn't take it anymore, so I suddenly shot off across the room and walked right up to him.

"I'm sorry," I sort of nervously whispered to him, "I hope you're OK. I didn't mean to hurt you out there today."

"Sure you did," he said real all matter-of-fact-like.

"I said I was sorry," my voice got sort of angry. "What are you doing here, anyway?"

Jeff gave me this totally shitty grin and cocked his head to the side all innocent-like.

"I just wanted to come here and wish you a Happy Birthday."

"Thanks. So - now you can go."

"I'm in no hurry," he grinned even wider. "We have until midnight."

"I told you I'm not going with you," I whispered really emotionally to him, leaning closer to his face.

"Just giving you one last chance," Jeff said all serious-like, his grin totally disappearing.

I took a deep, trembling breath and bit down on the side of my tongue.

"Jeff - please don't go to the police. Please! I'm begging you."

All of a sudden I noticed that almost everyone in the room was really quiet and just standing and looking at Jeff and me. I stared back at Jeff and he gave me this really piercing, intense look.

"We need to talk," he announced very softly. "Let's go outside for a minute."

I nodded "OK", and he turned and started limping toward the doorway. I numbly followed after him. We walked all the way to the end of the lawn area next to the edge of the bluff. For a moment, neither one of us said anything. We just looked out at the lights of the city. All I could hear was the electric buzzing croak of those damn frogs way down below in the forest along the creek. Einstein's fucking 'wise' frogs.

"You did it on purpose - didn't you, Niner," Jeff said with this painful look as he turned and really emotionally confronted me. "You planned the whole fucking thing."

"No," I kind of desperately cried out in protest. "It was an accident. I didn't mean it. I swear to God - I didn't mean it. It was an accident."

"Bullshit! That's what I wanted to believe last night. That is was an accident. I believed you. But then this morning I started thinking about everything and putting all this crap together. And then at the ceremony after the game this afternoon. Then I kind of knew for sure. You planned it. You planned the whole thing."

"What's the ceremony after the game got to do with it?", I raised my voice and helplessly held my hand up to my forehead.

"Everything," Jeff mumbled sadly. "They were honoring Kyle and giving his folks that memorial plague. Mr. and Mrs. Martinsen came out on the field and stood right in front of us. I kept looking at Kyle's dad. He looked just like that guy Steve last night at the Warehouse. The guy you killed."

"You're crazy," I mumbled, shaking my head.

"Or - more to the point - they both looked like Kyle - what Kyle would sort of look like in twenty years or so."

"So what?"

"So - that's why you went after him the way you did. You're angry with Kyle for killing himself. You're so pissed off at Kyle that you want to kill him for bailing out on you - his best buddy."

"You're so full of shit, Jeff! You're insane! You're completely out of your goddamned fucking mind! Kyle didn't kill himself! Don't say that! Don't ever say that again!"

"Of course he killed himself," Jeff gently said with a bitter little smile.

"No! He didn't! Stop it! Stop talking!"

"It was suicide, Niner. He deliberately was running out there in the traffic. He never did that before. Hundreds of times - he always ran on the sidewalk. He never ran in the traffic before. And that truck driver said Kyle saw him coming and he just ran right out in front of him. Kyle wanted it to happen."

"No!", I shouted, grabbing Jeff by the shirt and yanking him toward me. "Shut up! Shut the fuck up! It's not true! You're a liar! You're a rotten fucking liar! You've always hated Kyle!"

"I never hated Kyle," Jeff said really gently. "I loved him. Everybody loved him."

"Go on!", I angrily spit it out. "Go to the police! Go to the fucking police and tell them all this phony shit! Tell them all your lies!"

"Is it a lie that you killed him?"

"Go on - get the fuck out of here! I don't want to talk to you anymore! Get the fuck out of here!"

I let go of Jeff's shirt and shoved him away from me.

"That's why you set the whole thing up. When Reicher told me that you and Beth had dinner last night at the Warehouse and how you fed that homeless guy at your table, I started figuring out why you were so set on going back there when I met you on the apartment stairs last night. You'd just taken Beth back to her place, and you told me you were so depressed by Kyle's memorial service that afternoon that you really wanted to go out for some drinks. I wanted to go down the block to Tompkins, but you insisted we go down to the Warehouse in the Marina. You really insisted we go there. And when we went down there and went in, you insisted on sitting at the bar instead of at a table like we always do."

"You're so full of fucking shit," I angrily sputtered.

"And that guy Steve was sitting there all by himself at the very end of the bar. And you led me all the way down there and you sat down right next to him. There were a dozen empty seats at the bar, but you sat right next to him. And I didn't really think much of it then, but I remember now what he said to you. He said, "You kept your promise - you came back."

"You're fucking nuts."

"You saw him there when you were having dinner with Beth and her family. You saw this super handsome guy who looked like what Kyle might look like some day. He was probably giving you the eye as you ate, and you were so pissed off about Kyle that you played along with him. You probably stayed behind a little bit when Beth and the others left the restaurant, and you went over to the guy and told him you'd be back later when you got rid of your girlfriend. You probably told him to wait for you. I'm sure you did."

"Your crazy," I said in this totally bored voice.

"Now I know why you were acting so funny last night. You already had a couple of drinks at dinner and you had a couple more when we were at the bar. I know how you get when you're drunk. You always get super pissed-off. And you always get into a fight with somebody. I've seen it at all the parties we've been at. The more you drink, the more of a rage you get into. And that's why you insisted we go to the Warehouse last night."

"Why?", I asked him with this sarcastic sneer.

"Because you wanted a fight. Because he tried to pick you up and you wanted to beat the shit out of him for that. Because he thought you might be gay. You wanted to teach him a lesson - especially because he looked so much like Kyle and his dad. You've been angry with Kyle ever since the accident. You hate him for doing that to himself and leaving you behind all alone. That's why you never cried about it with all the rest of us. You've been mad as hell with Kyle, and when you went after that gay guy

Steve last night, it was to punish him for thinking you were gay and to punish Kyle for killing himself."

"I don't wanna hear anymore of this horse shit," I shouted, turning around and walking away from Jeff.

"Of course you don't," he said loudly as he followed after me and grabbed me by my arm. "You don't want to hear the truth. You never did. You've been running away from the truth for your whole fucking life."

I took a swing at him with my right fist, but he ducked and I missed him completely.

"Yeah - that's how you deal with everything, isn't it," Jeff said with a kind of bitter laugh. "Just like last night. You kept leading that guy Steve on more and more while we were sitting there at the bar. I could tell you were pissed at him and making fun of him, but he thought you were really on the level. He didn't realize you were just playing with him and setting him up. You even let him put his hand on your arm and kind of stroke it. I was sure you were gonna tell him to go fuck himself any minute, but you never did. You just kept playing him along like that."

"It was fun," I sort of arrogantly smiled.

"It was cruel. It was rotten, and it was mean. You made that guy think you really liked him. And when we left and went out to the parking lot, he asked you to walk down through all those palm trees to that hidden area behind the fence. I couldn't believe you went with him. That just blew my mind. And when you told me to wait for you in the car, I honest to god didn't know what to think. I'd had a couple of drinks too, and I just didn't know what was up with anything you were doing anymore."

"I just wanted to teach him a lesson," I said all defensive-like.

"Yeah - some lesson. You killed him."

"I didn't mean to! I keep telling you that. He grabbed me and start-ed to . . . to make love to me."

"What the fuck did you expect?"

"I thought he'd make a move and I'd clock him good - and maybe get in a couple of really good punches to his gut. I just wanted to teach him a lesson - that's all. I was feeling so shitty last night. And, you're right - I was pissed about everything. And I did have too much to drink. And maybe it does make me really mean when I drink too much, and maybe it does make me get into fights and all that shit."

"And you didn't think you might really hurt him bad?", Jeff asked me with this totally amazed look.

"I wasn't thinking."

"You should've known you could really hurt him."

"I wasn't thinking about fucking anything," I said all emotional-like. "I was just so fucking mad at everything. I just wanted to get back at some-body - everybody."

"For what?"

"For everything," I mumbled to myself.

"For . . . Kyle?"

I didn't answer him and just turned my face away.

"For Kyle?", Jeff repeated.

"I . . . . don't . . . . know," I muttered really sadly.

"And when you came back to the car all frightened last night and told me he tripped and fell and hit his head - that wasn't true, was it? I didn't believe it then, and I don't believe it now. He didn't trip - did he?"

I sucked in this really long, trembling breath of air and held it for a few seconds, then suddenly spit everything out.

"No. I lied to you. He didn't trip and fall. I pushed him. I pushed him really hard and he fell over backwards and hit his head on the concrete. I didn't mean for him to fall. I swear to god - I didn't want that to happen."

"Then why did you push him so hard?"

I hesitated and bit down on my lower lip.

"Because . . . he was so strong - so much stronger than I thought he'd be. I thought I could handle him. I know he was bigger than I was, but he was a queer, and I never expected a fag like him to get so rough with me. He grabbed me real hard and wouldn't let me go. I couldn't get away from him. And I kept telling him I was gonna deck him if he didn't let go of me, but he had his arms all around me and he was holding me so close and then . . . he started . . . ."

"Started what?"

"He . . . . started kissing me on the mouth - real passionate-like. And I tried to pull away, but he was so strong - I couldn't get him off me. I couldn't get my mouth away from his, and he was pressing against my mouth so hard it felt like he was gonna break my fucking neck. I just really went out of my mind and I just sort of panicked and I pushed forward against him as hard as I could, and he went flying backwards like he did. He was so surprised by it that he just fell right over on the back of his head. It was so horrible, Jeff. I can still see him stretched out there the way he was. I can still see him there. And all that blood. But I didn't mean it. I didn't mean it, Jeff! You gotta believe me."

"But you made the whole thing happen. You set him up."

281

"But I only wanted to hit him a little and teach him a lesson," I said in this really desperate tone. "I didn't mean to kill him. It was an accident."

"When you came back to the car and got me and we went over there, I couldn't believe it when I saw him on the ground in all that blood. I worked in a clinic last summer. Like I told you last night - since I'm a pre-med major, I got a lot of hands-on training. I knew that guy Steve was dead as soon as I saw him. I didn't even have to take his pulse. It was the way his eyes were set in that frozen stare. All the life was gone. I could tell as soon as I looked down at him. He must have hit his head just right when he fell. His life just got turned off like a switch. It happens like that sometimes."

"But I didn't mean to do it."

"You caused it. And you lied to me last night. You told me you didn't touch him. You said he moved backwards and tripped. You lied."

"But you promised we'd just forget we were there and you promised you'd never tell anybody."

"Yeah - I promised because I believed you. I believed the lie you told me. That it was an accident. And that you didn't have anything to do with it. But he needed the paramedics to see him. Just to make sure nothing could help him. That's why I drove off so fast and stopped down the way at that hotel and called 911 from the pay phone in the lobby. They probably got to him in a few minutes after that. But there was nothing they could do."

"So we did everything we could do, Jeff. Why can't you leave it alone? Why can't you leave it? Fuck! What good does it do now?"

"I told you this morning," Jeff said really harshly. "I heard on the news that they arrested this homeless guy. When the paramedics arrived they saw this homeless guy going through Steve's pockets.   He had Steve's wallet in his hands. They thought he mugged him."

"But . . . maybe . . . "

"And the police decided that the homeless guy hit Steve over the head to rob him. What else could they think? They arrested him and charged him with murder. It's an open and shut case. If you don't come forward and tell them what happened, this other guy is gonna get totally slammed for it. Life in prison - or worse."

"I wonder . . . ," I mumbled with this dead little laugh. "I wonder if he's that same homeless guy I shared my dinner with when I was there earlier with Beth. Be funny, wouldn't it? Sure be a joke on me. Maybe it was that same guy.   That really would be the fucking god damnedest joke in the whole fucking world. Don't ya think so, Jeff?"

Jeff looked at me with this really strange, puzzled look. Sort of like he was disturbed by everything I was saying.

"I don't know," he sort of whispered. "Does it matter?"

"No," I numbly gave a sharp laugh, shaking my head.

"We gotta go to the police and tell them what happened. And I gotta tell them or else I'm part of a crime. There's no way I can't go down there and tell them what really happened. How could I go on and live with my-self if I didn't tell them what I know - that it's a mistake - that the homeless guy didn't mug him and try to rob him. That he didn't kill him."

"And that I did," I stared at Jeff with a burning look.

"Yeah - that you did. You can tell them your story. Like you told me. That you didn't mean it. That it was an accident."

"And they're gonna believe that?", I bitterly laughed. "They're gonna believe me? No way in hell! They'll ask why I went off with him if I didn't want him to do what he did to me. They'll never believe me. They'll lock me up and throw away the key. Fuck! Kiss my life goodbye!"

Jeff narrowed his eyes and stared at me for a long time.

"You don't know that," he said. "Maybe . . ."

"Maybe fucking what?", I spit out. "Maybe I won't get life. Maybe I'll just get twenty or thirty years?"

"You don't know that," he insisted. "All you can do is tell the truth and see what happens. You have to do it. And the longer you wait, the rougher it's gonna be. The worse it'll look for you. You gotta go tonight. You gotta go with me, Niner.   If I go alone - they're gonna come and get you. They'll come here by morning and arrest you and take you away. And it'll make you look really guilty - like it wasn't an accident at all. Like you did it on purpose and were trying to hide it. You gotta come with me."

I didn't say anything for a minute. I just stared west toward the moon that was shining on the dark ocean in the distance.

"It doesn't matter anymore," I sadly mumbled. "Don't ya get it, Jeff? It just doesn't fucking matter anymore. It's over."

"What's over? What are you talking about? You've gotta go. You don't have any other choice."

"Yes I do," I said in this soft, firm voice. "I'm not going. Not now - not ever. And that's final. Don't ask me again. Don't fucking ask me again."

"OK," Jeff said in this really sad tone, his face sort of drawn in tight like he was in some kind of pain. "But if you change your mind, I'll be waiting in my car by the flagpole at the end of the mall. I'll wait there until ten minutes after midnight - then I'll go by myself."

He started sort of limping off across the lawn. When he was a short distance away, he stopped and turned back toward me.

"Did you know your dad was at the soccer game this afternoon?", he very quietly asked me. "He came toward the end.   After you got kicked out and left."

"My stepdad?", I asked with this really big surprise. "He was there? He and my mom were supposed to be here tomorrow. They're supposed to be flying in late tomorrow morning. Are you sure it was my stepdad?"

"No - it wasn't your stepdad," he said sort of gently. "It was your dad. You know - your real dad. The one you call Bob the Bastard."

I was totally amazed.

Then all confused and upset.

"Yeah - Bob the Bastard," I sort of snickered. "What the fuck was that asshole doing here? How'd did you know it was him? When did you ever meet him?"

"I met him last Christmas when he was here trying to see you. Remember - he left his Christmas present for you with me when you wouldn't see him. I know him. And he knows me. He came over after the game and talked to me."

"Big fucking deal," I angrily sneered. "That's just like him to miss almost the whole fucking game."

"He said he had an emergency with one of his patients and had to take a later flight. He made it as soon as he could."

"Yeah," I snickered. "His whole fucking life story. Never there for me. Everything's always more important than my crappy life."

"He said to tell you . . "

"I don't fucking want to hear what he fucking told you!"

285

"Tough shit! You're gonna hear anyway. He said to tell you that he really wants to see you - to wish you a happy birthday."

"He can go fuck himself!"

"I told him that you and I had some trouble we had to straighten out later tonight. I told him that we could swing by and pick him up at his hotel after midnight, and he could come with us."

"You told him all that, you asshole! We'll - I hope you two fuckers have fun at the police station. You two deserve each other. Fucking ass-holes! You both would like nothing better than to see me go totally down big time. You'll both get a great fucking laugh about it!"

"He's really worried, Niner. I saw it in his face. He said he'd stay up all night if he had to. He made me promise to come by tonight."

"Fuck both of you assholes!"

"And he asked me to tell you tonight - he didn't want to take the chance of spoiling your party by coming here. He knows how you feel. He said to tell you Happy Birthday, and that he hopes to tell you in person - that he'll see you later on."

"Right!", I said really sarcastically.

"And - he said to tell you . . . that he loves you."

I felt this sharp pain in my chest.

"And you can tell HIM to go fuck himself!", I yelled bitterly.

Jeff gave this really deep sigh.

"The flagpole," he said kind of casually as he continued walking slowly away from me, limping on his right leg.   "Ten minutes after midnight."

"And fuck you!", I shouted at his back.

I stood there for a couple of minutes. My mind was totally numb from listening to all this crap. All I was really aware of was that racket down below the bluff - that loud croaking-buzz of those damn fucking frogs down there by the creek. If Einstein was right - if these frogs were speaking to me and telling me their wisdom, I sure the fuck didn't understand their language. I stepped back from the edge of the bluff just a few feet and I was surprised to notice how I couldn't hear them anymore.

It was just still and completely quiet.

11:24 pm

I went back inside the Bird Nest and saw that the party was breaking up. Several people had gone, and a few were saying goodbye to Beth and passing by me and wishing me a Happy Birthday again.

Those fucking freeloaders up in the loft came skulking down and snuck out without saying a word. Some of them even snatched up a few cans of Coke and Pepsi and the remaining paper plates with cake on them as they quickly left.

Tom or Roy - whichever one of them it was - stepped up from the fireplace and grabbed a handful of chips and gave me this huge, fake friendly smile and went to give me a left-handed high-five. I just sort of ignored him, so he gave me this light little punch on the shoulder.

"Great party, Niner," he beamed brightly at me. "Just another half-hour now - you'll be officially twenty-one. You'll finally be legal. You'll be a man. You're the man, Niner. You're the man, bro."

He went out the door, then Beth's best friend Laura left, and then Beth and I were totally alone.

Moving over to the small table, I looked down at what remained of my cake. Most of it had been cut away. Only about a fourth of it was still there. The only writing on the top of it that was left was the word 'Happy.'

I stared at it for a minute or two. Then Beth came over and put her arms around me and went to kiss me on the lips.

I turned my face and pulled away from her.

"What's the matter?", she purred all sexy-like.

"Nothing," I mumbled.

"Then . . ", she smiled, trying to kiss me again.

I moved away from her.

"I just don't feel like it - that's all."

"Wow - that's a first."

She gave kind of this irritated little smile and went over and started putting the cake back in its box.

I sort of drifted toward the dark center window and stared out at the lights of the city.

"Thanks for the party," I quietly said in this totally numb, cold tone.

"Did you have a good time?"

I didn't answer her.

"Did you have a good time, Niner?", she repeated in a slightly louder voice.

I took a deep, hard breath.

"Why did you say you were my fiancee?", I softly asked her. "Why did you tell her you were my fiancee?"

"Who?", Beth casually sort of chirped.

"Why did ya say it?"

"Oh - you mean little Miss Genius?", she laughed. "What's her name? Debra?"

"Megan," I firmly told her.

"Megan. Poor Megan. Did you ever open that gift she brought you? You really got her good."

"What'a'ya mean by that?"

"Don't you think your seduction routine is getting a little out of hand. I mean - you're gonna be a father pretty soon. Those days are over."

That really pissed me off.

"I didn't say we were gonna get married," I raised my voice.

Beth put down the cake box and moved around the table and stepped towards me.

"You didn't say we weren't," she said very firmly.

"I don't know," I sort of sighed. "I haven't made up my mind yet."

"Well you'd better. I told you I can't wait any longer. I've gotta know tonight. Right now! I've got plans to make. Things to consider. You said you loved me. You said . . ."

"I told you," I said sort of helplessly, "I don't even know what love is. I don't know if I love you or not. I don't know."

"When WILL you know?", she said really impatiently and all kind of pissed off. "You keep saying that. When are you gonna make up your mind? When are you gonna know?"

I glanced over at her, and I hung my head down a little.

"Tomorrow," I said in this sort of dead whisper. "You'll know tomorrow. It'll be all over tomorrow. You'll know then."

Beth looked at me kind of funny-like.

"Tomorrow?", she asked with a confused expression.

"Yeah."

"Why do I have to wait to know . . . ?"

"Tomorrow," I repeated in a louder voice.

She sort of shrugged and went back to the table and continued stuffing what was left of the cake into its pink box. I followed after her.

"How do you know it's mine?", I just asked her sort of right out of the blue.

She snapped up her head and gave me this really hostile look.

"What the fuck do you mean by that?"

"Just that. You said you were three months along. That was right around the time that we made our pledge and got really serious about each other. But just before that - even the couple of weeks after I first met you - you were still going out with other guys. Sleeping with them. Weren't you?"

"Not really," she said all angry and defensive.

"What'a'ya mean 'not really?", I asked her kind of harsh-like. "You either did or you didn't."

"Why are you talking to me like this? I don't like the way you're talking to me. I'm not a fucking criminal on the witness stand."

That kind of really took me deep in the throat and I think I coughed a couple of times and lowered my head. Something over by the open doorway triggered my attention, and I glanced towards it with a jolt of surprise.

Einstein was standing there alone, and he looked really upset and disappointed. He had this kind of really sad and hopeless expression on his face.

"What do YOU want?", I asked him all annoyed and hostile-like.

"I want to talk to you," he softly replied.

"About what? To tell me how pissed off you are at me? To tell me what an asshole I am? Hey - stand in line."

"No, " he said lowering his voice even softer as he stepped into the room. "I'm really concerned about you. What's wrong with you, Niner?"

"Fuck - well, let's see. Where should I fucking begin? I know - how 'bout this?   Beth here is pregnant, and she wants me to marry her next month during Christmas break. How's that to begin with? Only I was wondering if the kid is really mine. That's what I was just asking her and trying to find out. So - take a seat, Einstein, and buy a fucking bag of popcorn and enjoy the show."

Einstein looked really startled by the angry stuff I was saying. He came over next to Beth and me, and he actually sat down in a chair.

"You're the father?", he gently asked me.

"I think so. I'm not sure. That's what I'm asking Beth. She sort of thinks there might be some other guys she slept with three months ago or so - just before we became exclusive."

"Not guys," Beth said really pissed. "Just one guy. And we only made love once. It was no big deal. We both were drinking and he wanted to and it just happened. It didn't mean anything. It was just that one

291

time. It was after the soccer party at Mike Johnson's house over on Fordham and you were playing pool with Chad and Dave, and he walked me home. That's all. And he kissed me and one thing led to another. It wasn't a big deal. Just that once."

My mind started spinning back to that party last August. I remembered it pretty well. It was just before the semester started, and I went there with Beth and we'd made out on the couch while everybody was dancing and playing music, and then I got in that intense pool match with Chad and Dave and Mike, and Beth wanted to go home, but I didn't wanna leave, so . . . so she . . . she left and went home . . . she walked back . . to her dorm . . . with . . . with . . .

I stared at her like I couldn't believe it. I was totally stunned.

"Kyle," I whispered.

Beth looked a little embarrassed. She tossed her hair back and assumed this really hard expression.

"Yeah. Kyle."

"That's impossible," I muttered to myself, shaking my head.

"He was all over me as soon as we got into the room," she said in this sort of mean, challenging tone. "He wouldn't take no for an answer. But he didn't even know what to do. I don't think he ever made love to a girl before. He was fumbling all over the place and it was pretty awful. He didn't even use a condom, and he came inside of me almost as soon as he started. It was horrible. And there was no way I'd ever fuck him again, so I never told you. I knew he was your best friend, so I never told you. I didn't want to make any trouble - and it was just that once."

I sort of staggered over and sat down in the chair next to Einstein. Leaning down a little into my lap, I put my head in my hands.

"Kyle," I softly said his name in a slightly trembling voice.

"Yeah," Beth said real emphatic-like. "Kyle. So what?"

"It's impossible," I whispered as I numbly shook my head.

"It's true. Why's it so hard to believe?"

I leaned back and shut my eyes for a few moments and took a really deep breath.

"Kyle was gay," I heard myself calmly saying.

Beth and Einstein stared at me like I was totally crazy. Then they looked at each other as if they were trying to make sense of what I had just said.

"You think Kyle was gay?", Einstein finally asked me in a very gentle and curious tone. "Why do you think that?"

I gave a really sad and bitter little laugh.

"I don't think it - I know it," I said very simply.

"How?", Beth asked loudly. "How do you know?"

I stood up and tightened every single muscle in my body and looked her right in the face.

"Because he was in love with me," I managed to say in this really choked voice. "He was in love with me."

Beth sort of blinked twice and stumbled over and sat down in a nearby chair.

Einstein opened his mouth but didn't say anything. He just left it open and his eyes got all sharp and tense.

"Kyle was gay?", he finally asked me in this weak voice. "Yeah. He was gay. I can see that now. A lot of stuff makes a lot more sense now. I understand it all much better now. And he told you he loved you? When did he tell you? Have you known a long time?"

I paced over to the window and looked away from them.

"I guess maybe I always knew," I emotionally started to explain. "Since the first day we meet a few years ago. There was just something different about him. Different in a really good way. And he treated me different than anybody else ever did. I never thought it was about sex. It never occurred to me that he might be gay. He was just different. Better. Better than anybody else I'd ever met. You know - he could feel what I was feeling inside. He always knew how I felt about things. And he always knew the exact thing to say to make me feel better. I felt . . I felt more complete when I was around him. He was sort of like my other self. My better self. We just kind of completed each other. But I never thought about it. I didn't want to. I just wanted to be with him all the time."

"You loved him?", Einstein quietly asked me.

"Uh . . I didn't want to think about it. I never thought about it."

"Never?", he asked incredulously.

"I didn't wanna."

"Then how do you know he was gay?", Beth asked very sharply. "If you never thought about it, how do you know how he felt? How do you know he was gay and in love with you."

I put my head in my hands and leaned against the wall next to the window.

"Because . . . that last day - the day he died," I could barely speak. "He'd been acting really weird all afternoon at soccer practice. We were all horsing around, and everybody was tackling each other, and Reicher tackled me, so I went and tackled Kyle. I can still see his face when I rolled over on top of him on the ground and held his shoulders down. He had the strangest look. Like he was all desperate and everything. He looked me in the eye with this incredible emotional kind of thing. I thought I'd hurt him, at first. I was kind of scared. I asked him if he was OK, and he said he was alright. So I got up really fast and pulled him up and we finished playing the scrimmage. Then, afterward, we went for a swim in the pool. Hardly anybody was there. I swam laps, but Kyle just stayed by the side in the lane next to me and watched."

"So just because he gave you all these loving looks you decided that he was gay and he had the hots for you?", Beth sarcastically asked me.

"After we were done swimming, we went in the locker room and showered and got dressed. It was totally empty. Nobody else was there. I made some kind of lame joke about something, but Kyle didn't laugh. He'd been really moody and quiet all day, so I didn't think anything of it. But when I started trying to talk to him, he looked away and didn't answer me. I was getting really uneasy. I didn't know what was happening to him. After a minute or two of nobody saying anything, I walked around him and looked him in the eye, and I asked him what was wrong. He started to cry. That freaked me out. He started to cry in this really gentle way. Just all quiet, and tender, and gentle."

I stopped talking and pressed my head against the wooden wall and closed my eyes again. I bit down hard on my lip.

"What did you do?", Einstein very softly asked me.

"I . . . I didn't know what to do. I didn't know what was wrong with him. I had this feeling. I started getting this feeling. I was sort of afraid to ask him what was wrong. But then he stopped crying and he started really slowly trying to tell me how much he loved me. I didn't want to hear that kind of crap at all - so I made a joke of it and kept cutting him off and making funny remarks and kidding him. He kept trying to tell me he was in love with me, but I wouldn't let him.   I wouldn't let him.   I didn't want to fucking hear it at all.   Finally he got kind of mad, and he yelled at me to shut up. Then he started saying that he loved me. He got really emotional and raised his voice and told me he loved me more than he'd ever love anybody in his life - that he was gay, and that he'd been wanting to make love to me ever since he first saw me. He said he felt like he was gonna die if he couldn't love me - make love with me. And then . . . and then he . . . he put his arms around me and he began running his hands up and down my body and he . . . and he held me tightly in this passionate embrace and he kissed me on the mouth - he kissed me all over my face and he kept coming back and kissing me passionately on the mouth like nobody ever kissed me before."

"Sounds like you put up quite a struggle," Beth angrily sneered.

Einstein gave her this sharp, critical look, then gazed over at me with this really gentle, sympathetic expression.

"And what happened then?", he softly asked me.

"Everything seemed to be happening so fast," I tried to remember as I took a deep, trembling breath. "Kyle was so . . . so kind of over-whelming. He was just all crazy with emotion, and he kept kissing me, and . . . it was so weird and kind of surreal - because I really hated what he was doing - but I sort of was feeling a little like I wanted it. Just a little - I was feeling that. But mainly I hated it.   I hated it. I hated the way it made me feel. And I hated him for doing it. And I kept trying to shove him away, and I was really pissed off and yelling at him to cut it out. But he totally ig-nored me, and when he grabbed the back of my head and pressed his mouth against mine and started giving me this really long, deep kiss . . I got so pissed that I totally lost it. I pushed him away really hard, and when he ignored me again and came back toward my face and tried to kiss me again, I just hauled off and smashed him right in the mouth. It really made his lip bleed. It must have really hurt, 'cause he stopped. And I started calling him names. Really bitter and mean-like. I hated him right then at that minute. I called him a 'worthless fucking faggot'. I remember I said faggot and 'rotten queer" and some other things. I couldn't help it. It just came all rushing out of me. It was like I didn't know what I was saying. I couldn't help it. And I didn't mean it. I swear - I didn't mean any of it. I didn't hate Kyle at all. I didn't. I . . . "

"What did he do?", Einstein sort of sadly asked me.

"He wiped the blood off his mouth and he just stood there looking at me as I called him all those awful names. He looked at me like . . . like I had crushed him - crushed something really deep inside him. Then he just turned all of a sudden-like and ran out the door of the locker room. That was the last time I ever saw him. The last time."

My throat tightened into a knot and I couldn't speak anymore. I twisted my neck and stared out the window.

"That was the late afternoon, wasn't it?", Einstein painfully mused to himself.

I slowly nodded.

"Kyle ran out of the locker room, and he kept running. He was supposed to meet Doug at the library. That's what they said. But he kept running - all the way out the front gate and down Lincoln Boulevard. That's why he wasn't on the sidewalk where he always jogged. That's why he was running out in the street. Out in the middle of the heavy traffic. He didn't want to be safe. He didn't want to be safe at all. He just wanted to quickly end his pain. That's why when he saw the truck - when he saw that big truck coming towards him, he decided to run right . . . "

"Stop it!", I shouted. "Shut up, Einstein!   Shut up!"

"You know it's true," Einstein firmly told me. "You have to face it. You can't pretend forever, Niner. You've got to face it. Kyle killed himself."

"NO!"

I put my hands over my face and sank down into the chair that was next to me.

"That's good," he said in this really comforting tone. "Let it all go, Niner. Go ahead and cry. You need to cry."

I angrily put my hands down and gave him a mean, sort of defiant stare.

"I don't cry," I sort of spit at him. "I've never cried."

"You need to learn," he said very gently.

"Fuck off. Not everybody cries. It's useless. What good did it ever do anybody. And anyway, I couldn't even cry if I wanted to. Some people just don't cry. And I'm one of them. Got it! So stop telling me shit like that!"

Einstein gave this really big sigh and stood up.

"It wasn't your fault, Niner. You can't blame yourself. Kyle just had this one lost moment. He just lost it and did something really stupid. It was just a stupid sudden impulse. He was just all confused and lost for that one moment and he felt he couldn't go on."

"I don't blame myself," I said really angrily. "I don't blame myself at all. I don't even think about it. I haven't thought about it for a second - not for one fucking second since it happened. And I'm not going to. Kyle was a jerk and an idiot, and he didn't give a fuck about the rest of us. He just wanted to hurt us. Well - he may have hurt everybody else, but he's not gonna fucking hurt me. Do you hear me, Einstein! Kyle's not gonna hurt me one little bit! He was a stupid jerk, and he's not gonna destroy me too. He's gone now - and good riddance! It's over! That's it! So - shut up!"

Beth sat there listening to all of this like she was in a bad dream or something. When I was done talking, she slowly got up and just walked out of the room and into the night.

Einstein stood up after she left and he paced over to the fireplace. He went to say something once or twice, but he seemed to have a second thought about it and he remained silent.

I just wandered from window to window and tried to calm down a little. My heart was really racing, and I was beginning to realize what I was going to have to do pretty soon. I'd made up my mind.

"Niner," Einstein firmly called over to me. "If you don't marry Beth, is she going to have the baby anyway?"

"Yeah."

"And they'll do a test. A blood test. And they'll be able to know who the father is."

"Yeah. I know. It's probably me.

"But what if it isn't?"

"Huh?", I said with a bit of surprise.

"What if it isn't? What if it's Kyle's?"

"What?"

"What if Kyle's the father? What then?"

The idea of that just kind of totally punched my brain like a boxing glove. I couldn't follow any of my thoughts. Everything was scrambled.

"I . . . I don't know," I mumbled. "But the chances of that happening are as . . . "

"Are just as good as the chances that it's yours. It just takes once, you know. Just one time."

I tried to think again, but couldn't. I just had this feeling in the pit of my stomach - like when I looked at those pine trees outside my window this morning. I just was feeling a lot of things, but nothing that I could recognize. Just all these things. Confusing and disturbing things.

"If it was Kyle's," I whispered all emotional-like.

"Yeah?"

"Then maybe . . . maybe he wouldn't be . . . he wouldn't really be . . . "

"He wouldn't be dead?"

I looked at Einstein with this amazed look, then got angry again.

"You're talking shit!", I spit at him. "The kid isn't Kyle's. You heard what Beth said. Stop making all this shit up. You're just fucking trying to cause trouble. It's not Kyle's, and Kyle's dead. He's gone for good! Get used to it."

"But if it was . . . "

"Shut up I told you! It doesn't matter anymore."

"But you loved him," Einstein suddenly said in this really dumb, matter-of-fact tone. "Niner - you loved Kyle as much as he loved you. Not in the same way. You didn't sexually want him. But you loved him just the same. Probably as much as you'll ever love anyone in your entire life."

I tensed my whole body and rushed over to the fireplace and held up my fist right in front of Einstein's face.

"One more fucking word," I shouted, "and I swear to god I'm gonna knock your fucking head off!"

Einstein sort of sleepily narrowed his eyes and gave this kind of really pleased-with-himself little laugh. It really confused me.

"Thanks," he said with a confident smile.

"For what!"

"Just thanks."

I angrily kicked at the carpet and backed away from him.

"Fuck! I swear to god, Einstein! You're the queerest son of a bitch on this whole entire fucking campus!"

"I don't doubt it," he said with a very gentle, amused laugh.

"Fuck! How do you survive around here!"

"It ain't easy."

"Fuck! Butting in to everybody else's business night and day! Why don't ya just keep your fucking big nose to yourself once in awhile!"

"Might be worth trying," he laughed again.

"Shit! I'm out of here! Just go fuck off!"

"I probably will," he laughed even louder.

Walking angrily off to the open doorway, I started numbing myself for what I knew I had to do later on.

"Where are you going?", Einstein called after me with this really worried sounding voice.

"To get my truck," I kind of barked back at him.

"Why?"

"To drive!"

"Where?", he asked really anxious-like.

"None of your fucking business!"

"Niner - let me go with you? OK?"

"No! No fucking way. Fuck off, I told you!"

"Niner - wait a minute," he said almost like he was afraid of something. "Stay a little while here by the bluff. Listen to the frogs for awhile. Listen to the wisdom of the frogs."

I turned around as I was walking outside and gave him the biggest snicker I think I've ever given anybody.

"You should be in a mental hospital!", I yelled at him with this huge bitter laugh.

"Niner?"

"And stop fucking calling me Niner - or Number Nine or any other goddamned, mother fucking stupid number! I'm not some dumb, worthless fucking object! I'm a person! I'm a human being! And I have a name! I have a goddamned fucking name! And nobody wants to call me by a name! Not one fucking person in the whole world ever says my name!"

He went to say something, but I just jogged off across the lawn and down along the winding street through the faculty parking lot. I just wanted to get away as fast as I could from all his crazy talk and his crazy ideas and his crazy frogs and all the other stupid bullshit he was always shoveling out. I'd had it once and for all with Einstein. What a fucking stupid jerk. I couldn't believe that I used to think he was so goddamned fucking smart. Shit!

I stopped jogging when I came to the edge of the Sunken Garden. I stood there for a moment and tried to sort of calm my mind a little and decide what I was gonna do next.

I remembered my truck was parked in back of McKay, so I decided to walk over and get it and take a ride.

To the beach.

11:47 pm

I walked across the lawn of the Sunken Garden and climbed up the steps of Regents Terrace. As I passed by the stone benches tucked beneath the flower planters on the second level, I hesitated for a moment and turned around and gazed up at the bell tower and the front of the chapel.

I knew instantly that this was the very last time in my life that I'd ever be seeing them. The last time I'd be seeing this view. My favorite view.

And even though the bells weren't ringing anymore tonight, I still wanted to look at the beautiful tower for one long, last time. You know - sort of say goodbye to it and all that sentimental crap.

So I moved over to the center of the stone benches and I sat down there. It was hard and cold. But it sort of fit my mood. I was really totally numb all inside now. I didn't feel sad. I didn't feel angry. I just plain didn't feel anything anymore. I was already there. In my mind - I was already half there. Halfway to those high waves in the ocean.

I just kind of leaned back and stared at the bell tower and silently said a calm goodbye.

I could feel my truck keys in my pocket pressing against the top of my right tight. It was a short walk to the McKay parking lot. I went to get up and start off for my truck. Part of me wanted to just instantly get down to the beach and out to the ocean and get everything over with. But, I hesitated, and leaned back again and stared at the clock on the tower.

I wanted to look at it just a little bit longer. I told myself that I'd stay here just two more minutes - then I'd get up and go to my truck.

Honestly, there was still just this really tiny little part of me that wanted to stay sitting there looking at the tower, and never leave. It wanted to stay there forever - or at least as long as it could.

But the rest of me knew for sure that I couldn't stay behind. Kind of like those guys in the huge memorial statue behind the chapel. The guys who were staying there behind. I couldn't be one of those anymore - and I knew it. I was part of the guys in the statue who were leaving - who had to go and couldn't stay. I was one of those departed guys now.

And I kind of thought for a moment how they'd be putting my name on one of those little wooden squares right there on the base of the memorial beneath all those statues. And I was thinking how funny it would be if they put my name right next to Kyle's. If they put my little square right next to Kyle's.

I kind of liked that. I kind of really did. And I started hoping that would happen.   That our names would be together right there pretty soon.

I liked that.

And it made me want to just jump up right now and run and get into my truck and drive really fast down to the beach.

When I went to stand up, this old man came down the steps over at the side of St. Robert's Hall, and he started walking across the terrace kind of right in the middle and in front of me. So I kind of sat back again and waited for him to pass by, because I didn't want to have to deal with him at all - like smile and say hello and all that horse shit. I wasn't in the mood.

And, besides - the closer he came, I could see that he was a really old guy and he was one of the maintenance guys - you know, the janitors at the school.   They all dressed in those blue uniforms sort of like they probably wear in prisons, and you can never talk to them because they can only speak Spanish, and they never know what to say to you or how to act. It's a real nuisance the way they're always swarming around and in everybody's way.   So us kids just always totally ignore them and pretend like they're not there - like they don't exist.

So when this old guy came walking close to me, I turned my head away and just stared toward the dorms across the way, then looked down and started thinking about what I had to do.

I kept expecting him to pass by me pretty quickly, because he was walking pretty fast like he was just off-duty and on his way home for the night.   But he really slowed down when he was opposite me a few feet away. And then he stopped completely and just stood there looking at me.

At first, I thought maybe somehow he knew me. Maybe it was some anonymous janitor that cleaned up something for me a long time ago. Some of these shit workers have memories like elephants. But I was really hoping that wasn't the case. I wasn't up for dealing with anybody at all. I just kept ignoring him.

But he not only stopped, but he took kind of this really shy couple of steps towards me.

Fuck!

I just kept silently saying to myself 'go away!' - 'go away!'

But he didn't.

He just kept fucking staring at me and moving a little bit closer, like he'd bought a goddamned ticket to look at me or something.

I finally glanced up at him and saw he was this ancient old guy - a Mexican guy with white hair and this goofy, moronic smile on his face.

Some of these janitors are really mental cases. Like this old guy, they're alway smiling and laughing and whistling and singing little songs. Shit!   They're either morons or senile with Alzheimer's or something. That's why we all stay away from them. With the shitty jobs that they have, they'd have to be nuts to act all happy all the time like that. Fuck!

This old guy came right up to me. Close enough to touch me. And he stood there staring down at me and all of a sudden he stopped smiling his crazy smile and he looked all concerned and everything.

I didn't know what to make of the whole fucking thing.

This old, ugly janitor just kept standing there right in front of me and looking down right into my face - and he sort of was all intense and worried looking and . . . and looking into my eyes so deeply that it seemed like he was almost reading a book.

Fuck!

I didn't say anything. I turned my head and glanced to my left and tried to completely ignore him. But, for some reason, I quickly glanced back at him - and I stared him right back in the eye. I gave him this real mean, hostile stare - and I was hoping it would make him fuck off and just go away.

But it didn't.

It just made something really weird happen.

This Mexican janitor guy leaned closer to me and he gave me this sort of really tender, concerned little smile.

"You . . OK?," he kind of awkwardly asked me in this really thick accent. "Everything . . OK?"

I was so surprised by his question that I just kind of locked into his really gentle eyes, and I didn't say anything.

He tilted his head a little and looked really worried. Bending even lower, he brought his sad, sensitive face even closer to mine.

Then he just softly asked me:

"What your name? What your name, son?"

And without even thinking - I told him my name.

I said my full name out loud in this calm, peaceful voice.

He leaned back a little and gave this big, friendly smile.

And he said my name. He said it very happily and proudly. Like it was the best name in the world.

Then he gave me this warm, wonderful expression, and he reached down and patted me on the shoulder, and he said really gently and firmly:

"It OK.   No worry.   It always turn OK."

Then he happily said my name again.

And he quickly walked off and started happily whistling.

When he came to the edge of the terrace and started down the steps, he turned back and beamed this huge smile and gave me a shy little wave.   Then he hurried on and disappeared into a basement door of Malone Hall.

I sat there totally paralyzed by something.   I couldn't move.

I felt that huge wave.   I didn't see it this time.   I just felt it.   And it came up higher and faster than any of the waves in the ocean.   And it started crashing right through me.   It crashed down right through me and crushed my gut and my heart and everything inside me.   And I couldn't breath for a minute.

I couldn't breath at all.

Then, all of a sudden, this incredibly painful howling, screaming, wailing sound started coming out of my throat.   The sound that a dying animal makes.   And it terrified me.

And I started to cry.

I really didn't understand what was happening to me.

But I couldn't speak and I could barely breath, and my whole body was shaking with these convulsions that came one after the other.   And I was sobbing so hard that my face hurt and all this water was streaming down my cheeks and my neck and getting my shirt totally soaked.

I tried to stop, but I couldn't.

I thought I was going to die.

I was making these loud, wailing sounds just like some kind of crazy lunatic.

I couldn't think and I couldn't feel anything except my heart. And it didn't feel like the heart I always had. It felt like something totally new and different. It had this deep crushing pain that it had never had before. It was like it had just sort of sprung out of something - really painfully sprung forth from something really hard, and now had become something really tender and soft and sensitive.

And I kept sobbing and sobbing and putting my hands to my eyes and trying to wipe away some of the tears. But there were so many that the palms of my hands got soaking wet.

There was nothing left inside me now.

Just this sharp brutal pain that was slicing downward from my throat through my chest and my stomach.

As I kept bitterly weeping, I really thought I was gonna die.

Then the pain sort of spread out through my body and started hurting a little less and a little less until I could stand it now, and I suddenly knew it would be OK.

In a couple of minutes I stood up very slowly, and that made me feel better.

I was still crying a lot, but I could breath now, and I could speak.

"Kyle," I tremblingly called out his name through my sobs. "Kyle. I loved you, Kyle. I'm sorry. I didn't understand. I didn't understand. I'm sorry, Kyle. I loved you! I loved you with all my heart!"

Then I sobbed bitterly again for several moments and lost my breath again and couldn't speak.

I dried my eyes with my hands and stepped forward a little bit across the Regents Terrace and looked up at the bell tower.

It was a minute after midnight.

Suddenly something just exploded right out of my gut, and I bitterly sobbed again, and then I heard myself saying something loudly in a really painful voice that really surprised me:

"Dad! I love you, dad. I love you.   Help me, dad! Please help me, dad!"

And I cried hard again, and I shook my head and took several deep breaths, and then I started feeling a little better.

And I gazed up at the bell tower and gave a painful little smile.

And suddenly I could hear the frogs way down there in the creek. I could faintly hear them chattering.

They must have been almost a quarter mile away - but I could hear them. I could hear them talking to me.

I could hear their wisdom.

And I sort of tenderly smiled through my tears.

"Those frogs," I said softly.   "Those damn frogs."

-

-

-

-                                    **- END -**

Manufactured by Amazon.ca
Bolton, ON

18492120R00175